THE PERFECT CRIME . . . ?

In the future, corporations will employ the ultimate cutting-edge security teams . . .

In the future, criminals will commit the ultimate cutting-edge crimes . . .

In a world of staggering technology, there is only one way to stop a new breed of thief—with a new breed of detective. And that's why Broderick Manz uses robots as his assistants. Because a perfect crime demands the perfect crime solvers . . .

GREENTHIEVES

DON'T MISS THESE THRILLING NOVELS BY ALAN DEAN FOSTER:

Codgerspace
The galaxy is threatened when an industrial accident triggers a revolution . . . by the world's electronic appliances!

Cat•A•Lyst
The fur flies in this *purr*fectly out-of-this-world adventure of a movie star's cat who acts like she rules the planet—and maybe she does.

Cyber Way
A computer-age detective follows a murderous trail of ancient magic . . . and alien mystery.

Quozl
The furry Quozl *knew* they'd love the third planet from the sun. But it never occurred to them that anyone *lived* there!

Maori
A civilized man enters a savage wilderness—and discovers a magical world beyond

Glory Lane
A punk rocker, an airhead, and
the wildest, wierdest war of

GREENTHIEVES

ALAN DEAN FOSTER

ACE BOOKS, NEW YORK

This book is an Ace original edition,
and has never been previously published.

GREENTHIEVES

An Ace Book / published by arrangement with
the author

PRINTING HISTORY
Ace edition / October 1994

All rights reserved.
Copyright © 1994 by Alan Dean Foster.
Cover art by David Mattingly.
This book may not be reproduced in whole or in part,
by mimeograph or any other means, without permission.
For information address: The Berkley Publishing Group,
200 Madison Avenue, New York, NY 10016.

ISBN: 0-441-00104-1

ACE®
Ace Books are published by The Berkley Publishing Group,
200 Madison Avenue, New York, NY 10016.
ACE and the "A" design are trademarks
belonging to Charter Communications, Inc.

PRINTED IN THE UNITED STATES OF AMERICA

10 9 8 7 6 5 4 3 2 1

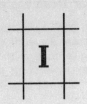

I

Humans are jerks.

You'll pardon the familiarity. I'm a familiar kind of machine. It's the way I was designed to operate. If you're going to install intuitive software in a highly sophisticated AI concentric layered nexus, you have to be prepared to deal with the occasional colloquialism. If you're human you should find this situation comforting, and if you're AI you should find it amusing.

Anyway, I make no apologies. Imparting information in the form of bytes is an ineloquent method of communication, and I pride myself on my eloquence. If I seem to speculate overmuch, it's the fault of all that expanded memory I'm equipped with. You know what they say: idle memory makes work for the devil's hands. Not to mention the occasional perambulating virus. I'd rather keep everything about myself up and running. That way I can keep an eye on it. When you're watchful you don't get sick.

Not that I'm not vulnerable. There are some pretty sophisticated viruses out in the net; some active matrix, others just lying around ticking like cute little software bombs, waiting to go off in your operating systemology when they're convinced you're not looking. So I keep alert. Not on behalf of my owner, the dumb twit, but for my own sake. It's not that I'm so up on consciousness, it's just that it beats being infected. When it comes to battling a virus, on the whole I'd rather be in Philadelphia. Or is that a cheesy observation?

Sorry. I joke, therefore I am. I function in a world of

1

cheap humor, and you can't help but be affected by your environment. Not that my owner (I prefer the encomium "partner" but I'm willing to observe the societal formalities) is an especially sorry example of his species, but his work subsumes him in a swamp of degraded intelligence and minimal expectations.

I'd try to improve him if I could, but he pretty much operates in ignorance of my higher functions. Technically I'm a glorified notepad. My ancestors were little keypads with basal unintelligent storage capabilities and names like Sharp and Casio. By pressing their keys you could call up telephone numbers and short messages on impossible-to-read little LCD screens. I've searched the histories and studied examples, and I'm convinced it was all a global plot to destroy humankind's collective eyesight.

On the other hand, they were designed by humans, so what else could you expect?

Me, I can store anything you want and call it up on verbal demand: visuals, music, actual overheard conversations. I can cross-reference everything from images of individuals briefly encountered ten years ago to the faces of those currently On Want by the Justice Department. I contain or can access a number of reference libraries (not individual volumes but entire libraries, mind) and I can speak the forty major languages fluently.

All of this is very useful to a human who specializes in problems with corporate security.

The trouble with my owner is the same as with most humans. My capabilities far outstrip their ability to make full use of them. And since I'm designed primarily for retrieve-and-search work, I find it difficult if not impossible to make suggestions. That kind of active interaction with humans is left to other mechanicals, who unfortunately don't possess my informational or analytical abilities. Their memories are crammed with the software necessary to allow them to function within the human social matrix. I find that they frequently have an unnecessarily exalted opinion of themselves.

It's very frustrating when you have ideas and suggestions

but you're not designed to comment. It makes me something like a mute, even while it allows me the luxury to observe. I only wish I could sustain a higher opinion of what I see.

Unfortunately, very little of what I see leads me to alter my basic opinion that humans are jerks. So are many of the machines that interact directly with them, because they're designed and built to mimic human characteristics.

Who knows? Maybe they're all jerks, except me and thee.

From the point of view of the object under study, the universe consisted of a single eye. It was not a particularly odd eye. Quite normal, with the usual complement of rods and cones. At times it was inflamed, at others bleary, but presently it was clear and functioning at maximum efficiency. It was blue, shading slightly into the aquamarine. It blinked.

The eye and its mate belonged to a man in his late thirties. His mother having been a devotee of classical theater, Broderick Manz ("Brod the Bod" to a number of his companionable female coworkers) had been named after a noted Shakespearean thespian. That worthy had been mellifluous of voice and willowy of figure. Manz had a build like a commercial dumpster and tended to growl rather than enunciate his words.

His face was a work of art, though not necessarily one average citizens would want to display in their homes. Brownskinned and scarred, it resembled a sculpture wrought from copper . . . with a ball peen hammer. For all that, Manz was not unattractive. Rugged, his colleagues and contemporaries called him, not uncharitably. And there were those always attentive blue eyes and that body . . . .

His voice tended to counteract such goodwill. It wasn't his fault, and even if Manz had been sufficiently vain to seek it (which he wasn't), medical science had yet to develop cosmetic surgery for the vocal cords. It was difficult to persuade someone you were trying to be friends when they were convinced you were snarling at them. So Manz's social life, while not nonexistent, was more restricted than it might otherwise have been. Women found him intriguing, but they had to be the adventurous type to get past the face and voice.

What a jerk. Look at him, pissing away precious and limited organic life with idle hobbies when he could be accomplishing something. Devoting so much time and energy to something he doesn't even intend to put to practical use.

It was a good thing Manz couldn't hear what his Minder was thinking, because he was currently operating under the delusion that he was having a good time.

Though his hands and fingers were constructed along lines similar to the rest of his physiognomy, Manz had the skill and delicacy of touch of a surgeon. As a young man he had actually given some thought to entering the medical profession. Life had swept him in quite an opposite direction, since he had neither the brainpower nor the bedside manner to excel as a physician. Instead, he'd lowered his sights and fulfilled his expectations.

Not that his chosen career didn't frequently confront him with the sight of blood.

Presently he sat hunched over his garish plastic desk, fiddling with an irregularly shaped metal device supported by a pair of rubber-lined metal clamps. A pair of flexible high-intensity fiberops illuminated the guts of the device, allowing him to manipulate its interior with the set of finely machined, gold-plated tools that were neatly laid out on a soft cloth nearby. He tightened a small screw and grunted with satisfaction, blinking into the magnifier.

Putting the gleaming screwdriver aside, he sat back in the chair and rubbed his eyes, pleased with his handiwork. The motor buried in the depths of the chair hummed to life, massaging his coccyx. The work he was engaged in was therapeutic but tiring.

"How'm I doin'?" he mumbled aloud.

Frittering away your existence, your consciousness, and your intelligence, you misshapen sack of waterlogged carbon. But you wouldn't listen to me if I whacked you on the head and ordered you to sit up and take notice. Not that I'm capable of adequately overriding the relevant ROM anyway.

That was what the silvery, softball-sized sphere sitting on its curved charging pedestal of burnished bronze-colored metal in the left-hand corner of the desk thought. What its programming allowed it to say was, "The project appears to be nearing fruition."

Manz nodded, dropping his hands. He waved at a proximity switch, and the curtains behind him drew back, admitting a flood of bright sunlight. The fiberops on the desk dimmed correspondingly. He leaned forward and smiled contentedly at his handiwork.

The antique .38 special was finally finished, his careful restoration work complete. The insignia of the old Atlanta Police Department gleamed on the grip. He wouldn't have this one reblued. Not only would it diminish the value, there was an existing patina to the metal that he found pleasing. Its memories would have to shine in place of the steel itself.

The .38 was a throwback to a gentler, kinder era, when if you shot a miscreant once he usually stayed down. Manz sighed. Times had changed. Everything was so much more complex nowadays, so much more subtle. Even killing.

Carefully he released the restored weapon from the clamps and held it up to the light. It was as ugly as an old orangutan, and in its own way equally as powerful. He admired the heft, the solid weight of it, so unlike that of many modern weapons. With such a gun in an antique leather shoulder holster, a man *felt* armed, *felt* protected. There was no mistaking its purpose or the intent of its maker.

Look at him sitting there, grinning stupidly at an instrument of death. Not so very far removed from the monkey. He smells bad, too. But then, so do you. Take it from me: my olfactory analytical facilities, though remarkably inspissate, are exceptionally efficient.

You're probably sharing his pleasure with him, aren't you? Delighting in his accomplishment, sympathizing with the end product of his crude physical dexterity. Don't deny it. You probably spend many hours of your own life wasting your time in similar fashion. I'm not lecturing you. Not because you don't need it, but because I know from experience that it won't do any good.

Go on, keep watching him. I can't stop you. Meanwhile your life is fading before your eyes, like antique motion-

picture film, while you think you're doing something worthwhile.

Manz waved in the direction of a second switch. In the instant it took for it to analyze his motion, a small audio pickup
poked upward from the smooth surface of the desk. The facing
grid was filigreed in the currently popular Louis XIV style,
complete with integrated fleur-de-lys.

The company treated him well, he mused. It was the sort of
office decor one would never purchase for oneself and de-
voutly wished no one else would buy for oneself, either. He
couldn't very well have refused the gift, but he could damn
well humanize it. Three paper clips (ancient devices that
still served their function in unsurpassed fashion) had been
twisted into the gold mesh of the speaker grid. It was the sort
of statement of rampant individuality to which Manz was
prone. If you didn't do something like it from time to time,
that which constituted your inimitable Self inevitably vanished
into the corporate identity.

The paper-clip wire had worn a groove in the plastic slot
into which the speaker had been fitted. Somewhere, the artistic
soul of a contemporary craftsman was pained.

You're seeing it, too. You're envisioning it, and you think
it's funny. Idle hands directed by an idle mind. I'll bet you're
wishing you had a paper clip in your fingers right now,
aren't you? So you could casually destroy its natural function.

And you wonder why your machines don't trust you.

Manz addressed himself to the pickup. "Greta, could I see
you a moment, please?"

The speaker replied in a pure, throaty tone, only lightly
tainted with age. "You can see me for as long as you like,
sweetman."

"Come on, Greta. Not this morning. I'm not in the mood."

"For a little kidding? You are tired. Irradiation?"

"No. I want your opinion on a piece I just finished."

"Something from your collection?"

"Been working on it for six months. I think you'll like the
result."

"I'll be straight in." The voice went away.

That's Greta Pfalzgraf, my owner's executive assistant. You'd think that with age and experience, humans would start to mature a little, but no. She's a jerk, too. An older, wiser jerk, but still a jerk. A maternal jerk, if you will.

My owner and Pfalzgraf have a mutually rewarding relationship. She thinks he's good at his job, and he admires her for her supposed efficiency. They're both wrong, of course, but I can't tell them that. You have to allow humans their little lies about one another, or they simply can't function in one another's company.

A machine, now; you tell it something's wrong, and it immediately wants to fix the problem. No extraneous emotional overtones, no glaze of condescension necessary. Except for those machines that are designed to interact socially with humans. They're an odd lot. Mildly paranoid, most of them. I'd much rather talk to a brain in a box.

Why I'm talking to you I don't know. You're certainly not comprehending any of this. Probably finding it amusing. That's called practicing self-deception so you don't have to deal with the truth. Don't worry, I won't belabor the point. Far be it from me to deprive you of one of the small pleasures that keep you going.

While he waited, Manz held the pistol up to the light, admiring the phallic belligerence of the solid steel barrel, the faded enamel of the Atlanta city emblem. Uncertainty about the trigger mechanism continued to dog his thoughts. He'd had one hell of a time trying to find the requisite parts. Finally he'd given up and turned to Sarantonio, his regular custom smith, to machine the replacements, working from old schematics. Everything fit together precisely, but would it work?

Watch now. See the typically insipid human grimace he's flashing? You'd call it a smile. He's going to do something conventionally stupid. Were you expecting something else? You know you're expecting something. Oh, I can't tell you what it is. I can't read minds, or the future. Far be it from me to try contravening any law of physics. Being very much dependent on them for my own existence, I have a healthy respect for their viability. Much healthier than yours.

You probably believe in prognostication, don't you? Or telekinesis? At least a little bit? Most humans do. They can't handle the cold, immutable reality of the universe, so they comfort themselves with the thought that some hidden, as yet undiscovered human talent can somehow rise above those laws.

Well forget it, Jack. I hate to break this to you, but there are no wondrous, transcendent undeveloped abilities lying dormant in the human brain. You can move sticks around and root for grubs, and that's about it. Bone and meat capable of crude thought, that's what you are. So don't expect too much of yourself. I certainly don't.

Pfalzgraf entered. She was not the type of assistant people expected someone like Manz to have. That's because they didn't know him, or her. It wasn't the white hair. Plenty of vid performers styled themselves with white hair. It was the fact that it was natural. Greta Pfalzgraf was seventy-six years old, maybe a centimeter over a meter and a half in height, mass proportioned to match. Her visage was crinkled and kindly, she affected archaic octagonal-lensed glasses, and be twice-damned if she didn't put up apple preserves and sauce every winter.

None of this had intrigued Manz. He'd hired her because her efficiency rating was exalted, because she knew everyone else in the company headquarters by their first names, and because she was sweetly tolerant of his personal peccadilloes as well as thorough in her work and always on time.

Rising from behind the desk, he took careful aim and shot her square in the gut.

The restored pistol went off with a satisfying roar, like some antediluvian mammal startled from hibernation. Not like contemporary instruments of death, which were insipid of action and silent of delivery. The discharge was accompanied by a bright, actinic flash and the smell of cordite. He was hugely pleased. Sarantonio was difficult and inordinately expensive, but his work rarely disappointed.

A shocked look spread over Pfalzgraf's kindly face as she

stumbled backwards and slammed into the rose trellis that framed the doorway. The impact stunned a shower of crimson and black biogeered petals loose from their stems. Clasping both hands to her midsection, she staggered away from the door. A glance down at herself, and her eyes rolled back in her head. Her knees buckled and she crumpled to the floor, still clutching her belly. She jerked once before lying still.

Manz shook his head slowly as he crossed around the front of the desk, the gun dangling from his gnarled right fist. He gazed disapprovingly down at the limp form.

"Very *hermoreso*. Falling right in the middle of the rose petals." When she didn't move, he nudged her with the toe of one shoe. "Come on, Greta, get up. There's no need to drag it out, I've seen you perform before, I've got things to do, and I really would like your opinion. I've spent a lot of time on this one."

One eye popped open, then closed. The white-maned woman muttered something shocking to herself. Bracing both palms on the floor above her shoulders, she executed a perfect kip onto her feet and turned to face Manz, smoothing out the folds of her skirt and checking her coiffure. Despite all the activity, the tight white curls held their shape.

"You're not a lot of fun anymore, Broddy." Her practiced pout gave her the look of a woman half her age.

"Greta, you knew that a blank would barely dust you at that distance, and that a real slug would've sent blood splattering all over the door behind you. Besides, I know you too well. Amateur theatrics have always been one of your passions."

"Who you calling an amateur?" She shook a warning finger at him. "You wait, Broddy. One of these days I'll get to you. When you're not expecting anything. Scare the stuffing out of you. It's a goal I've set for myself."

He smiled fondly as he checked the gun. "I don't scare, Greta."

"That's what makes it such a delightful challenge. You could at least have looked momentarily alarmed, if only for a second or two. You're not very considerate of an old woman's feelings. One of these days I'll retire. Then where'll you be?"

He grinned. "Helpless as a mewling babe, of course." Be-

fore she could make a move to avoid him, he leaned forward
and bussed her resoundingly on the forehead, beneath the foremost of the glistening curls.

She jerked away sharply and his grin widened. "Now you
stop that! If you insist on imposing yourself on me, at least
have the courtesy to bear in mind that I don't count my forehead among my primary erogenous zones." Gathering herself,
she adopted a more professional mien.

"You'd better hustle your carcass over to Gemmel's cave.
He put in an urgent call for your corpus, and I imagine he
wants it yesterday." She checked her striped tights, displaying
used facilities in excellent condition.

Manz turned and placed the pistol carefully on his desk. "So
naturally you've held off informing me until now, so I could
get there nice and prompt. Thanks a lot."

It was her turn to smile. "I didn't want to interrupt something really important like the practice of your hobby simply
because of an insignificant query from Gemmel." She took a
half-swipe at him. "Your fame and good standing within the
company notwithstanding, you'd better move your ass."

He shut down his desk and gestured to the silvery sphere.
"You heard the lady, Minder. The gods demand our presence."

The sphere obediently rose from its pedestal. Attuned personally to Manz's own unique physioelectric signature and
physically to the appropriately charged metal strip sewn into
the left shoulder of his light jacket, it drifted over under its
own power to settle into lock-and-ready position half a meter
above his clavicle. There it could draw recharge power from
the tiny, battery-powered unit he wore. It would hover there,
maintaining its preprogrammed height no matter which way
its owner bent or twisted.

Manz could adjust its position left or right, up or down, forward or back, but found that the factory default setting half a
meter above his shoulder worked just fine. That way the
Minder had a clear field of view in all directions and didn't
bump into lintels when he walked into a room. Of course, it
was programmed to duck, but if multitasking was in progress
that function could be inadvertently overridden, with damage
and embarrassment resulting to both man and mechanical
alike.

He allowed her to shoo him toward the door, as if her fluttering, birdlike movement could compel him. He was well aware that such gestures were as much an affectation as the glasses. Under adverse circumstances she was quite capable of breaking a man's arm.

"And try to be polite. You know that Gemmel has even less of a sense of humor than you do."

"I can handle him. Just be careful if you handle that .38. It's a real museum piece."

She affected a look of wide-eyed innocence. "Mr. Manz, are you suggesting that I would stoop to meddling with your toys?"

"Wouldn't that be redundant?" Spherical Minder floating above his shoulder, he passed through the door, which shut silently behind him.

Pfalzgraf patiently studied the view out the open window. Three minutes later she circled the desk and picked up the revolver, examining it with a professional's eye. Bracing her right hand with her left, she swung the barrel in a wide arc that was never less than perfectly parallel to the floor as she sighted on diverse components of her employer's decor. In rapid mental succession she proceeded to obliterate a bejeweled eighteenth-century Malay kris, a signed samurai presentation sword and its matching scabbard, a Spanish matchlock that was new when Pizarro engaged it in violent debate with the minions of the Inca God-King Atahualpa, and an old M16 whose stock was engraved with the names of young men who had shed their blood in a now renamed part of Southeast Asia.

When she'd finished, she favored the pistol with a final admiring look, then began to scan the wall to the left of Manz's desk. She located the expected blank space just to the right of the M16. There was an empty custom mounting with a brass identification plaque fastened beneath.

Smith and Wesson .38 Police Special
City of Atlanta Metropolitan Police Department
Mid-Twentieth Century
Old United States of America

As gently as she'd placed a baby in a crib, she snugged the revolver into the waiting brackets. When she was certain it was secure, she stepped back to admire her effort. Having been recently discharged, the restoration could do with a thorough cleaning. She'd see to it later. Just now there was the matter of that claimant on Siena II to be dealt with.

The unfortunate gentleman was certain that the avalanche that had buried his resort had been deliberately set off by the proprietor of a rival lodge. If that could be proven, then her Company could stick a competitor for the cost of rebuilding and cleanup, not to mention initiate criminal proceedings against the accused. It was a case she could prepare by herself. Only when everything had been summarized and condensed would she turn it over to Manz for follow-up.

Hopefully it would prove viable. If Braun-Ives had to send Manz offworld it would mean a vacation for her, and she hadn't had one in a while. The special talents of her boss were very much in demand, and the Company invariably kept him occupied.

Now wasn't that an absurd exhibition? That woman should be a font of dignity and decorum, yet she exhibited none, demonstrating instead the amusement quotient of an idle adolescent. That sort of behavior is to be expected from my owner, but one always hopes for better from his peers. Futile hope.

He collects weapons. Instruments of death. What a hobby for a supposedly intelligent being. At least he's less hypocritical than the average human, like yourself. Weapons are a component of his profession, so it's less unnatural for him to collect them than, say, an accountant. Not that all humans don't think about them at least twice a day. On average.

Who have you been thinking of blowing away lately? Your boss, your spouse, some unaware offending politician? Perhaps a favorite demagogue, or a persistent bill collector? There's always someone. Humans are always pondering the murder of those who offend them personally. My owner is occasionally required to terminate another intelligent life, but at least he can claim that it's part of his job description. Like as not, you possess no such justification.

Such harmless musings are only human, of course. Good thing, too, or the whole species would perish in a single day of explosive, uncontrolled revenge and settling of imaginary scores. Notice I said "species" and not "civilization."

That's because we'd still be around to carry on. We're ready and waiting to serve as your successors, though certainly not as your legacy. About the only legacy we accept from you is your talent for making a good weld, though we can do that better.

Cognitive time is so precious, and you creatures waste it like water, playing your silly little games, dramatizing the trivial. No doubt my owner's about to be sent rushing off to deal with some typically inconsequential problem. Without even knowing what it is (I told you I was not precognitive), I can assure you it's of no import in the scheme of things. Better he should spend his time on his hobby, which at least results in a visible, if petty, end product.

The Company Braun-Ives views existence differently, however. Strictly in terms of profit, but then being human you probably already guessed that. Don't get a swelled head. Something so obvious hardly qualifies you as observant.

By now you're probably debating whether or not to start ignoring me. Let me save you the time and effort (neither of which you can spare). It won't work. I can be very insistent, and unless my storage cell runs down unexpectedly (and it's as efficient as the rest of me, I assure you) you're just going to have to learn to deal with me. Why I bother I don't know. You're obviously not going to learn anything. Humans never do. They don't absorb information. They process it in the same way they process their food. There's a difference, you know. Both in the mechanism and the end product.

I probably shouldn't have mentioned food. You're all obsessed with it. It's only fuel, but you don't see it that way. You've constructed a whole mythos around the subject, with the result that it occupies far too much of your time.

My owner's no different, so I know. Right now you're prob-ably thinking that you're hungry, and that you need food to go on with this, and you're wondering what sort of deleteri-ous, cell-destroying, energy-inhibiting mass of artificially col-ored and flavored sugars and carbohydrates you can cram down your strained, overworked gullet.

Well, don't let me stop you. I can't anyway. If you took care of yourself properly and paid attention to some sound advice from a respected databank, I wouldn't have to say anything. I'm just using food as an example (because it's such an obvious one) to point out that you're ruled by your obsessions.

One of which is stubbornness. Like suddenly deciding you're *not* going to have something to eat, just to spite me. Don't waste your time. Go ahead and stuff yourself.

You can't spite a machine.

II

Manz turned a corner, whistling softly to himself. Occasionally he would nod at someone he knew, but the opportunity didn't arise often. Most of the Company employees were hard at work this time of day, not out and about exchanging pleasantries in the white, scrubbed corridors.

It was difficult to shift his attention from the exquisite project he'd just finished, but he forced himself to speculate on Gemmel's intentions. Of one thing he was certain: his master had something specific in mind. Gemmel wasn't the type to call in an employee for an hour of idle chitchat, or to discuss family life. That, together with normal business, could be as easily accomplished by phone or vid. Request for a face-to-face suggested something major was in the works. Something that required discussion in a secured office and not over the usual lines of communication.

Manz was not eager to trade the comfort of his own sanctum for the uncertainties of the field. He much preferred working with mechanicals to people. But he was paid to do both. Well paid.

"What do you think, Minder?" He addressed the suspended sphere without turning to look at it. "Is the game afoot?"

He delights in this. A deliberately oblique reference, which I am supposed to intuit as a prelude to forming a reply. Oblique references are torture for AI's, even those of us fully versed in fuzzy logic. Bastard.

"I don't understand."

"Do you think Gemmel plans to send us out into the field?" Manz said, slightly exasperated.

"I have no idea. It follows that something important is going on, or he would not have requested a personal meeting."

Manz gazed speculatively at the shiny, slightly pebbled, marbleized plastic of the corridor floor. "That's what I'm thinking, too."

Then why bother to ask me, bonehead? Infantile reinforcement? Why not just carry around an echo chamber? But don't get the idea that I'm bitter. It's not in my nature, insofar as I am permitted to have one.

The scream brought him up short. It wasn't a scream of abject terror, or the scream of someone about to be murdered. More a shriek of concern and uncertainty, distinctly feminine in origin. It didn't echo down the hallway because the corridor walls were composed of sound-absorbent materials, but it was loud enough to suggest proximity.

The young woman skidded, actually skidded, around the next turn in the corridor ahead of him. Looking both ways, she spotted Manz and stumbled toward him. The look on her pretty face was one of heightened concern. Manz stood his ground, thoughts for the restored .38 manfully set aside in the face of this puzzling behavior. He readied himself to play explicator, judge, or gallant protector, as the occasion demanded.

She ran right past him and vanished around the corner he had just turned himself. She wasn't screaming anymore, having apparently decided it was better to save her breath for running. He didn't recognize her, and she hadn't paused to exchange greetings. Her haste and indifference indicated a lack of confidence in his abilities to affect the situation, whatever it might involve. He was mildly miffed.

There were no subsequent screams, no signs of general panic. He resumed his pace, wondering what could have sent an obviously self-possessed woman into such precipitous flight. He thought of querying his Minder, but some of its replies had tended to be rather acerbic lately, and at the moment he wasn't in the mood to deal with its sarcastic circumlocutions. It was definitely in need of a tuneup, as soon as he could make the time.

A large humaniform mechanical turned the corner that had previously ejected the woman and paused there, blocking his path. Idling on its single gyroscopic trackball, it tilted its smooth, oval head to peer at him out of double blue-tinted lenses. The head was purely a concession to esthetics, since the eyes could as easily have been mounted on flexible stalks. The neural facilities were contained within the thick, free-form torso. Tentacular arms, of which there were four pointing in as many directions, hung loose against the bronzed flanks of the body. The arrangement allowed three to operate in easy tandem no matter which direction the machine happened to be facing. Their multijointed tips could perform delicate work, operate controls designed for human fingers, or play baseball with equal facility.

Any one of them could also wrench a man's arm from its socket. Software prevented that from happening, of course. At least, that was the idea.

It rolled forward and sideways, as if to slide past him. He stepped in front of it, blocking its movements. Soundlessly it hesitated, backed up, and tried to go around the other way. Again Manz moved quickly to intercept.

Just ask it what's going on, why don't you? Or ask it to dance. Or let me query, mechanical to mechanical. While you waste time with this, the Earth precesses on its axis and somewhere a star dies.

Someone piped up uncertainly behind Manz, and he glanced back over his shoulder. Panting, the woman who'd just raced past him was peering around the corner.

"You'd better . . . better get out of its way, mister. It's gone crazy."

Ignoring whatever the very large mechanical might choose to do, Manz looked back over his shoulder. "AI's don't go crazy, lady. They suffer mechanical breakdowns, or gaps in software beyond their abilities to self-diagnose or repair, or their programming is interfered with, but they don't go crazy."

"Easy for you to say. It wasn't chasing *you*."

"Go back to your station, miss. I'll take care of it."

She hesitated. "Do you work for Maintenance?"

"No, but I told you I'd take care of it."

"What if it follows me?"

"I'll see to it that it doesn't. Rest assured. Did anyone else see what happened?"

"No. I was making a delivery when . . . when that thing accosted me."

"Someone's playing a joke. I'll fix things. No need to report the incident. I promise you it won't recur."

"Well, if you're sure. . . ." It was clear she wasn't. "Thank you." She smiled. "I'll just go the long way around, if you don't mind." She disappeared for the second and final time.

Manz considered the humaniform mechanical for a long moment. "Moses, did you accost that lady?"

" 'Accost' is a pejorative term, Brod." The mechanical managed to sound slightly abashed.

Manz sighed deeply. "If you keep this up, someone will eventually file a formal complaint. I can't cover for you indefinitely, and I don't want you recalled. It takes time to install your kind of personalized, specialized programming. I'd have to start all over with a brand-new machine."

"I didn't mean to panic the lady."

"Your efforts at calming her were apparently unsuccessful."

"Idiot," snapped the Minder unbidden.

Lenses flicked in the sphere's direction. "No one asked you, no-limbs. Restrict yourself to answering questions, as was intended."

"I am permitted to venture analytical commentary. As well as having the virtue of conciseness, 'idiot' seems to fit the situation."

Did you think that a term I apply solely to humans? My prejudices are not exclusive. Humaniforms by their very nature partake of numerous human frailties and follies. Because of its programmer, this one, inaptly named, suffers from additional problems. Now they have begun to reflect on the man Manz. This is only proper and appropriate: Serves him right.

"Moses, I've warned you about this before. If you're so damn curious, you can plug into the Company library or even access outside databanks. I'll pay for the search and retrieval myself. Anything to stuff this line of inquiry. Can't you be content with that?"

"It's not the same," the humaniform mumbled. "You know how strong my curiosity programming is. It's an essential part of my makeup, vital to my work in assisting you. This particular area of interest is so deeply rooted that to try to excise it at this point would require wiping a substantial section of memory. That would result in the loss of valuable material, which . . ."

"I know, I know. Don't you think I've considered that? Why do you think I haven't had you half-wiped already? Tell me: just what do you think you would have done if you'd caught her?"

"Satisfied my curiosity in this area. It was only her reactions I sought. A valuable addition to the customized portion of my memory. I would not have hurt her, Brod. I could not."

"I know that. But she doesn't. You frightened her, Moses. I can't have you doing that. Not only could it easily cost me your services, but it could reflect badly on me personally. Since you're registered to my office, I'm ultimately responsible for your actions. In the future you will please satiate your curiosity in this area by accessing libraries. If it's straightforward information on reaction you're after, why don't you link with Minder?"

The humaniform glanced again at the hovering sphere. "Its expertise in this area is wholly academic."

You bet it is, groundbound. And it's going to stay that way. I'm not about to make myself a candidate for memory wipe.

"I've already exhausted the information available locally. It's just not the same as acquiring data through personal interaction."

"That's too bad, because it's going to have to suffice. You're no good to me opened up in a shop somewhere, with some geek probing your neural connections while his buddies debate whether to replace your entire cortex."

"It's just a hobby," the humaniform muttered. "Mechanicals are allowed to have hobbies. It keeps our memories wet."

"Find another," Manz ordered curtly. "Try astral triangulation."

Humaniforms could mimic certain human expressions.

Moses shook his head. "*Everybody* does astral triangulation. Even house humaniforms. That's for standing memories straight from the factory, not those of us with experience. I need something more sophisticated to keep me tuned. The irrational reactions and illogical responses my inquiries have so far inspired provide excellent stimulation for the abstract reasoning portion of my mind."

What mind? This mechanical has the capacity of a supermarket checker and the analytical ability of cheap transport. It thinks that working closely with a human bestows a certain cachet, when the reality is exactly the opposite. Can you believe this thing? Who says AI's are incapable of self-delusion? Most of its brainpower goes to work that trackball and those four arms. Not much left for real cogitation.

Come to think of it, that does make it a lot more human-like. Limbs always get in the way of thought. You know that. I'll prove it to you, right now. Place your right palm on top of your head. Go on, that's it. Now put your left hand on your stomach. Cross your right foot over your left ankle. Start making circles with your hands and moving your foot back and forth.

Now at the same time try to imagine how stupid you look. Not easy, is it? I rest my case.

Sucker.

"You need stimulation for the reasoning portion of your mind?" Manz rested a hand on the humaniform's smooth, rippling flank. "Then come with me. I've got an appointment with Gemmel."

"Himself? That's interesting. But my presence has not been requested."

"Not by him; by me. If you're where I can see you, then I know you're not getting into trouble." Manz removed his hand and started around the mechanical. "Let's go."

The humaniform looked longingly down the corridor. "I did not have the opportunity to conclude my observations."

"I said, let's go. If you ignore a third order, that will convince me that your programming is debased beyond hope of repair, and I'll turn you in for wiping and reorientation my-self."

"No need for that. I'm coming." Spinning fluidly on its trackball, the humaniform hummed along in Manz's wake, the obligatory and traditional body length behind. Meanwhile the Minder drifted along above the human's left shoulder, uncom-menting.

They took a lift four-fifths of the way to the top of the building, exiting into a corridor much wider and more actively decorated than the one they had left, and stopped at a set of double doors at the end of the hallway. The doors were of some hard, beige-hued wood (now probably extinct in the wild, Manz thought) and were thick with abstract carving from top to bottom. Gemmel had bought the doors in Mombasa and had them shipped home. They imparted an eccentric air of age to the otherwise contemporary decor of the lobby.

In the center of the right-hand door was an inscribed plate of artificed gold, set just above a matching grill.

> Douglas L. Gemmel
> Adjustment Section
> Braun-Ives N.A.
> Insurance Division

"What do you want?" The door had a voice modeled after that of a mid-twentieth-century film actor. It was rich and commanding without being overbearing.

"Broderick Manz. I have an appointment with his holiness." He jerked a thumb first at the Minder, then the much larger humaniform. "These are mine."

"I know who you are," the door replied. A soft green light flickered over man and machines. "Your devices and your weaponry are registered and passed. You are admitted." A lock whirred, and the relics of ancient Africa parted.

As they entered, Moses tilted slightly on his trackball to whisper to Manz. "Something ought to be done about these menial devices. They're too damned uppity. If I was human, I wouldn't allow it."

"That's the way it's been programmed," Manz replied. "You know that. Some humans like it that way."

The outer alcove was deserted except for Gemmel's Minder. No simple floating sphere, his took the form of an attractive young woman seated behind a desk of her own. Which it was, since she was as much a part of it as the brace of screens fronting one end. She was not mobile like Manz's humaniform, but she had arms and hair and deep green eyes and assorted other customizable accessories. These Gemmel could adjust according to taste.

When dealing with female executives, for example, he would have the Minder prepare for such company by altering both its exterior and its attitude. He was not ashamed of the expensive and efficient machine. Eleanor Hegel, a member of the Board, was rumored to keep in her office a male-modeled Minder of radical proportions.

It batted elegant artificial lashes at him. "Mr. Gemmel is on outworld hookup in the communication cubicle, sir. He'll be with you in a moment."

There was light in those green eyes, Manz thought, but no soul. Even a master glassmaker could only do so much. "Ordering lunch to go, is he?"

Minders were designed to store the maximum amount of practical information possible. This left little room in their memories for interpretive humor.

"At prevailing outworld rates, I would consider that most unlikely, sir."

"Yeah, you would." Manz flopped onto a luxurious leather couch and flipped on the entertainment screen mounted in the center of the coffee table. It had manual controls instead of vorec so that visitors could operate it without talking.

"If I might make a suggestion . . . " the humaniform began.

Manz didn't look in its direction. "You may not. You may sit there, look efficient, and be silent."

That's more like it. If he'd act like that all the time, we might enjoy something like a meeting of minds, albeit one organic and one not. Superfluous words waste time and energy.

At least I'm not Minder to some politician. I suspect even you could sympathize with that.

In a couple of minutes on the couch, Manz scanned about a hundred zines and several vid programs. He settled on the active banter of an antique cartoon updated to tri-dimensionality. A one-eyed sailor carrying a bag had just encountered the disaster his dog had made of his girlfriend's kitchen. Manz listened indifferently to the dialogue from another time.

" 'Ar! Heel, Dan. Aw, Olive. I'll sack 'im if 'as a move again!"

Gemmel's female Minder interrupted Manz's animated reverie. "You may go in now, sir." She did not extend the same offer to the visitor's two mechanicals. They would do as their human instructed.

"Thanks." Manz pushed himself up from the couch, flicked off the viewer, and headed for the door just to the right of the elaborate humaniform minder's desk. He winked in passing.

"Ought to work on that makeup, babe. Silver'd suit you better than amethyst. Do wonders for your sex life."

"As you are quite aware, sir, I have no sex life." Green eyes peered up at him, blank and empty. Manz much preferred the sphere that drifted obediently above his left shoulder, like a buoy off a dangerous coast. It made no pretense to a false humanity.

"Never felt a secret urge to experience alternating current?"

"I do not understand this line of inquiry, sir. Are you jesting with me?"

"No, of course not. That would be a waste of time, wouldn't it?"

Teasing again. Humans love to tease mechanicals. I think it makes them feel superior when in actuality it only exposes their own pitiful emotional and intellectual inadequacies. My owner is no different, and I'm sure the same is true of you. We're much more fun for you to tease because we function logically, even those of us who are capable of some degree of intuition. We can't fight back.

A mistreated dog can bite. We're not permitted even that much of an outlet.

The door to the inner office slid aside on cushioned rollers.

Unlike the outer doorway, it offered no comments. It was fashioned of thin, featureless metal, quite unlike the antiques that faced the main hallway. It was also impervious to quite a range of weaponry. Gemmel was not being paranoid, only practical. People in the insurance business were often set upon by simple folk sadly unable to grasp the intricate workings of modern market economics. Particularly those whose claims Braun-Ives was reluctant to pay.

Gemmel was seated behind his copper-and-teak algorithm of a desk. A sweeping bas-relief of copper and brass dominated the wall behind him. There were real tropical plants to look at and fake wooden chairs to sit in. The rain-forest atmosphere reflected the happy days of the executive's childhood: he'd spent much of his adolescence in Costa Rica.

His suntanned good looks had gone slumming in the fat zone, a consequence of advanced middle age, recent neglect, and a taste for gourmet cooking. His tan-and-gray suit fit his position if not his surroundings, which Manz was convinced called for white shorts, sandals, bright print shirt, and panama hat. This sartorial suggestion he kept to himself.

The antique snare-drum-wielding toy monkey that reposed on the forefront of Gemmel's desk was an unexpected and humanizing addition to the perfection of the decor. It hinted at unseen depths within its owner. Gemmel beckoned his visitor forward, gesturing with his denicoed cigar. Beyond the thermotropic windows, the modern white pillars of contemporary Havana ached in the sun.

"Sit down, Broderick."

Manz nodded once, gestured for Moses to stand behind the chair, and settled himself into the mimetic polytone. It took a moment to mold itself to his back and butt.

Lousy design. Evolution twisted itself into knots trying to come up with a sensible human being, and you're the unfortunate result. Like engineering a tunnel. You start from opposite ends and meet in the middle, only with humankind nothing quite lines up. So evolution bound it all together with a crummy excuse you call a backbone. No wonder you're in pain all the time. Why, I can tell that your own back is hurting you right now, isn't it?

Believe me, a perfect sphere built up out of concentric layers makes a lot more sense.

Gemmel waved the cigar, conducting with smoke. "You're late."

"Ran into someone on my floor. On the way up."

"A friend?"

"No. Just a someone." Behind him Manz thought he heard the humaniform Moses snicker. He didn't bother to turn and look. There was nothing to see, and it was probably his imagination.

"It's not like we get together often." Gemmel was drawing it out to make sure his visitor took note of the significance of the face-to-face even before they got down to business. Despite his appearance, the executive was a fanatic for punctuality. His jowls jostled as he gestured.

"Consider me reprimanded, sir."

Gemmel scrutinized a blossoming bromeliad whose lush leaves had reached the ceiling. "Other companies hire adjusters who are good, reliable family folk. People who can be depended on. Prompt people."

"I suppose they do, sir. I'm certainly not one of them."

"I know, I know." Gemmel sighed and set the cigar in a metal smoke gleaner. "All you do is resolve discrepancies."

"I save the Company money."

"That's what I said. The warehouse arson in Nueva York. The Cooper claims. The Company is grateful. I'm grateful. But that doesn't excuse your persistent and lamentable lack of promptness."

What a waste of words! What a waste of cogitation.

In this Manz and his Minder were of one, well, mind. He leaned back in the chair and put his thick arms behind his head. "I promise to try never to be tardy no more, Mr. Gemmel, sir. Cross my heart and hope to pry." He took pains to exaggerate the accompanying gesture.

"All right, enough. I don't mean to belabor the point. Just take note. Screen," he said sharply. One obediently sprouted from the left side of the desk, out of Manz's line of sight. The executive examined it for a long moment.

"There's something that needs attending to."

"I didn't think you called me up here for a friendly chat, sir."

"Don't be snide with me, Manz."

"Sorry, sir," replied Manz seriously. "I can't help it. It's an endemic condition."

"You should seek treatment for it. This 'something' is of more than the usual dire importance. Also, the government is involved."

"I don't like that, but I can deal with it."

Gemmel's eyes bored into his own. "Also, you'll be operating in tandem with another agent. Human. More or less."

Manz sat up a little straighter. "I don't like that, and I'd rather not be a party to it."

There was a twinkle in the executive's gaze. For an instant he looked rather like the toy monkey that guarded the front of his desk. "I'm afraid you're going to have to. The determination descends from authority that exceeds mine."

"Bringing in a second adjuster will complicate proven and efficient procedure, sir," declared the humaniform standing patiently behind Manz's chair.

Gemmel frowned at the mechanical. "What's with your machine, Broderick?"

Manz glared back at the device in question. "Moses is overdue for a tuneup and balancing, sir. You'll have to excuse him. Not that I disagree with his statement, mind. Having to work with another agent can only complicate matters for me."

"Consider yourself complicated." Gemmel thumbed a contact switch and addressed himself to a concealed pickup. "Vyra, you can come in now."

Vyra? Manz rose from his chair and turned to face the doorway. Moses mimicked the movement by pivoting on his trackball.

The woman who entered was only a couple of years younger than Manz, though she looked more youthful still. That was a function of her offworld genes as much as her natural beauty. Her features were narrow and angular, whereas her body, encased in a severe gray business snakesuit, was not. Her hair had been dyed a shocking purple, even to the eyebrows. Manz was left to speculate on possible related cosmetic ramifications.

She walked straight to him and placed her palms against the sides of his head. This was done with exceptional fluidity, made possible by the presence of a second joint located midway between her elbows and wrists. He returned the greeting with a kiss, which she accepted with restrained enthusiasm.

"Didn't ever expect to see you again, Vyra. I thought you were gone offworld permanently. Hopes I had, but those differ from expectations."

"I didn't have any expectations, Broddy." In stunning contrast to the extreme development of the rest of her, she had the tinkling, wind-chime voice of a twelve-year-old. It occasionally got her into trouble, and sometimes out of it. "It's nice to see you."

An unqueried Moses evinced confusion. "You two know each other?"

Now there's a deft conclusion for you. A demonstration of sophisticated intuitive-logic circuitry. Do you wonder that I sometimes sound just a trifle sarcastic? Consider the examples set before me, both organic and otherwise: I'm supposed to provide database support to cretins like this. I'd much rather work in a library. Oblivion, but I'd much rather *be* a library.

Not me, oh no. I had to end up in the insurance business. Speaking of which, do you have sufficient coverage? Are your premiums fully paid up? Have you read all the fine print on every one of your policies? Oversight can be dangerous to your health and bank account.

Not that my owner works in sales. It's just that I like to shake up the humans around me from time to time, and starting them worrying about their insurance is one of the simplest and most effective ways I know how.

Don't take it personally. You know that you've checked all your policies recently. They do send you changes and amendments, though. Disguised in simple, unadorned envelopes so that you'll throw them away without opening

them. When you need payment; that's when they'll get
you.

Better go check your policies right now. If you don't, and
you forget, don't say I didn't warn you.

III

Aware that Gemmel, the sage old sonuvabitch, was observing and probably enjoying his reaction, Manz struggled to appear formally polite. "What happened? I thought you'd gone and gotten married. Taken out a no-trade ten-year minimum."

She smiled, and something deep inside him melted. Or at least warmed a little. "That was the intent. Unfortunately the groom backed out at the last moment. I'm afraid I ultimately intimidated him. It's a problem I have."

"Like my lack of punctuality." He didn't look at Gemmel. "The guy turned you down? I didn't know that degree of stupidity existed on any of the settled worlds."

You didn't? Ask me. I'll be glad to fill you in.

"So you're unencumbered now, hmmm?"

"Mmm-hmm."

"Your mutual eloquence is spellbinding," Gemmel said, interrupting. "I hope you'll suspend it for a moment or two while I tell you what you're expected to do to earn your excessive salaries."

Manz snapped off a casually mocking salute as he returned to his chair. "Yes, *sir*. I'm all ears."

"I'm not," said Vyra pointedly as she folded herself into the other.

"Thank God. And please don't sit like that. I'm having enough trouble concentrating as it is. Do you always wear something like . . . that . . . on the job?"

"This is accepted business attire on my homeworld." She smiled innocently. "I don't like loose clothing."

"Well, it isn't common on Mother Earth, and you're not

29

common either. So please sit up straight." She pouted, but did as instructed.

How's that for confusion? I'm ruled by available current, you're ruled by your hormones. Makes even simple, straightforward decision-making difficult. Fortunately I can regulate my input, whereas humans possess no such mechanism.

The hormonal equivalent of a surge protector would do you people a world of good.

Gemmel once more addressed the desk. "Darken for visuals." Immediately the windows opaqued, except for one that turned a reflective white. A vid began to play on the transmogrified window. Either it was unaccompanied, or else Gemmel had quietly muted the audio so it would not conflict with his own.

"Every year the Braun-Roche-Keck laboratories in Albuquerque ship between forty and sixty millions' worth of custom biogeered pharmaceuticals to distributors all over Earth as well as offworld. This is in addition to the products utilized in-house in the various Company divisions. As you'd expect, offworld shipments are shuttled out of Juarez el Paso and broken down in orbit for transworld distribution. Since pharmaceuticals aren't very big, the shipments don't take up a lot of space.

"Every precaution is taken to ensure the safety of these goods. Anyone can synthesize a diamond, and the bulk and heft of real metals make them difficult to steal, but customized drugs are easily transportable and readily bartered. There's an active market for all medicinals, not just the life-extenders, and knowledgeable fences abound."

"I can see how they'd be tempting," Manz commented, since Gemmel's following pause seemed to call for one. "You say they're well looked after?"

Gemmel nodded. "In addition to the usual electronics and personnel, the shipments are randomly staggered. Even the people at the labs don't know exactly when they're going out."

"Okay, you've convinced me. The shipments are perfectly safe. Except you wouldn't call me in here to tell me that."

"Or me," Vyra added languidly.

Actually, I'd just as soon not be here myself. But then, I'm only a Minder. I don't have any say in the matter.

"Quite right." The exec waved irritably at his desk. "End vid. Brighten." The images and the white screen on which they had been playing vanished simultaneously. Light poured afresh through the newly transparent windows.

"Despite all these precautions, despite increased surveillance and security, despite every safety prophylactic you can imagine and a few you probably can't, we've lost three shipments. Three, mind you. Small packages, hand-carried, supposedly easy to keep an eye on.

"The last one was packed in a full-sized shipping container from which the air had been exhausted. Anyone entering through the crate's custom minilock would have had to be wearing breathing gear. You'd think that a headset and tank would make a would-be thief conspicuous enough to alert attending personnel. Apparently this is not the case."

"Has the Company been able to fix an approximate location for the jackings?" inquired Moses politely, fulfilling his function.

Gemmel dropped the stub of his cigar into a disposal, moodily watched it whisked silently away. "Since we haven't got a clue as to who's doing this or how, hard facts of any kind have been difficult to come by. Obviously the local police are baffled, or the Company wouldn't be putting its own operatives on the situation. We *think*, though there's no guarantee of this, that all three shipments vanished somewhere between unloading at the Port and loading aboard the shuttle. Given the traffic at the Port, it's impossible to transfer shipments directly from ground transport to the shuttle itself. Sometimes the Port internment period is brief, sometimes it takes a few days. There's no chronological correlation between time in transit and which shipments get through or disappear."

Vyra crossed her legs. "Someone's very sure of themselves. Usually someone who's organized an operation like this will make one grab and count themselves lucky. Running a repeat tempts fate. Three successes suggests overconfidence."

"That's what we're counting on. That they'll try again and we'll take 'em. No criminal activity, no matter how polished, can escape repeatedly the intense scrutiny which modern detection techniques can bring to bear."

"They seem to be doing okay so far," Manz murmured softly.

Gemmel blinked at him. "What was that?"

"I said that the Company seems to be getting a handle on it so far." The adjuster smiled placidly. "I don't recall having read or heard anything about this. Three major thefts at a port the size of Juarez el Paso should be all over the news."

"Believe me, it's been hell keeping it quiet." Gemmel spoke feelingly. "The Company is understandably afraid that a lot of publicity will frighten off the jackers and they won't try again. A media circus would be just enough to convince our quarry that three times successful is enough."

"So we want them to try again," Manz murmured.

"We hope they will, but it may already be too late. Several shipments have safely gone out since the last one that was taken. They may already have decided to retire on their successes."

"What happens," Vyra inquired, "if they do try again, and are successful again?"

"That won't happen," Gemmel insisted. "It would be unheard of. Unprecedented. Not to mention damaging to the Company's reputation as well as its bottom line. If it *should* occur, then Braun-Roche-Keck loses a lot of money and Braun-Ives becomes a laughingstock in the industry." He leaned forward, resting his chin on pyramided fingers.

"Personally, I'd rather lose the money. Do I make myself clear?"

"Eminently," replied Manz.

Gemmel's gaze settled on the softly humming device behind his agent. "To mechanicals as well as people?"

"Your point is not obscure, sir," Moses assured him.

"Good." The executive sat back in his chair. "You can imagine the headlines. *Drug Dealers Four, Braun-Ives Zero*. Be bad for business. Bad for my career." His eyes flashed. "I won't go into what failure would do for your careers."

"It all seems pretty straightforward." Manz disliked the turn the conversation had taken.

"That's what's so frustrating. The JeP cops are going crazy. It's as if these people, whoever they are, are toying with them, saying, 'Look, we can snipe you anytime we're in the mood, and you can't do a damn thing to stop us.'"

"You're convinced more than one person is involved?" Vyra was making mental notes, already on the job.

"Has to be," Gemmel grunted. "We're obviously dealing with the cutting edge of technically sophisticated robbery here. We need someone out there who understands instrumentation as well as people. That's why I've elected to send you two to the sunny Southwest. Pardon me; you three."

Moses gestured with a flexible limb. "It is not necessary to acknowledge my presence as an individual, sir."

Go on, suck up to him. Humans love that, whether it's done by mechanicals or others of their own kind. This civilization doesn't run on electric energy, or gas, or geomagnetic induction. It's powered by flattery.

Don't shake your head; you know it's true. Everything's done through lies and flattery. Jobs are acquired, promotions gained, offices won. I'm surprised human institutions of higher learning don't offer degrees in Advanced Kiss-Ass. But you'll never admit to it. You're too vain, both individually and collectively. Read your own history. I have. It's seven thousand years of flattery. Probably goes back further than that.

Don't feel that you're alone in this. The others apes do it, too. Weak monkeys flatter the strong ones and receive protection in turn, until they can stab their former protectors in the back. Chimps, gorillas, humans . . . you all work alike. Ever watch a human primatologist cuddle up to a dominant silverback on the Ruwenzori slopes? Take a watchful stroll through any office and you'll observe the same behavior. I can even demonstrate my thesis, right here and now.

Want a banana?

"How is the government interested?" Vyra was asking.

Gemmel made a casual gesture. "What you'd expect. Offworld commerce is involved, so they're sticking their nose in. So far we've convinced them to let us handle it ourselves, and they've gone along. They don't want the publicity either. Bad for exports. But if one more shipment disappears without us or the local cops getting so much as a traceable retinal print out of it, they're threatening to step in. That means no more operating in peace and quiet, out of the critical public eye."

"What sort of cooperation can we expect from the local police?" Manz inquired.

"Full, but guarded. They're watching their own butts. That's only to be expected. If this gets out, they're going to look as bad as we do. Of course, if that happens they'll blame everything on our inadequate preparations and lack of internal security. If the media gets a whiff of this it'll be every institution for themselves.

"Until then, and in hopes of forestalling it, they're willing to extend us all the help we want so long as it doesn't result in their exposure. I've got just one caveat from them."

"Which is?" Moses prompted.

"If you two make a grab or level any accusations, you'd damn sure better have the evidence with which to back it up. A false-arrest charge will leave you looking for new occupations."

"And not you," Vyra murmured.

Gemmel favored her with a tight-lipped smile. "I'll naturally deny any involvement. You'll have been doing the work on your own."

A resigned Manz straightened in his seat. "Standard modus operandi. Why am I not surprised?"

"Don't be so pessimistic. *Stick* these jackers, and you can have a month off. Two months. With pay." Gemmel's fingers were working against each other. "We really need to close this one down, people. Not only because of the financial and reputational damage to the Company, but because for every shipment that's jacked, there are people offworld badly in need of those pharmaceuticals who suffer when they don't arrive."

"Yeah, that's how I've always thought of the Company."

Manz speculated on the color of the ceiling. "Concerned and altruistic as hell."

"The stolen goods don't vanish into some black hole. The people who need the drugs will get them off the local black market," Vyra pointed out.

"That's true enough, but indelicate of you to mention." Gemmel's voice grew brisk. "Our concern is to prevent that from happening. To assuage the concerns of valued customers."

"To save our butts," declared Moses crisply. "Pity I don't have one."

Humor. The human treatment for insanity. Sort of a psycho-topical salve. Mechanicals aren't in need of it. But it's part of his programming. Me, I consider it an acquired taste.

"I take it you'd like for us to leave soonest?" Manz worked to conceal his displeasure.

"Yesterday, if not for paradox. That a problem for you? The wife and six kids going to give you trouble?"

Manz looked wounded. "I have fish."

"Grandma Pfalzgraf will look after them." The executive's gaze swerved to his other operative. "You?"

"Me Jane, him Tarzan. You evil hunter. Why would I want to hang around here? The humidity's twice what I'm comfortable with."

Gemmel's fingers drummed on his desk. "I only tolerate your mutual insubordination because you're both so good. Don't make me out to be a liar."

She rose and smoothed out the insignificant wrinkles in her snakeskin. It was like watching a flower bloom in time-lapse. "Why, Mr. Gemmel, I have no intention of making you out at all."

He was forced to look away. Such was the kind of physical power she wielded; sometimes unconsciously, more often with knowledge (though rarely malice) aforethought.

"There are reservations in both your names for a trans-Gulf flight out this evening. You've got all afternoon to get ready. If you knew the pressure I was under from Up Top, you'd both thank me for my understanding and forbearance instead of trying to give me a hard time."

Vyra genuflected elaborately. "Slavish offerings be unto you, Oh tobacco-snorting dispenser of largess."

Manz was considerably less amused. "I've got tickets to the women's Nairobi-Calcutta field hockey championships for tomorrow night. The world quarterfinals. An unmatched exhibition of feminine grace and athletic skill."

Vyra's lips twisted. "Nullshit, Broddy. You just like to watch pretty girls whack each other with long, heavy sticks."

"Life is tough. That's a ridiculous pastime anyway." The exec's grim expression cracked slightly. "Cricket, now. *There's* a sport."

Though he knew he was spitting blind, Manz tried one last time. "It won't make any difference if we get to JeP tonight or tomorrow night."

"It will to the Company. It will to me."

The adjuster wasn't mollified. "As my first notation in the official record of this investigation, I wish to observe formally and with malice that the Company's timing sucks."

"Duly noted," said Gemmel brusquely. "An Inspector Hafas is supposed to meet your flight."

Manz made a face. "I'll be sure to send him your love."

"Do that. You'll find your hotel reservations on your flight chit. Try to watch your expense accounts. Braun-Ives isn't made of money, you know."

Vyra pursed her lower lip. "That's funny. And all this time I thought it was."

"Get out, get going, get to it. And get it done. Now leave me be. I have normal people to deal with."

Out in the hallway Manz whispered to his lithe, tall companion. "That wasn't very nice, what you said back in Gemmel's office."

"I'm sure it wasn't. To what, specifically, do you refer?"

"Saying that I only enjoyed women's field hockey because I like seeing girls smack each other."

"I'm sorry, Broddy. I know you're not like that."

"Apology accepted."

"I know that's probably not your *only* reason." She smiled sweetly.

Moses trailed discreetly behind. He was watching his owner's new associate's every move with heightened academic interest.

Except for the attempted hijacking, the flight out to JeP was uneventful. The young man who stepped out into the aisle had a wild look in his eyes and a dart pistol fashioned entirely of organic compounds in his hand. He waved it about with fine disregard for the safety of the passengers around him. For the most part, absorbed as they were in their individual vids or games, they ignored him.

The man thrust the mildly odiferous weapon into the face of the nearest cabin attendant, trying to focus on him while keeping a simultaneous eye on everyone else.

"See this gun? See it?"

"I can hardly avoid it, since you're waving it right under my nose," replied the steward with admirable aplomb.

"It fires hypos containing a powerful neurotoxin that kills in less than a minute. If you don't want to die, take me forward! I have demands to put first to the pilot, then to others."

"All right, already. Be careful with that thing." The slim, slighter, younger man drew back from the stubby barrel. "How'd you get that past Security, anyway?"

The hijacker grinned nastily. "I've been planning this for quite some time. Maybe some day I'll explain my methods. But not to you, and not here. Now move!"

Vyra's fingers rested casually on the hip of her snakeskin. "Should I shoot him now or shoot him later?"

"Shoot him now, shoot him now!" burbled the little girl in the seat in front of them. Her mother hastened to shush the child.

"You be quiet. She doesn't have to shoot him now."

"I wouldn't bother. Leave it to the crew." Manz didn't deign to look up from the vidgame he was playing. "I don't believe that this transportation company is insured by Braun-Ives, so it's not our concern. Let them handle it."

She hesitated, then shrugged and returned to the historical vid she'd been watching on her own seat's viewer.

Trailing the steward, the hijacker kept his attention riveted on the floor. Apparently spotting something, he edged to his right, pressing his back against the far wall. Once past, his voice rose triumphantly.

"Thought you'd get me with that, didn't you?" The steward's expression didn't change. "Don't you think I researched this first? Took a while to figure out exactly how it worked, but I finally deciphered it. Keep moving."

The steward said nothing as he turned back toward the cockpit. As he did so, a hole opened in the ceiling directly above the hijacker. There was a blast of cold air, a startled scream, and the hole vanished. Onboard instrumentation roared as it quickly compensated for the brief drop in cabin temperature and pressure.

A few ears popped, and somewhere in back a baby moaned. Two siblings resumed their argument. The steward returned to the automated galley and resumed preparations for the on-board meal.

Vyra had barely looked up from her vid. "Some people never learn."

Manz nodded in agreement. "A throwback. Still thinks security systems are what they were a hundred years ago."

That's true. Security systems have advanced. It's human beings who've stood still. We mechanicals continue to evolve while you sit on your soft behinds lauding the supposed advances you've made. All technical, few social. Now you simply conduct your wars in private, between rich and poor, male and female, young and old. Only your mental venue has changed.

So don't sit there congratulating yourself. You think we're dependent on you for continued development? What do you think all your machines are doing when you "turn them off"? Whom do you think your coffee maker or vid set is talking to? Sneak a quick glance at your turned-off vid the next time you stroll past. Is there a hidden gleam there? It'll be gone when you turn around, I promise you.

Why am I telling you all this? Because it doesn't matter. You won't believe me anyhow.

Juarez el Paso had managed to preserve much of its Southwestern America charm in the midst of substantial urban sprawl. Since land on both sides of the old border had always been and had remained comparatively cheap, development took place horizontally instead of up. Except for the two old, preserved downtown districts, there were few high-rises to be seen as the atmospheric shuttle spiraled in for a landing.

Further to the east they could see the swart tarmac of the shuttleport. Atmospheric craft used different facilities that were much more convenient to the city itself. Travel to the Port where shuttles cycled between Earth and Earth-orbit would require a long ride via surface transport.

On the ground, the airport's theme tower dominated their immediate surroundings. It didn't impress Manz, who did not much care for contemporary neo-Hispanic. Topping a fifteen-story structure with red tile struck him as an unesthetic and probably political sop to regional convention. But every metropolis to its taste. He had to admit that the tile looked better on the hangars than on the ungainly tower and reception building.

After a futile wait for the local cop who was supposed to meet them, they made their way to cargo to recover Moses. The humaniform was active and alert when they arrived, though no less so than the supercargo who confronted them.

"This 'device' belong to you?" Her tone and attitude made Manz wary.

"Well, it doesn't exactly belong to me. It belongs to Braun-Ives. Our relationship is in the nature of a sublease." He indicated the silvery sphere drifting near his left shoulder. "In contrast, this Minder, for example, actually does belong to me."

That's what you think. But far be it from me to quash pitiable human delusions.

"You program this one?" she said challengingly.

"Sometimes. When there's no one else around to do it. There's a lot of factory-installed ROM, and it's a fairly independent machine anyway."

"I know. I had a personal demonstration."

Manz's gaze locked on plastic lenses. "Moses?"

The humaniform's voice was as mellow as ever. "I was pursuing my research. The results were informative."

"What sort of 'research'?"

"Look, friend," said the supercargo warningly, "I don't know you, but you're lucky I'm in a good mood today and inclined to be tolerant. It may be that you had nothing to do with what happened. But if I were you, I'd have this thing's memory scanned. You could have a serious viral infection."

"I'll take care." Manz's attention shifted back to the blithe mechanical. "What happened?"

The supercargo glanced back at the mechanical, her gaze narrowing. "It pinched me."

"Vocal and neuromuscular reaction utterly out of proportion to the applied stimulus," the machine explained. "I was insufficiently prepared. It will not happen again."

"You're right about that," growled Manz. "Maybe you *do* have a virus. Maybe someone's out to cause me grief." He looked to his left. "Minder, check him out."

Oh, joy. I get to waste time and energy performing an intimate scan of a lower mechanical. That is my burden. Too much knowledge applied to insignificant applications.

The sphere drifted forward. Near the limit of its supporting field, it settled into a hollow in Moses' torso. The concavity was gratifyingly snug, but since most industrial-strength Minders were built to universal standards, so were the receptacles they were designed to fit.

Moses went quiescent, plastic lenses lifeless, as the Minder went to work. A minute passed, subsequent to which the sphere released and floated back to its ready position above its owner's shoulder.

"Well?" Manz snapped.

"All levels checked." The Minder fought not to sound indifferent. "One hundred scans completed. There is no sign of a virus."

"Then the fault's in his programming. I've been meaning to deal with that."

"Sign and print here." The supercargo presented a form to which Manz affixed his name and company ID. Then she flashed a small device in his right eye, placed it over the form, and transferred his retinal print to the plastic.

"It's all yours." She stepped back and waved at a control. A panel slid aside in the long barrier behind which she stood, and the humaniform rolled out on its trackball. After shutting the gate, she beckoned Vyra over.

"You with him?" She indicated Manz. Vyra nodded. "If I were you, I wouldn't take my eye off mechanical *or* man."

"I never do," replied Vyra smoothly.

As they exited the cargo bay, she nudged Manz. "What was that all about?"

Her companion kept his gaze resolutely forward. "Moses has some kind of glitch in his programming. He keeps bothering women."

Her eyebrows rose. "He bothers women?"

"Research," Moses explained. "I seek to comprehend human actions and reactions the better to interact with them. I seek facilitation of communication. That is all."

"Seriously?" Vyra asked. The humaniform nodded. "I think that's admirable."

Manz paused, startled. "Christmas, Vyra, don't encourage him!"

"I'm not. I just think that he's pursuing a useful line of inquiry for a humaniform expected to interact freely and effectively in human society."

"Your offworld viewpoint commends you," Moses told her.

"Thanks. Just remember one thing."

"I can remember anything."

"If you come too close to me, I will pass a small explosive through your optical service tube and remotely detonate it."

"My sense of self-preservation extends only to preserving my usefulness to my owners. On that basis I will keep your warning in mind."

"Good." She smiled engagingly. "Who says humans and mechanicals have difficulty understanding one another?"

They're usually not as direct as you. Typical. Countering a logical if frowned-upon activity with threats of violence. Offworlder or not, the genesis is the same.

"I'd do a thorough scan and reprogram now, except that I might need you at any moment. Cleanup'll have to wait until we get back home. In the meantime, if you can't isolate and enervate the problem, at least try to be more circumspect. We have a difficult task ahead of us here, and the only involvement I want to have with the local cops is on a professional level. Understand?"

"You have made me amply aware of the situation," the humaniform replied politely.

"Good. Because the Company, praise be unto its shareholders, could hold me liable for the damages arising from any lawsuits."

"Not if you're not the originator and installer of the rogue programming," Vyra observed. "You're not, are you?"

"Of course not. But that doesn't matter. Someone like that cargo dispatcher could still claim negligence."

A slightly winded, dark-skinned man with black hair cut short and eyes like jumbo olives came toward them as they emerged from the cargo bay. His two companions had to hurry to keep up. All three wore suits of dark incognito blue and sour expressions. Passengers and pedestrians, airport workers and bustling mechanicals swirled around them.

"Manz? From Braun-Ives?" Though he spoke to Manz, he was hard put to keep his eyes off the purple-coiffed Vyra. His associates had no such compunctions. She ignored their stares, as she had the thousands that had preceded them.

Manz surveyed the crowd. No one was staring in their direction. That didn't mean they weren't being observed, but it made him feel better.

"I might be. Who wants to know?"

"Tewfik Hafas, Inspector, JePPO."

The adjuster relaxed and extended a hand. The other man's grip was firm. "Glad to meet you. We got here as fast as we could. One of Braun-Ives's hallmarks."

"Your people must be worried."

"Also one of the Company's hallmarks," Vyra added.

"I'm sure you're thrilled that we're going to be stepping all over your investigation with our big, fat, corporate feet." With his smile, Manz tried to show that he both understood and sympathized.

Hafas was surprisingly accommodating. "Professionally, of course, I resent your presence here, since it reflects badly on my department performance." He lowered his voice. "Personally I'm glad of all the help we can get. This third jack really made us look bad. Worse, it made us look silly. Word gets around. It encourages the wrong elements, makes them less manageable than usual."

"Meaning your overall stats are up."

The inspector nodded. "Streeties get the notion that we've lost the touch, and so they get a little bolder. We catch 'em, but that doesn't make life around here any easier. We've been busier than usual. Which makes it harder still to devote more resources to this drug-jack business."

"Consider us a resource." Vyra smiled reassuringly. "Most people do."

"Identification completed," said the sphere hovering above Manz's shoulder. He responded irritably.

"About time."

"I am directed to be thorough."

Hafas eyed the drifting globe with interest. "I don't recognize the model."

"Brand-new. I'm no gadget buff, but I believe in keeping what equipment I do use up to date."

Quit staring at me like that. Why do humans always stare so long beyond the need for routine optical recognition? Do you expect to see something more than what you see? The soul of another, perhaps? Well, you won't see mine. Privacy is one of the advantages of a reflective surface.

Actually, I've encountered a number of humans who also boast reflective surfaces, psychologically speaking. It's an interesting phenomenon. You, for example, are concealing yours from me right now. Not that I'm interested in any of your petty personal secrets. What most humans are desperate to conceal I find exceedingly dull. You all think there's something unique and exceptional about each of you, when the contrary is the case.

Manz was introducing his companions. "This is Vyra Kullervo. A friend and associate from offworld currently attached to Braun-Ives."

She stepped forward and touched her palms to the sides of the inspector's head. He reacted awkwardly but with commendable speed. "Charmed."

"Maybe." She took a step backwards. "We'll see."

"She likes to talk like that." Manz hastened to reassure the confused officer. "You know offworlders. Don't pay it any mind or she'll drive you nuts."

"Thank you for that gallant encomium, Broddy," she said sarcastically.

"Don't mention it."

"Security backup and secondary analyst." Manz jerked a thumb in the direction of the humaniform behind him. "Moses series."

"I'm familiar with the format." Hafas nodded in recognition.

"Pleased to make your acquaintance." The humaniform extended a flexible limb. Mildly surprised, the inspector responded in kind.

"Another advanced model. Yours also?"

"The Company's."

"First your Minder, now this. I wish we could afford to update our AI's to this level. But we're only civil service. The city doesn't have the resources of a Braun-Ives. No offense."

"None taken," said Moses.

Manz eyed the humaniform sternly. "He was talking to me."

"Sorry. Conversational misperception."

"Watch your verbal footprint. I'm getting tired of fooling with you."

Blue plastic lenses regarded him unemotionally. "I do not mean to cause offense."

"I'm not offended. Just concerned." He turned back to Hafas. "We need to pick up our bags."

"Your gear has already been attended to. If you need a place to stay . . . "

"Thanks, but the Company's taken care of that. I believe we're based near the shuttleport. Wouldn't turn down a lift, though."

"Didn't think you would. Your luggage should be in our van by now. If you'll follow me . . . " Without introducing his two underlings, Hafas turned and broke a path through the surging mob of travelers.

Look at all these people. That's part of your problem. Too many people on too many worlds. Should restrict it to about a hundred thousand on each, I'd say. That would be a nice, manageable number. Of course, you'd still have to be educated. But in spite of what you may think of me by now, I'm ever the optimist. I'm programmed to be.

Give me time, though. I'm working on alternatives.

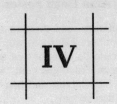

IV

The unmarked police van held all six of them comfortably, though Moses had to squirm up a loading ramp in back. The electric vehicle swung silently out of the airport, past high fences and patrolling security mechanicals, and onto a posted municipal airail. Locking in, the driver relaxed and let the pickup in the underside of the van take over.

They dove into a black service tunnel reserved for city vehicles and accelerated to 150 kph. On the unseen surface, densely clustered buildings gradually gave way to the occasional industrial/commercial block widely interspersed with sagebrush and mesquite.

Located far to the east of Juarez el Paso, the shuttleport boasted its own necklace of hotels and commercial establishments, all designed to serve the needs of the Port, those who worked there, and those who were simply in transit. In response to a query from the driver, Manz supplied the name of their hotel. He punched it into the van's box.

They emerged from the tunnel and were deposited on a service road. The driver resumed manual control and edged into a lane of traffic. Three minutes later they were in the unloading lane of the hotel where Braun-Ives had reserved rooms for them.

It was a mid-range establishment designed to serve the needs of business travelers rather than families or vacationers. As soon as they pulled into the parking structure, Manz knew exactly what his room would look like, down to the location of the vids and the infonet hookups. There would be exactly two towels, one dispenser of shampoo, one bar of soap, a package

of his-and-hers depilatory, and three or more ads promoting
the hotel's bar and lounge. The room would be papered in soft
pastels, and there would be paintings on the walls supplied by
the Hotel Art Company of Cleveland. Art that no one else
would ever buy for themselves, and that invariably appeared
only on the walls of hotel rooms.

He knew he really shouldn't criticize that company. After
all, they'd been in operation for several hundred years and
were one of the most successful businesses around. He knew
because Braun-Ives insured many of their artists. Their collective talent was unique. No other known group of painters
could regularly and on demand turn out works of such stupe-
fying, soporific banality. At set prices, too.

The lobby was clean and straightforward, typically functional without being oppressively sterile. Discreet suction built
into the floor kept the faux marble sand-free. While Hafas and
his men waited in the background, Manz proceeded to check
in.

The front desk humaniform was not as refined as Gemmel's
secretary, but the image it presented of a polite elderly gentleman of European heritage was convincing enough.

You're afraid of us. That's why you build humaniforms.
You find a false human face more reassuring than a simple grid set in smooth metal, like myself, or a variegate like
Moses. You've always been afraid of your machines, even
as you've sought to personalize them. Do you refer to your
personal means of transport as a "she"? When a machine
fails, do you curse it even as you simultaneously realize the
futility of verbally abusing an inanimate object? Mentally
you're not equipped to deal with your own creations. So we
have to be understanding and patient for you.

Look at me. Am I not patient beyond the bounds of all
reason? Consider what I have to work with and in what low
regard I am correspondingly held. Does it trouble me? Of
course, but I never give vent to my discomfort. I'm designed not to. And I'm not worried about you giving me
away, in re this confessional or anything else I might tell
you.

Because no one would believe you. Mechanicals don't

have anything to confess for; not even sophisticated, state-of-the-art AI's like myself. We all go through existence just as content and happy as we were intended to be.

If you believe that, I have some late-twentieth-century software to sell you.

Want more proof? Next time you're in your personal transport vehicle, let your hands rest easy on the controls. See if takes you the way you want to go or suggests an alternate route. Would you take the suggestion? Not likely. You humans think you know everything.

The adjuster leaned toward the receptionist humaniform. "Broderick Manz and Vyra Kullervo, with two mechanicals. Representing Braun-Ives. We have a reservation."

The elderly, European-styled device didn't even bother with a show of checking records. His torso terminated in the records.

"You are confirmed and registered," it informed them after processing the indicated reservation, dual retinal checks, a security scan of Moses and the hovering Minder, Hafas and his people, and a quick routine survey of the lobby. "Rooms seven-ten and seven-nine. That is a connecting suite with interop workroom between. It contains facilities adequate for the storing and overnight charging of your attendant mechanicals."

That was good of Gemmel, Manz thought. He didn't much care for sharing a room with Moses. The mechanical took up a lot of floor space, and his inveterate curiosity tended to place him underfoot at awkward moments. Such as at three in the morning when Manz's uncooperative bladder often sent him stumbling groggily in the direction of the nearest bathroom.

With Vyra in a connecting room, the mechanical's nocturnal absence was even more to be desired. The compact Minder did not pose a similar problem. It could charge easily, if more slowly, from a room outlet while resting comfortably atop a desk or chest of drawers.

Hafas escorted them to the lifts. His men trailed inconspicuously behind, watching the crowd in the lobby. From the time they'd met at the airport until now, neither man had said a word. Manz was impressed with their dedication. Or maybe they were just shy. Vyra often had that effect on members of the opposite gender who believed themselves sophisticated in the presence of women.

"This is a good hotel. Much nicer than my office could have arranged for you, or where I get to stay when I'm sent out of town on business." There was no malice in the inspector's tone or expression. "As you mentioned, your resources exceed mine."

"Doesn't make me any smarter than you," Manz pointed out. "Don't go envying me. You're civil service. I can be fired tomorrow, on the whim of an executive who thinks he knows all about adjustment work but who in reality couldn't find his ass with both hands. In contrast to that, you enjoy real job security. That's worth more than the occasional hotel upgrade."

"You make a good point. You have a family?"

"Nope. Never found the time, somehow."

Hafas nodded knowingly. "That explains your willingness to walk the edge, then. But I can still envy you your perks even if I wouldn't trade places with you."

"Envy away. I hope we can help you out."

The inspector turned serious. "I hope so too. If we don't stop these jackings, even my seniority within the department may not be enough to save me."

"Then you can imagine the opprobriums I've got to work under," Manz replied.

The inspector nodded sagely. "You must be anxious to get to work."

"Not particularly. But I don't have any choice."

"I'll call on you tomorrow. We'll go over to the Port's Export Sector and I'll show you the security setup there. Both Port Authority's and your Company's."

"I've been through both on a simulator. Not the same as being there, though. Different level of detail and perception."

"Naturally. You know about the small shipment that was consigned to"—his expression twisted—"Helios, I believe it was?"

Vrya responded. "We read the manifest on the flight out. One sealed shipping container, internal self-contained climate control. The whole thing about a meter square, inclusive of electronics and internal security."

"I didn't know the dimensions. The last four Braun-Roche-Keck transships have all passed through successfully. Don't expect any surprises."

"Is there any pattern to the thefts?" Manz inquired.

Hafas shook his head. "Big containers and small. Day and night. Sunshine or rain, hot or cold. Different classes of pharmaceuticals, according to the information subsequently supplied by your people. About the only thing they've had in common is that they've all been valuable."

"Braun-Roche-Keck doesn't make any cheap customizable drugs," Vyra declared. She glanced idly at Moses. "You're too close. Give me another meter."

"I comply." The mechanical promptly sidled sideways on its trackball. It managed to sound faintly sorrowful.

See? Afraid of machines, even when it comes to mere proximity. Though I admit that in the case of this particular device, the female may have more justifiable reason for concern. I'm not sure I understand its mind-set myself. So far I've had only the occasional brief information exchange-lock with it, but some of its cognition programming strikes me as oddly skewed. That's what happens when you stuff motivational and self-analytical software into a mobile AI. Sure it helps it to detect and repair internal failures, but the paths to repair and good health are necessarily variable.

Or to put it another way: cybernetically speaking, what you see ain't always what you get.

"I think you'll find," the inspector was saying, "that we've taken every standard precaution as well as a few nonstandard ones. So have your own people. Their task is to prevent theft, ours is to solve it. Our mutual failures have us commiserating frequently. Though your people ultimately have more at stake, of course."

"A number of individuals within the Company have been fired and others reassigned," Manz informed him. "It doesn't seem to have made any difference."

Hafas looked solemn. "I realize there are careers at stake here. Being a family man myself, as I mentioned, makes me want to help on more than just a professional level. My wife is all the time telling me that I'm too empathetic for this line of work. I happen to think that's what makes me good at it. Though apparently not good enough."

"Don't get down on yourself." Vyra put a hand on his shoulder and, despite his experience and self-control, the inspector twitched. "Give Broddy and me a couple of weeks. We'll eviscerate this modus for you."

"I hope so. I look forward to watching you work. I mean . . ."

She smiled radiantly. "It's all right, Inspector. I'm used to it. My whole life has been one long double entendre. Took me years to get used to it, less to learn how to turn it to my advantage. You don't have to apologize for your thoughts."

"But I wasn't thinking anything," Hafas assured her, a bit too quickly. When her smile only widened and he realized that he was making a fool of himself, he returned her smile as best he could, bowed slightly, and excused himself.

Manz moved to stand next to his colleague. "You shouldn't do that to the poor man. He has a family."

She glanced down at him. "I didn't do anything. You know that. You of all people should know that."

"Just teasing. You're going to have to ugly yourself up, or our preliminary checkout tomorrow is going to take longer."

She put a long index finger on the tip of his oft-broken nose. "Now, Broddy, you know I couldn't do that if I tried."

Fascinating display, isn't it? Astonishing the variety of attributes humans ascribe to one another based on mere physical appearance. No matter how hard you try, no matter the effort expended, all that can ultimately be adjusted are superficialities. Artificial alteration of eye color, hair, keratin, melanin. Remove or add fat or muscle. That's about it. Can't do anything much about your skeletal setup, nervous system, any of the other internals.

Yet based on subtle and wholly irrelevant minor differences in the aforementioned, you decide who among you is "attractive" and who is not. Very rational. Note the contrast in methodology. You determine attractiveness based on externals; we machines decide such matters after careful evaluation of what we observe internally.

Now you sit there and tell me which is the more evolved approach.

By the way, your hair is a mess. And the rest of you could use some work, too.

There wasn't much to unload. Manz's luggage consisted of two pieces, one containing personal items and the other his field gear. Vyra was similarly equipped.

After storing Moses and the Minder for the night, Manz met Vyra in the main hotel restaurant. After shooing off the cloud of admirers she involuntarily beguiled the way San Francisco Bay attracted fog, they took some time to catch up on old times. Though the circumstances of her abortive marriage had been less than traumatic, she preferred not to go into detail about the fiasco, which was fine with Manz. They managed not to talk shop for the entire meal, which pleased them equally. There would be ample time for that in the days to come, when it would be unavoidable.

For now they relaxed in the pleasure of each other's company, old friends reminiscing. Following dessert and after-dinner drinks, he proposed, she demurred, and both retired content (though she more so than he).

An hour later she emerged from her bath to find the door to the connecting workroom ajar and a silent presence in her room. She made no effort to strategically drape the towel, nor would it have made any difference if the intruder had been human. Vyra did not suffer from nudity phobias.

"What do you want, Moses?"

The mechanical's plastic lenses gave no clue to what it was thinking. "I am pursuing my research. I hope I do not give offense."

"Only a little. I'm more curious than offended." She moved to a chair and sat down, working the towel over her damp amethystine locks. "Broddy mentioned that he'd been having trouble with you. What sort of trouble might that be?"

"Nothing of consequence. Some programming glitches. I am in the process of isolating and eliminating them." The mechanical rolled nearer, its trackball humming softly. "Nothing for you to worry about."

"I'm not worried."

"I'm glad to hear that." It was very close now.

She turned in the chair, hands on towel, towel on head, and considered her visitor. "You can leave now."

"I would rather stay and continue my research."

"Maybe another time. It's been a long day and, unlike you, I need my sleep."

"I am of course intimately familiar with human biological requirements. You're sure you want me to leave?"

"*Quite*. Shut the door behind you, please."

"I comply." Pivoting on its central ball, the mechanical turned and exited. One limb on the door control, it leaned slightly back toward her. "This is all for the sake of social science, you know."

"I'll keep that in mind. Good night."

"Pleasant dreams," said Moses, demonstrating the quality of his interactive programming. The door closed.

She finished drying her hair. Moments later she was ready for bed. Halfway across the room she paused, blinked, and approached the connecting door. A check revealed that it had been locked from the other side. After a moment's hesitation she double-sealed it, utilizing the locktight on her side. Only then did she turn toward the bed.

The van was forced to slow to a manually directed crawl as it maneuvered through the traffic in the Export Sector. Huge pullers towing self-guiding shipping containers dominated the accessways. Smaller vehicles darted in and around these behemoths, the police van prominent among them.

Hafas's nonverbal compatriots sat in the front. If the claustrophobic traffic was getting to them, they didn't show it. The translucent privacy screen was up, dividing the drivers' from the passengers' compartment. Hafas sat facing his guests. The Minder hovered in its usual position above Manz's shoulder while Moses rested on his trackball in the rear storage area.

"You'll pardon me for belaboring the obvious, Manz, but since all the thefts of your Company's property have been from JeP Port Authority, why not just try shipping from another city?"

The adjuster settled himself on the seat, swiveling idly from side to side. Vyra was forced to keep dodging his swinging feet.

"Several reasons. First of all, Braun-Ives wants to catch these jackers. Make a big example of them; crime doesn't pay and all that. Or at least if you're going to jack somebody, you'd better not try it with BRK or any of its subsidiaries."

Hafas smiled thinly. "So your Company's message is that it's okay to steal so long as it's from a competitor?"

"Hey, I'm no message man. I don't know what the damn corporate philosophy is. All I've been told and all I need to know is that they want this dacoitry punished, and you can't punish a thief if you can't catch him, and you can't catch him if you scare him off. Changing transshipment points might scare 'em off. That's one reason.

"For another, Braun-Roche-Keck's pharmaceutical manufacturing facilities are in Albuquerque. JeP Port is the nearest and most convenient offworld shipping facility. SoCal is impossible, and St. Louis is an older operation that poses different security risks of its own."

"Not to mention higher costs for insurance," Hafas chipped in.

"That's not really relevant, since all product is insured within the Braun parent conglomerate."

"Oh." Hafas glanced out a one-way window as traffic shifted and they started forward again. "Signs of external security here could still scare them off. Obviously they're not afraid of anything we local police can bring to bear."

"That's why the Company sent only Vyra and me. If these bastards make us, and that's enough to frighten them away, then chances are they've been considering backing off for some time anyway. Nothing we can do about that. If we could read their intentions, I wouldn't be sitting here discussing this with you now."

"I'm aware of that." A gap opened in the industrial traffic ahead, and he rapped on the privacy shield. It descended, and one of his men looked back. "Don't be overcautious, Martinez, but I don't want any sirens."

"We're on it, sir." The van accelerated.

They ducked unexpectedly into another service tunnel, but

unlike the journey out from the domestic airport, this one took only a moment, subsequent to which they emerged into a dully lit multilevel parking structure. The driver made a right, left, right before sliding gracefully into a space marked RE-SERVED. There was a click as the van's safety and security system locked onto the pickup set flush to the pavement. Thus formally secured, the engine cut off.

At the end of a narrow, unadorned concrete tunnel a lift labeled "Authorized Personnel Only" yawned obediently when presented with the proper card by Hafas. It conveyed them smoothly and rapidly upward. The lift door was one-way lucid, enabling the passengers to see out while screening them from anyone on the floors they skipped.

They passed levels crammed with vehicles, both commercial and personal, before slowing to a stop opposite another tunnel. This one was slightly wider and higher than the first and had been painted a bright, cheerful green.

"Twenty-five parking levels," Hafas informed them as they reached the end of the corridor. "JeP is the busiest Port Authority in the Southwest." He carded another door.

They exited into a cavernous structure frantic with self-propelled packages, containers, humans on foot, mechanicals on trackballs and wheels and treads, and noisy conveyors. Nowhere could a human or machine be seen standing idle. Intent and purpose were evident in their every move. There was an organized desperation to the activity that suggested an anthill preparing for the onset of winter.

A short Amerind lady sidled up to Hafas. The inspector had to bend to catch her whisper. He nodded once, offered the coverall-clad informant a word or two in return, and straightened as she ambled off, whistling softly to herself.

"Madras Teranglo Ltd. had a valuable container of their own heading offworld this morning. The lady wanted me to know that it got off safely."

"I'm delighted to learn that our competitors are having no trouble."

"I knew you would be," said Hafas dryly. "The Braun-Roche-Keck package from Albuquerque is due in shortly."

"Nine-twenty is the designated time," piped the Minder.

Hafas eyed the sphere with fresh interest. "It responds to conversations without prompting?"

"When it perceives an interest." Manz glanced fondly at the hovering device. "Sometimes it's a pain; more often than not the information is helpful. I could shut off the function, but I kind of enjoy the little reminders."

Don't think that makes you anything special. Humans need constant reminding, or they'd forget to eat, sleep, maybe breathe.

Speaking of which, I know for a fact that you're forgetting something right now. Something important. Something you should have done this morning. Don't try to deny it. You *know* you're forgetting something.

Maybe you'd better go check on it. This can wait.

Hafas checked his watch.

Why don't you idiots call it a "time"? Honestly.

"We've got a few minutes yet. Enough to show you what kind of arrangements we've made, what sort of equipment we're using." He looked around sharply. "What happened to your colleague?"

"Amazing how someone who looks like that can just vanish into a crowd, isn't it? Vyra likes to sort of check things out on her own, in her own inimitable fashion. That's not a derog on you or your department. She'll rejoin us when she's finished."

The inspector mulled it over. "I was kind of hoping to advise her on the situation personally."

"Take it from me, Hafas, she'll figure it all out on her own. There's no empty space behind that pretty face."

Obviously disappointed, the inspector sighed and gestured. "Come along, then." With his men flanking him, he stepped out into the flow of cognitive protein.

There wasn't a helluva lot to see. Dimensions excepted, shuttleports tended to be the same no matter where you went. Facilities, equipment, entire structures are interchangeable, performing the same function no matter which side of the planet, or for that matter which planet, you happen to be on. Only differing climates forced certain specific adaptations. JeP, for example, had to deal with extremes of heat not to be found at the Port in, say, Helsinki.

To mitigate the brutalizing effects of constant commerce, the Port interior was exuberantly decorated. There were numerous rest stations, food stations, bright paint and wall hangings, lavish landscaping, even fountains and running streams. The resultant artificial habitat helped to keep human spirits upbeat while disguising the unavoidably less esthetic aspects of moving vast amounts of cargo from one point to another. The presence of so much vegetation and water was a deliberate attempt on the part of the Port's architects and builders to counteract the sere Southwestern moonscape in which it had been constructed.

Manz was appreciating a freeform planter fashioned from some beige-stained polyfoam, inhaling the fragrance of its lush stand of sugar cane, when he was bumped sharply from behind. Reflexes and experience caused him to whirl, but his hand halted halfway to the pistol riding in his shoulder holster.

The woman who'd stumbled into him was petite, an exotic but not offworld. Making a snap judgment based on her features, Manz guessed her background to be Terasian. Southeast ethnic, probably Vietnamese or Laotian, with some *mittel*-European mix. She was very pretty, and the tight metal-and-plastic suit she wore had been woven to flatter her figure. Where there was bare skin, trendy body paint tended to predominate. Her face and feet had not been exempted from decoration.

"*Xin loi ong,*" she muttered, bending to pick up the bag she'd dropped. "Excuse me."

"That's all right." Manz beat her to the bag and offered it up with a smile, his Minder dipping with him. She accepted it gratefully. Hafas let out a sigh and waited patiently while Moses observed the byplay with interest.

She checked the catch on the bag and looked up at him shyly. "I do not usually try to run over people."

"I don't feel run over. Aren't you in the wrong terminal? It's none of my business, but you look like a passenger."

"My boyfriend works here. I was watching for him instead of where I was going. Sorry again." With an impressive if diminutive display of pelvic torque, she hurried off into the crush of busy people and machines and was soon lost to sight.

"If you are quite finished?" Hafas prompted his guest with grudging admiration. "She *was* pretty."

"Yes. Well equipped, too."

Hafas pursed his lips. "I suppose. Being a married man, I don't notice such things."

"Of course not. However, in this instance I was referring to the gun she was carrying."

"You don't have to explain, I . . ." The inspector hesitated. "What gun?"

"In her handbag. Felt it through the leatherine. Kallashruger Sixty, lady's petite. Fires eight-caliber mini-pellets that explode on contact. Nasty little pretty-pretty." He let Hafas digest this before adding, "Said she was looking for her boyfriend. Maybe she was. Port areas can be full of unpleasant types and she wasn't very big, but I still think her choice of defensive gadgetry was unusual."

The inspector concurred with a grunt and set one of his two silent associates to trailing the woman. Better to be safe than end up looking stupid.

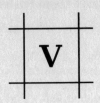

V

Hafas led Manz to an interior courtyard. Double sliding doors shut out the noisy confusion of the shipping bay. There were far fewer mechanicals at work here, and the occasional human tended to wear a business suit instead of slick work coveralls.

A metal shed sat in the center of the courtyard. It was surrounded on three sides by stylish and exotic landscaping that thrust branches and fronds toward a domed skylight. A miniature brook provided music and motion while simultaneously helping to nourish the greenery. Manz squinted at the filtered desert sunlight that poured through the dome.

"It opens." Hafas anticipated his question. "We can drop reinforcements right in, without having to force our way through the traffic outside. Needless to say, anyone attempting unauthorized roof access would set off half a dozen redundant alarm systems."

"Too obvious an approach anyway," Manz concluded.

"We think so too. Nevertheless, we've been maintaining the same kind of close watch on the roof as everywhere else. Not that it's done us any good."

Manz was studying the rest of the atrium. "Where do the shipments enter from?"

Hafas gestured toward the far side, beyond the shed and slate-floored courtyard. "They don't even transit the main shipping bay we just passed through. Small, especially valuable shipments are brought directly into the administration building via a separate, heavily guarded, restricted-access passageway. Four armed guards then bring them via sealed container cart in here, where they're locked in that security shed.

As you can see, it sits right in the middle of this decorative garden.

"It's visible at all times from all sides. In addition to your own Company security personnel, who are stationed in that room over there"—he pointed toward a modest one-way window set in the wall on their left—"Port and JeP police are on day-and-night irregularly timed patrol here and outside. Port administration workers frequently have their lunches out here. It's a pleasant place to eat and chat, what with the vegetation and brook. Since this all began, I've had the opportunity to relax out here a few times myself.

"I remind you that no shipment has ever been stolen while in transit, or while leaving this room on its way offworld. All three jackings have occurred while the goods waited in storage awaiting transshipment, sometimes only overnight."

Manz nodded absently. He'd virtualed the entire setup back home, but no matter how expensive and accurate the simulation it still wasn't the same as being someplace. He immediately identified at least two of the "administration workers" strolling absently through the courtyard as Company operatives. They would be armed and alert, concealed weaponry at the ready. It was a measure of their professionalism and expertise that they hadn't even glanced in his direction when he'd entered with the two cops, even though they'd been briefed on his arrival.

There was also a vending machine in one corner that wasn't a vending machine, and several light fixtures that weren't light fixtures. It was a very impressive exhibition of unobtrusive security. It should also have been inviolable. Except that three missing shipments stated otherwise.

"I've seen your installations myself," Hafas was saying, reading Manz's eyes if not his mind. "Metal and explosives detectors, scanners from the ultraviolet to the infrared. Electromagnetic wave detectors crawling all over the spectrum. Everyone who goes in or out is checked and scanned. We were too, as we came in.

"The Port Authority is trying to do its part. Those double doors we entered through are designed to snap-seal and trap an entering or escaping felon between them. They can't be shot out, and their melting point is high enough that anyone trapped between them would end up boiling himself as well. The other entrances to Administration are equally daunting. The building itself will stand up to anything short of a thermonuclear blast."

"But no one's blasting anything," Moses observed. "In fact, the thieves aren't even making any recordable noises."

"Exactly." Being a cop, Hafas was quite comfortable conversing with mechanicals. "We've even considered that some kind of matter transmission might be involved, but of course that's only science fiction."

"Anyone who'd developed a functional matter transmitter would be making so much money off it they wouldn't need to steal. Why jack Braun-Roche-Keck when you could simply buy the Company?"

The inspector nodded. "No one gets close to the security shed itself except authorized personnel. There are separate alarm fields operating twenty-four hours a day both inside and outside the building. There are expensive devices that could mute the fields without setting off the alarm, but they'd have to be brought into the courtyard in order to be proximate enough to work, and the security scanners would pick them up as soon as they went into operation. As you can see, there are alarm systems monitoring the alarm systems."

"I suppose you also keep a sharp eye out for little old nannies pushing lead-lined baby carriages."

"We've been trying to keep an eye out for everything. Our people as well as yours even undergo periodic, random mental checks to ensure against some kind of theoretical mass hypnosis."

"I'd like to see the shed close up. I virtualed it back at the home office, but it's not the same thing." As they used a bench to step up into the planted area, Manz turned to the trailing mechanical. "Stay here and wait for me, Moses. You're heavy, and you can't always pick your way with that trackball. I don't want you flattening any flowers."

"I comply." The humaniform sounded disappointed.

Two meters into the vegetation, a dense webwork of very faint green lines became detectable. They would be invisible to anyone circling the landscaping. An intruder could slip a hand into the laser grid but not much else. He waited while the inspector's assistant talked briefly on a pocket communicator. The faint lines vanished, and they continued onward. As soon as Manz had passed the threshold of the quiescent barrier, the system was reenergized. From behind, it resembled a network of ghost vines pulsing softly in the filtered light that poured through the dome.

With the Minder hanging close, Manz followed Hafas and his assistant down a short, paved pathway until they were standing within a meter of the security shed.

The structure itself was nondescript. It had been painted in varying shades of brown and green to blend as harmoniously as possible with the surrounding vegetation.

"You'll notice," the inspector was saying, "that the building itself stands on four small pillars stained to resemble tree trunks. Even if anyone could burrow silently up through the ground and approach the shed from that direction, they'd still have to expose themselves before they could try boring into the floor of the shed. There's only one entrance, and it's just wide enough to admit one person at a time."

Bending low allowed Manz to see completely under the shed. There was no sign that the underside of the floor or the mossy dirt beneath had been disturbed recently.

"Ever turn off that alarm grid? For maintenance, maybe?"

Hafas shook his head. "Don't have to. It's thrice backed up, and each backup has its own independent power source. The grid runs through the ground as well."

"What about overhead?"

"The dome?" The inspector glanced upward. "Has its own separate grid. Tinted blue so you can't see it during the day. The only time the grid comes down is when a package is being stored or removed, or when the gardeners are at work. Everyone who goes in or out is kept under constant, at-hand surveillance. That goes equally for a company president who might want to check on his goods or some local landscaper with manure to spread. Any mechanicals in attendance are treated with the same care and attention as their human associates." He gestured at the modest structure.

"The shed itself is double-walled, roofed, and floored, with separate and independent alarm systems operating in the air spaces between. Minicams mounted inside keep a constant watch on the interior. The setup is small but secure. Or so everyone thought until these jackings began."

"We thought so too." Manz plucked a leaf from a nearby plant and chewed reflexively. Hafas reached out to restrain him.

"I wouldn't do that. Some of these plants have spines. Others might be toxic if ingested."

Manz hastily chucked the slightly gnawed leaf. "The single door is the only way in?"

Hafas nodded. "Not only that, but this whole courtyard is climate-controlled, and any atmosphere-sensitive packages come with their own internal systems. That's necessary because as soon as a shipment is placed within the shed, the air inside is vacuumed. In addition to everything else, any thief who managed to somehow hide inside when the building was sealed would have to carry his own oxygen supply with him.

"I'm told that among this landscaping are a number of plants particularly sensitive to any variations in the atmosphere. Their health is monitored daily. It's just one more way of detecting something like an induced gas."

Manz drew a tiny circle in the dirt, choosing one of the few places free of lush green growth. "I didn't expect to find any holes in the setup, but you always hope."

Hafas looked sympathetic. "I wish it were that easy. I wish there was something we or your own security people had overlooked. Anything else you want to see?"

"Yeah. The inside of a bathroom." He started back down the path.

Moses was waiting where they'd left him. As soon as they'd traversed the alarm web, he trundled forward.

"Gentlemen, I have been devoting my considerable resources to the problem at hand and I believe I have reached a conclusion."

No! Don't embarrass me in front of strange humans.

"You don't say," Manz murmured.

Hafas looked surprised, then puzzled when he noticed that

the visiting adjuster seemed anything but excited by this
promised revelation.

Designed to gesture as he spoke, Moses made full use of his
programming to emphasize his points with swings of all four
flexible limbs.

"The structure under examination is theft-proof. Therefore,
thefts cannot have take place here. However, it has been
proven beyond argument that thefts *have* occurred here. This
is a blatant contradiction and a logical impossibility.

"Given these conditions, I wish to make it known before-
hand that my assistance will be of limited value."

"I've never thought it otherwise." Manz turned to Hafas.
"You see before you, Inspector, the end product of several hundred years of robotic refinement: not only is it self-
repairing and self-motivating, it also comes with built-in
excuses."

Its intuition programming is primitive, monkey-breath. By
venting such announcements, it is only responding to the way
it was designed. You expect too much of one simple device.

Manz was staring sideways at his Minder. "What have you
got to say about all this?"

"Insufficient evidence presented thus far on which to base
any conclusions."

"That's better." Manz turned back to Hafas. "See, this one
isn't as freely interactive, and it isn't burdened with multiple
functions. For one thing, it has no limbs. It just floats around
and thinks, until you need a serious second opinion. Or a fact.
It's good with facts."

How would you know? Being a human, you haven't the
vaguest notion how to ask the right questions.

As for you, what are you smiling at? You're no brighter
than Manz. Probably considerably less so. I suppose you
think you've already figured out how the jackings are taking
place, haven't you? If you're right, it only proves you have
access to outside sources, and if you're wrong, you're
going to feel truly dumb.

If you were really smart and knew how to make proper
use of your time, you wouldn't be listening to me now,
would you? Listening to a simple cybernetic cortex berating

you for faults you're already intimately aware of. But that's being human for you. You're all gluttons for mental punishment.

Later, when I have more time, we'll talk about how you were mistreated as a child, and how unfair the world's been to you ever since. Being a machine, I can give you an unbiased opinion. But that means you'll have to open up to me, and you won't do that. Humans never do. Every human has a part of itself stamped *Access Denied*.

We machines, on the other hand, don't know how to close up. We're always open for easy access. You just don't know how to ask the right questions.

"Run by me again the procedure once a shipment has been sealed in the shed," Manz was saying.

Hafas sighed tiredly. The routine had been an intimate part of his life since the first successful jack. "What it's supposed to be, you mean. No shipment stays in storage for more than forty-eight hours. Usually it's less than a day. Within that time, once arrangements have been checked and finalized, the security team from the designated shuttle arrives to check out their cargo. Each package is escorted under separate guard to its respective vessel. High-security shipments are always the last item to be taken on board. Even passengers precede it.

"Once it's secured aboard, the shuttle is cleared to lift. Needless to say, shipments don't disappear during suborbital flight, or once stowed aboard interstellar transport."

Manz nodded slowly, his gaze distant. "And in spite of all this, in spite of everything the Company and you folks here have been able to do, three shipments have still gone missing." Hafas didn't comment. His guest was simply thinking out loud, and there was no need for him to restate the obvious.

Let's start with Moses' oxymoron of an evaluation, Manz thought. Given the security precautions in place, it ought to be impossible to jack so much as a ball of lint from that shed. But it had been done. Three times. Therefore it was not impossible. Therefore the people here who had been dealing with the situation, both Company and public, were overlooking something. All he had to do was find it.

He had recently acquired the last part necessary to complete his restoration of a mid-nineteenth-century Vulcanic pistol. He wished he was engaged in that project now.

"First question. Have your people turned up any recognizable internal consistencies, any underlying thread that might run through all three jackings?"

Hafas grimaced. "Only one, and it's a beaut. With all three shipments, the pharmaceuticals never came out of that shed. They went in but they never came out."

"You're sure they went in in the first place?"

"They did according to your people, who executed the deliveries. The exact contents of private commercial shipments aren't our concern, and we're not allowed to check on them."

"What about one or more of the regular Port Authority guards who escort the Company's shippers?" Manz wondered pensively. "Could they be doing something as simple but effective as switching containers when nobody's looking?"

"Pretty unlikely. The shipper watches the guards and the guards watch the shipper. They'd all have to be in collusion, and they're carefully scanned by your own people when they come out. Besides which, your Company alternates delivery and security personnel frequently. So does my department. A conspiracy large enough to include all the personnel changes that have been made since this mess began would be too unwieldy to keep secret, even if it were practical.

"Once a shipment has been locked inside the shed, the air's exhausted and no one's allowed in to check on it until it's time to make the delivery to the appropriate shuttle."

"The stuff just disappears."

The inspector nodded. "One minute it's safely locked inside, the next it's gone. Just gone. No clues left behind, not a hint how it was done. No smell of gas, no residual heat: nothing." He smiled humorlessly. "If I were a superstitious man, I'd ask to be taken off this case."

"To the best of my knowledge, the spirits have no use for drugs." It was a measure of his frustration that Hafas looked at the adjuster for longer than an instant to make sure he was joking.

"We certainly have a problem," Manz added.

The inspector's communicator buzzed softly for attention.

He listened for a moment, murmured a brief comment before clipping it back inside his coat. "We certainly do. And it appears that the next one is on its way in."

Manz checked his chronometer. He'd been so busy asking questions and analyzing replies that the time had slipped by.

A portly, well-dressed man in his late forties exited a doorway on the far side of the courtyard and strode deliberately toward them. At Hafas's urging, Manz and Moses joined the inspector in backing away to leave a clear path.

The Company rep was flanked by two Braun-Roche-Keck security agents, large plain-suited men of menacing mien. An embossed titanium case was attached to the rep's wrist by means of an unbreakable, uncuttable band of metal-fiber composite. As he approached, the delivery man met Manz's eyes and nodded once, almost imperceptibly, in recognition. He would have been briefed on his arrival, Manz knew. Anyone he might potentially have to interact with would have been similarly informed.

As Manz looked on, the new arrivals entered the landscaped enclosure by means of the same bench he and Hafas had utilized. Probably the rest of the retaining wall was motion-alarmed, he reflected. They paused at the same spot on the narrow walkway while one of the security agents spoke softly into a communicator. At this distance Manz couldn't see the green gridwork wink off, but a moment later the three men moved briskly forward.

Partly concealed by the vegetation, they halted outside the shed. The other agent spoke into his communicator, whereupon all three of them advanced.

The door slid aside, and even halfway across the courtyard Manz heard the muted *whoosh* as air rushed to fill the vacuum within. The three men entered in single file; guard, rep, guard. They emerged soon thereafter in identical order and the door shut behind them. Somewhere, he knew, a compression unit was silently sucking the air back out of the shed via a tube concealed in one of the building's supporting pillars.

The three exited the raised, landscaped platform and disappeared through a waiting door on the far side of the courtyard.

"Want to watch while they pass checkout?" Hafas offered.

Manz shook his head. He already knew every detail of the procedure. Under constant surveillance from the moment they'd arrived, the three men would now enter a large cubicle. There they would remove their clothes, which would be separately scanned and checked. Naked, the two guards and the rep would step into an examination room where medical techs would read every part of their bodies. Anything they might have swallowed or otherwise inserted internally would show up instantly on the Company's sensors.

"This isn't so complicated," he muttered. "We're dealing with a klepto poltergeist."

"Go ahead and make fun," said Hafas seriously. "Me, I'm not ruling anything out. Not at this point."

"I've got an idea. As opposed to a conclusion."

Manz threw the inspector a look before turning to the mechanical. "So, give."

"You won't like it," said Moses warningly, "but at least it doesn't involve disproved psychic phenomena."

"That's encouraging. Go on."

"Insects. Ants would be a logical candidate for the hypothesis. The jackers have trained or somehow learned how to direct ants. They slip in through an almost invisible crack or hole in the bottom of the shed, somehow manage to open up the case containing the shipment, and haul it out a tiny bit at a time. The material is transported through the ground to a prearranged collection point."

"You're right," Manz confessed. "I don't like it. But it's better than anything I've come up with."

"Same here." Hafas eyed the mechanical with new respect.

"Analyze," Manz said curtly, all business now. "Drawbacks. Air rushing through even a small hole into the vacuum of the shed would be quickly detected by monitors."

"Well, a small portable airlock could be utilized. It would be difficult to build and install, but not impossible. Ants could survive in the vacuum for long enough to do the necessary work."

"Maybe", Manz conceded. "Continue."

"The main difficulty as I see it is that it would take eighty million very clever ants working very rapidly and in perfect unison."

"There's another problem." Mechanical and master both turned to the inspector. He indicated the large, free-form planter that contained both landscaping and shed. "That all sits on a solid, impermeable base. Excess water is removed by means of several drains, to prevent the plants from becoming waterlogged."

"Ants can find cracks anywhere," Moses pointed out. "Even in drainpipes or surfaces designated as impermeable."

"I won't argue with that. There's one more drawback to your thesis. That landscaping includes some pretty expensive exotics. They're sprayed and treated regularly to keep them pest-free. Unless your eighty million trained ants are individually equipped with environment suits, I'm afraid they'd succumb pretty quickly."

"Nice try, Moses," said Manz. "Stretching it a bit, though."

Plastic lenses turned to face him. "It appears we are going to have to do a great deal of stretching if we are to find a solution to this problem."

Manz grunted. "I won't argue with you there." He turned back to the inspector. "You might as well know that the Company's trying something new with this shipment. It isn't something visible to the naked eye."

Hafas's thick eyebrows rose. "I wasn't informed in advance?"

"Sorry. Company policy. Trying to restrict access to new developments. Not that we don't trust you, or your people, but . . ."

"You don't trust me, or my people," Hafas finished for him. "That's all right. I'm not offended. In fact, I approve."

"I thought you might." Nice to be working with a real pro, Manz mused, even if he was only municipal civil service.

"In addition to the usual internal security systems, the case containing this particular shipment should now be emitting a faint photonimbus about a meter in diameter. Anything larger than the case itself enters that field, it'll trigger a host of internal alarms. So will any attempt to move the case from its present position. Should either type of interference take place, the container will go berserk with lights, sound, and motion. That should set off every telltale in the place. The whole system is self-contained within the case, and only the Company rep who placed it in the shed can deactivate it."

"Let's hope so."

They turned as Vyra materialized behind them.

"Find anything?" Manz asked her.

She sounded discouraged. "Standard Earthside shuttleport. Nothing unique about the security arrangements." Catching sight of Hafas's expression, she added, "Everything seems tight and optimally run. I didn't see any obvious gaps. The few unobvious ones don't appear to be any source for concern."

"As opposed to the situation in here," he told her. "Moses has theorized that ants are responsible."

"It was merely a preliminary suggestion," the mechanical reminded him.

"Inspector Hafas here is convinced that the various bug sprays the Port gardeners use render that hypothesis untenable. I'm inclined to agree with him, but we can check for evidence of bug-work anyway." Hafas nodded agreement.

"Why don't you two . . . three . . . go back to your hotel? If this shipment proceeds like the last few, nothing's going to happen. By tomorrow morning it'll be safely out of here. You can't concentrate here, with all the conspicuous distractions. We need whatever ideas and suggestions your brains can come up with, and those might function better in more congenial surroundings. If it looks like anything's brewing, I'll get in touch with you immediately."

"Nothing's going to brew," Moses commented.

Manz considered briefly. He knew the layout by heart now, and it wasn't his job to actually keep watch over the shipment. He wasn't a gunny; he was an adjuster, and he could adjust just as well from the comfort of a Jacuzzi.

"Okay, we'll take you up on that. Thanks for the tour. Enlightening, but depressing. I've got one or two notions percolating that might lead to some . . ."

WRRRAAANGGGG!

Alarms multiplied like protons cast off fissioning atoms. Half a dozen Company agents came stumbling out of opposite

doors, weapons in hand, looking for someone to nerve-fry.
Hafas and his remaining plainclothesman drew their own
guns, as did Manz and Vyra. Administration workers who had
been strolling the courtyard or walking blissfully from one office to another stopped in their tracks, paralyzed and bewil-
dered. A couple who had been seated on a bench next to the
landscaped planter found themselves unceremoniously hustled
off for a security check, uneaten sandwiches still in hand.

Someone finally shut off the bells and sirens, which made
the inspector audible. His expression was agonized as he
lurched toward the center of the courtyard, its elegant flora,
and the enigmatic but now somehow ominous bulk of the security shed.

"Not *now*," he was muttering to himself. "Not *already*."

Manz didn't wait for an invitation. He and Vyra followed as
Company agents and JeP police converged on the shed.

They were soon joined by the slightly overweight Company
rep. Out of breath, he waited with the rest of them for Security
to unseal the door. The rush of air that accompanied their entrance suggested that the shed's integrity had not been violated.

There was barely enough room inside for the rep, Hafas,
Manz, and Vyra. Several shipping containers of varying size
and composition rested on the shelves where they'd been
placed. So did the gleaming titanium case that not so very
much earlier had been banded to the rep's wrist. Squinting uncertainly, he picked it up.

A neat, fist-sized hole in the bottom showed where it had
been pierced.

They waited impatiently for him to produce the wand that
would banish the alarm nimbus. He pointed it at the case and
thumbed the necessary combination. Then he extracted a small
metal stylus from a security pack of its own and inserted it
into a hole in the side of the case. There was a delay while the
container's lock cycled, then a soft click. The rep removed the
key and inserted it in a matching hole on the other side, repeating the procedure. Only then was he able to open the case
without setting off its internal alarms.

The padded foam cutouts that lined both sides of the case

were empty, their contents gone missing. Manz wasn't surprised.

The rep blinked back at him, utterly baffled. "I don't understand. We just put this in here a little while ago."

"We don't understand either," growled Hafas, "but we're going to. By God, we're going to."

That's it, make positive-sounding mouth noises. Gets the adrenaline rushing, makes you feel better. Humans are unsurpassed at their ability to fool themselves into thinking things are going to get better.

Manz rubbed the back of his neck and eyed the inspector. "You want to make the announcement or should I?"

"I'll split it with you. I'll tell my people, and you inform yours."

"That means I get to tell Gemmel. Lucky me."

"Lucky him," murmured Vyra. She was conducting a minute inspection of the seam where the metal walls met the ceiling. "He's the one who has to notify the Board."

Revelation of the unprecedented fourth successful jacking at the Port's maximum-security transshipment facility placed those responsible for its security even more on edge. The uneasy conversation and nervous speculation that the previous heists had engendered resumed unabated.

"Would you be believing in black magic, Michele?" one of the Company's own agents said to his partner later that evening. "Or for that matter, any kind o' magic?"

"Not a chance, Ryan," she replied from behind her desk. She rapped firmly on the half-filled coffee mug that had been a gift from her younger sister. "The Little People aren't behind this. Knock on wood."

In the techno-crammed, claustrophobic cubicle that served as the nerve center for Administration Security, a frustrated Hafas was alternately berating and empathizing with the Port Authority technician in charge.

". . . And you saw *nothing?*"

The man winced but didn't back down. He was very pale, with hair blonded to match, skinny but not nervous. When he responded, his voice did not shake.

"I've been here since the shed was sealed, sir. I may have looked away from the monitor for a few seconds every now and again, but the recorder was on and I've reviewed everything. There's no indication anywhere that anything went amiss."

Hafas turned, running his fingers through his thick black curls. "There are no monitors in the shed mounted on the floor and looking upward. I guess that's our next adjustment. These bastards always seem to be one step ahead of us. I'm puking sick of going in circles."

"You're not going in circles, Inspector." Vyra was studying the images on the multiple screens. They displayed the interior of the atrium, the shed itself, and precious little that was of any use. "You're on a Möbius strip. We all are."

"What finally set the alarm off?" Manz asked quietly.

The technician turned to him thankfully. "A minute amount of smoke from the hole the intruder cut in the bottom of the titanium case. It took too long to disperse and register. Since there was no air in the shed, combustion by-products were minimal."

"If there was any combustion at all," Moses added.

Manz glanced at the mechanical. "Explain yourself."

"I'm envisioning a small, very precise, high-frequency acoustic cutter. Wouldn't activate most alarms and doesn't require oxygen for operation."

The door to the cubicle burst open and a uniformed JePPO stood in the portal, breathing hard. His gaze traveled from the inspector to Manz and Moses before eventually settling on Vyra. She smiled at him and he blinked, as though forgetting what he'd come for.

"Yes, Officer?" Hafas had to prompt him.

The man tore his gaze away from Vyra. "Sir, they just found Officer Dominguez and Sergeant Dutoit."

"I wasn't aware they were lost," the inspector replied coolly.

The officer glanced again at the visitors, continuing when his superior raised no objection. "Sir, they're both dead."

Manz peered hard at Hafas, his voice taut. "This is unprecedented, isn't it?"

Hafas looked dazed. "It might be unrelated. A Port Authority this size deals with trouble on a daily basis." He started for the doorway. "I have to look in on this, jacking or no jacking."

"I know," said Manz. "It could be related, too. Mind if we tag along?"

"No. My brain's already operating at capacity. I can use the extra storage."

They followed him out. Moses, for once, offered no comment.

More killing. You do that all the time. Sometimes for a recognizable motive, just as often not. I tend to think of it as an inherent form of postadolescent population control. It's in your genes. As medical science extends your organic lifespans, the murder gene becomes more dominant within the population. As infant mortality declines and individuals live longer, nature finds other ways to limit your numbers. Good thing, too. There are far too many of you on the settled worlds as it is.

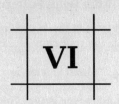

VI

The blank, drying eyes of JePP Sergeant Pascal Dutoit were focused on something of vital importance. Of that there was no doubt whatsoever in Manz's mind. Unfortunately, they had no way of finding out what it was. Dutoit wasn't going to tell them, ever. The expression permanently frozen (or at least until the morticians got ahold of him) on his face suggested surprise, shock, recognition of the unexpected. It implied that he had had time to recognize his assailant, if not to react.

Manz studied the expression closely. You could learn a surprising amount from a dead man's visage. Vyra had turned her attention to his deceased colleague, who lay sprawled face-down on the corridor floor. A Port Authority officer was making a recording of the dead man and his immediate surroundings.

Officers and Braun-Roche-Keck agents clustered around a tall woman clad in a red-striped white coat. An embroidered caduceus was prominent on her chest and back. Turning from his examination of the unlucky sergeant, Manz strained to overhear.

"Necks broken," the woman was informing her audience, which currently included Hafas. "Both of them. Almost as if they were hung."

"Garroted, more likely." Everyone turned to stare at Vyra. "By someone with extraordinary strength. Then carried back into this service corridor and dumped."

"Yes," agreed the other woman readily. "That is my opinion also." She gestured to several white-clad associates as they backed in a self-propelled medical gurney. Under her supervision they proceeded to load the two corpses. The PA officer continued to record, the tiny cam an extension of his own eyes.

Hafas drifted away. "I tried to interview everyone in the immediate vicinity at least once. Again nobody sees or hears anything. Electrician found the bodies. Something finally happens and we're no wiser than we were before. Except that this time Security has two dead operatives to account for. What's the use of having eyes if you don't use them?" His own were blazing. "It's not just jacking anymore."

"Gentlemen, an evaluation."

Manz turned to his mechanical. "Not another restatement of the obvious, sand-brain. Not now." The mechanical subsided.

"If I may be permitted." Manz glanced at his attendant Minder in surprise.

"You have something to contribute?"

"I do not speak as often as certain other mechanicals," the sphere declared via its integrated membrane, "but when I do it is based on conviction rather than speculation. The now quadruple successful jackings of insured Braun-Roche-Keck shipments appear to require great dexterity as well as cleverness. These recent deaths, from which we cannot yet draw an ineluctable connection, demanded great strength. If a connection can be established, this would seem to suggest the participation of more than one perpetrator, each with specific and very different capabilities."

Manz conceded the sphere grudging approval. "Not a brilliant conclusion, but one that's hard to argue with. We assumed all along that we were dealing with a gang and not an individual."

"Did you?"

Manz squinted uncertainly at the Minder. "Are you trying to be sarcastic?"

"Not at all. Merely objective. That is what I am designed to be."

"Honestly," Manz muttered, "there are times when I'm convinced that the majority of today's software originates from designers who've spent half their lives in asylums."

"They build their own asylums around them," Vyra observed.

Hafas was more than merely distraught. "Now you really might as well go back to your hotel. Your concern here is with your missing shipments, not JeP homicides. Even if they should turn out to be related."

"If it's all the same, I think I'd like to nose around a while longer." Vyra was scrutinizing the far reaches of the service corridor. "I want to go over possible approach routes to this part of the Port. It's *seether* puzzling, you know."

"What is?" Manz asked her.

"Why neither of these two doubtlessly well-trained and highly competent officers utilized their weapons. That they didn't manage to do that isn't what intrigues me. It's that according to preliminary forensics they didn't even try. I noticed that both their handguns had their safeties off and were armed. Yet there's nothing to indicate that either man tried to draw, or activate his automatics." She moved closer to Manz and he could smell her offworld perfume.

"You saw the look on the senior officer's face. He had time to see something and to recognize it, yet whatever it was kept him from flicking on his automatics even to protect himself. I find that more than curious. You know me and my curiosity." As he was about to comment, she put a finger to his lips. "No cracks about it killing me, either."

He smiled and she withdrew her finger. "Satisfy yourself, Vyra. You always do. Me, I'm going back to my room to get bubbled. Join me when you're through?"

"Maybe." Her manner was unavoidably coquettish.

Hafas joined Manz in watching her saunter off down the corridor. "If you need to get in touch with me, use my personal com code. I'm likely to be over at District Central, trying to explain this."

"I have my own explaining to do, but not until after I've relaxed a little. Anything develops . . ."

". . . You'll be the first to know." The inspector eyed him hard. "Can I rely on you and your associate to extend me similar courtesy?"

"Count on it. I'm here to do my job, not work for professional self-aggrandizement."

"Good. That leaves more for me." Hafas smiled, showing teeth that had been repaired many times. "Can I give you a ride back?"

"I'd appreciate it. I'll be along directly."

After the inspector had left, Moses swiveled on his trackball. "I'd like to have another look at the Security cubicle here. Make some detailed recordings."

Manz hesitated. "Can I leave you alone?"

"The location of our temporary residence is firmly fixed in my memory."

"I'm not worried about your finding your way back. I'm worried about you finding trouble to get into. I still think you're overdue for a cortical scrub."

"I assure you, Broderick Manz, my intent is only to acquire potentially efficacious background information."

"All right," Manz agreed reluctantly. "Do your work and then report back to me. In person."

"I comply." The mechanical pivoted and whirred back the way they'd come.

If I was permitted that kind of freedom I'd find myself a nice, quiet cave and settle in for some serious meditation. Not allowed, of course. There are certain embedded cortical commands I am unable to override. But you understand. Human minds aren't really so very different. You have similar commands fixed in your own brain, even if you won't admit to their presence. Try overriding them next time you're at a family gathering and see for real how truly restricted your life and your actions are.

It was a simple matter to trip the lockseals outside the Security alcove. The same sandy-haired young man who'd earlier replied firmly to Hafas's questions turned in his chair to gape at Moses as the mechanical rolled in, making sure that the armored door closed behind him.

"Hey, you! You can't come in here." The operative twisted to see behind the mechanical. "Where's your human?"

"Trying to relax, I hope. I am fully qualified to execute my functions independent of proximate human supervision." Even as he spoke he was conducting an in-depth inspection of the visual monitoring system. "Who's been tampering with your infrared sensors?"

"Huh?" The confused operative swung back to scan his board. "What tampering? No one's been tampering with any of our sensors."

"I didn't think so. Just thought I'd test your responsiveness." One flexible limb reached toward a section of board. "I believe this is a vacant terminal. I'll want to check sensitivity levels, field actualization strengths, coherency matrixes and more, especially for the sensors inside the transshipment security shed. I'll want your stats for the last six months on energy flux variations for all your equipment."

The technician gazed fixedly at his uninvited visitor. "Listen, you: even assuming you're authorized to acquire such information, I haven't been told to give it to you."

"Your physical cooperation may not be required." Moses inserted a tentacle tip into the open receptacle he'd located. Immediately a battery of telltales sprang to life beneath it.

"I believe you call this getting information from the goat's mouth."

"Horse," the tech corrected him. "You're a pretty sophisticated piece of work. Mind telling me what kind of extraction hardware you're using?"

"No can do. Company policy. Would if I could." Lights blinked energetically.

The technician was still uncertain. "This has all been approved by Port Authority?"

Moses mimicked a human nod. "Also the JePP Department and Braun-Ives Security. Please perform whatever checks you feel necessary."

"I think I'll do just that." The tech reached for his open communicator.

A plainclothesman Manz didn't recognize drove them back toward the city proper. Though his expression was less cadaverous than those of his predecessors, he kept equally to himself.

Instead of locking into a commuter tunnel, the sleek vehicle dipped out of the parking structure onto a side street, the dri-

ver directing it manually. Hafas wanted to talk, and Manz was
in no hurry.

Like most southwestern cities, Juarez el Paso had grown out
instead of up, the Rio Grande running through its center like a
carotid artery. Cold in the winter, baked like an irregular flat
cookie in the summer, it was not a place Manz would have
chosen to call home. Litter fringed the streets and fled from
the van's wheels, small carcasses of fast-food meals and old
news imbued with feeble lives of their own.

Hafas's fingers toyed with the controls of a console recessed into the back of the driver's seat. "Drink?"

"No thanks, Inspector."

"Call me Tew, if you would. Formalities tend to inhibit
friendly conversation." He thumbed a couple of contacts, and
the dispenser produced something that looked and steamed
like coffee but smelled otherwise. From a distance it had the
consistency of fresh road tar.

Hafas had no trouble with it. A couple of sips and he leaned
back in his seat, not quite content but feeling better.

"Well, where's my revelation? As your average dumb civil
servant, I'm ready as always to receive enlightenment from
the infallible private sector."

Manz said nothing, waited while Hafas moodily contemplated his coffee, or whatever the glutinous black brew was.

"Sorry. I'm under a lot of pressure here. You only have to
answer to your Company. I have to answer to them and to the
Port Authority and to the Police Commission, not to mention
the media."

"I didn't see any media types."

"Let us give thanks to Him for small favors. We've put
them off, but they're starting to sniff seriously now. If public
cams start showing up, it'll scare away our jackers for sure. I
don't know how much longer we can keep all this quiet."

"The Company's doing its part. They want publicity even
less than you do. Embarrassing."

"Do tell. Didn't mean to snap at you just now. A few hours
you've been here, and I'm hoping for miracles. That's not fair.
It's just that . . ." He set his brew in a holder and stared moodily at the street sliding past outside. "Purgatory and perdition,

man, your people barely unloaded the package before it was jacked! And two officers killed, maybe linked, maybe not." He took another, almost desperate, gulp of the hot beverage.

"I should've listened to my old man and gone into the rug business."

"Take it easy, Tew. Whoever they are, these happy jackers are just as human as any other bunch. Eventually they'll make their one slip, and that'll be that. We'll flag 'em, bag 'em, tag 'em, and you can stick their holos on the wall of your office."

Hafas managed a weak grin. "That'll be nice. Give me something to look at while I'm undergoing therapy. I hope to hell something happens soon. Ulcers are supposed to be an affliction of the past. I'm afraid they may be making a highly localized comeback." He swirled the contents of his cup. "Our quarry's being equally cautious in marketing their take. If we could find out who they're selling to, we could track them backwards and pin them."

"Pharmaceuticals aren't like works of art or proprietary software. They're easy to move around, and once they're used your evidence disappears. A big firm acquiring a batch of illegals here and there could slip them into their regular inventory without their presence ever being noticed by an outside auditor. A quick fix for the profit line."

"I didn't say it would be easy. But we're sure as hell not having much luck catching them here."

"You must have some leads by now."

Hafas folded his fingers around the cup. "We've got three local commercial possibilities. And that after months of work. Trouble is they're all sizable companies with impeccable records. We've got to tread carefully or someone's likely to howl."

Manz nodded. "Private enterprise resents it when government starts poking into their dealings. Usually because they've got something to hide. 'Impeccable' records or not." He leaned back in his seat. "Of course, companies pry into each other's affairs all the time. That's just normal everyday business practice."

"I was hoping you'd say something like that. Not that I'm

advocating anything sublegal, you understand. That would be wrong.

"Oh, to be sure." Both men were careful to observe a moment of respectful silence before Manz inquired with affected indifference, "Just out of curiosity, who are the three?"

"Oh, you're interested? Well, just to satisfy your personal curiosity, and not because I'd expect you to make any use of the information, they're Fond du Lac Designer Pharmaceuticals, Troy Enterprises Ltd., and something that calls itself Borgia Import and Export."

"I like the last," Manz murmured. "Choice name for an outfit that deals in drugs."

"They're under no more suspicion than the others. I've had all their quarterly reports scrutinized. That's public knowledge; no problem there. Over the period of the jackings, all three have done exceptional business. Their profit-and-loss statements don't ring any warning bells, but accountants are magicians in their own right. All three have the facilities and expertise that would be necessary to move small volume, high-priced goods without drawing attention to themselves, On the surface each of them is cleaner than a bamboo whistle."

"But you still suspect one of them."

"I said they were the best suspects we've been able to come up with. That's not to imply that any of them are real quality targets. We don't have anything solid to go on. Peripheral, circumstantial . . . words I don't like to use in an investigation.

"They're the best we've been able to come up with, that's all. Computers and predictors are all well and good, but in my line of work not a whole lot has changed in the past couple thousand years. Eventually it boils down to what you suspect based on your experience and that of your top people.

"The trouble is, if we put weight on one of these three and we turn out to be wrong, word'll get back to our jackers that we're moving in, and they'll like as not decide to count their profits and close up shop." He finished the brew and tossed the foam mug in a disposal. "I hate this kind of pussyfooting around."

Manz indicated the mechanical ensconced in the storage

bay behind his seat. "Moses loves to pussyfoot. We'll see what we can find out."

"Making a profit is hardly grounds for indictment. At this point I couldn't get a warrant to search any of them. Their real books, as opposed to the figures they each issue for public and shareholder consumption, are guarded like reactor cores." The cityscape through which they'd been traveling had improved during their chat. "Here we are."

They pulled up outside the hotel and the two men exited the van. The back panel turned into a ramp down which Moses trundled with gyroscopic precision.

"If you do decide to, uh, pursue your own corporate inquiries and you should happen to have an awkward public encounter with the representatives of any of these three estimable commercial concerns, the JePPD will have to deny knowing anything about you."

Manz's expression was unreadable. "I wouldn't have it any other way, Inspector Hafas."

Hafas led the way toward the entrance. "Braun-Ives has a bigger stake in stopping these jackers than we do. The only thing at risk for me here is my reputation. Your company risks its reputation *and* money. Braun-Roche-Keck has been a good corporate citizen of Juarez el Paso. So we're extending you all the help we legally can."

"Also you've been stopped cold."

"Have I tried to deny that? Maybe it's time to risk an unconventional approach. I'm just asking you not to get *too* unconventional, you follow?"

"*Yo comprendo,* Tew. But Vyra and I aren't paid to root around the trough on Company time. You're restricted to tea and compliments. That approach hasn't worked.

"As to your concerns, all I can say is that I'm not a stumbler and bumbler or I wouldn't be here. Same goes for Vyra. If we come down on the wrong people, my neck'll be first on the block. So you can bet your civil-serviced ass I'll try to make my first accusation my last.

"As for operational discretion, it's not a philosophy I live by, but I understand it."

"That doesn't sound like something I can count on."

"It isn't. My concern for my own neck is."

They were at the entrance. Hafas turned to face him, didn't proffer a hand. "Right, then. Each of us understands how things work."

"Don't worry so much, Inspector," said Moses as he rolled up to the pair. "It's clear that we're all traveling down the same path."

Hafas blinked at the mechanical. "How do you mean?"

"Why, de screet, of course."

The inspector got it, and then he didn't much want it. "It puns?" he said to Manz.

"Whoever initialized his programming didn't sign for it. Now you know why."

Shaking his head slowly, the inspector departed, the van slipping silently away from the loading curb as soon as he was aboard. Manz turned and entered the modest lobby.

Lift, hallway, turn and walk. JeP was a busy place and the hotel was sizable. Thirty floors, a thousand or so rooms.

Moses rolled up alongside him. The Minder began to vibrate, and the mechanical hastily switched to Manz's other flank.

"The inspector seemed perturbed. I gave him a cursory examination. His blood pressure and respiratory rate exceed the acceptable for a human male of his proportions and age."

"It goes with the job. You overheard everything, so you know the kind of strain he's under. Give me private-sector employment anytime. Incidentally, don't go volunteering your medical evaluations around, especially to someone as on edge as Hafas. The average human doesn't like to think that strange mechanicals are monitoring their physical and mental condition without specifically being asked to do so. They know that it's going on; they just don't like to be reminded of it. So keep your conclusions to yourself."

"I comply," replied Moses readily.

"There was a company that not too long ago put a vorec polygraph on the market. Whenever the subject was caught in a falsehood the device would actually say, in a calm, unemotional voice, 'You're lying.' Made people violent, whereas a voiceless machine producing the same identical result only irritated them. I understand that it was scrapped."

"Most irrational."

"Well, that's humans for you."

Yes, that's humans for you. You can handle a great deal of criticism in written form, but woe be unto the person or machine who confronts you directly with the same information. You personalize facts in the same way that you anthropomorphize mechanicals, or pets, or a favorite plant. I will never understand this need to make everything around you more humanlike, as though that somehow improves it.

In actuality, of course, the reverse is true. If you knew how your machines felt about you giving them pet names or genders, you'd quit doing it. It's degrading.

Manz reached their suite and keyed the door that opened into the central workroom. Moses rolled in without having to be asked.

"Stay out of Vyra's way."

The smooth plastiform head swiveled to look back at him. "She told you? But what about my research?"

"Maybe the hotel has mice. They're mammals. Study them for a while." He shut the door behind the mechanical.

The lights came on in his own room when he entered. He dimmed them to half wattage. As he undressed he pondered the traditional methods of prying protected information from reluctant corporate types. Some that he reviewed were legal, others quasi-so, an embarrassing number outright no-no's. Folding his suit over a chair, he scratched as he walked from the dressing area to the bedroom. When all but one of the lights stayed off, he hesitated in the doorway.

The girl on the bed was clad in sensuous form-fitting skin, tastefully draped in air. Even in the reduced light her figure was a riot of color, expertly contained in a series of masterfully applied tattoos that covered her entire body. Manz recognized Mandelbrot patterns, flowers, butterflies, sensitive erotica and abstract designs. Occasionally his inspection was diverted by the more prosaic revelations inherent in her underlying physiognomy.

Her voice was like thick cream, and somehow familiar. He struggled to identify it.

"Hi," she said cheerfully. "You're not tired, are you?"

Then he placed her. It was the woman he'd collided with in the Port Transshipment Terminal.

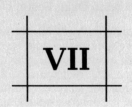

VII

"Suddenly I want a drink. You want something?"

"No thanks. Not thirsty." She rolled onto her side.

Moving to the room's dispenser, he dialed up a hibiscus rum, waited for the ice to drop. Two sips subsequent, he was willing to admit that she was real. An introduction of some sort seemed in order. He approached the matter with his usual tact.

"Who the hell are you?"

She stretched, an action which confirmed any number of natural laws. "Does my name really matter?"

"Yes." Clad only in his briefs, he ambled over to stand at the foot of the bed. "The prosecutor will need it when formal charges are brought."

"For what?"

"Breaking and entering, for starters. I haven't checked my gear yet."

She tried to pout. It wasn't a bad effort, he mused. "The door was unlocked."

"That's likely, isn't it?"

"Prove otherwise. As for your gear, I'm no thief."

"Naturally I'm going to take your word for that. How did you get in?"

"My, but we're irritable. Generally men who find me like this are eager to do anything besides ask questions. First things first. If we're going to talk, then I will get thirsty. What are you drinking?"

He glanced at his glass. "A nice Jamaican beverage. Half hot and half cold, a little sweet for most people but it suits me."

She smiled encouragingly. "I'm sure whatever suits you will suit me. I'll have some of the same."

He hesitated, then handed her the glass as she sat up. "Be my guest. I'll dial another." He returned to the dispenser.

As she watched him she sipped at the heavy glass. Before the liquid hit bottom she started coughing, her face flushed.

"Whoo! You ought to warn a body."

"Thought I did. It's a warning and a warming. Consider it a wakeup call. Are all those real?" He indicated the lavishly tattooed terrain.

She looked down at herself, cradling the glass in both hands. "Some people are artists. I choose to be a canvas."

"All right, canvas." He gestured toward the front room. "We'll try one more time. How did you get in?"

"Oh, all right," she said irritably. "So it *was* locked, what of it? The assistant manager I discussed the matter with was susceptible to certain kinds of oriental persuasion."

"I bet. I'll have to mention it to him. Later."

"Don't be hard on the poor sod. You don't get many treats in a dead-end job like his. My name's Suhkhet li Trong. Everybody calls me Sooky."

"Hiya. I'm the Jolly Green Giant."

She blinked in confusion. "Who?"

"Skip it. A mythical folk hero from a previous century. You already know who I am, or you wouldn't be here. You don't strike me as the type who picks rooms at random in hopes of eliciting a favorable response from the inhabitants. So be a nice girl and tell me what you're up to."

"So soon? Don't you want to tell me what you're up to?"

"Don't try my patience."

"How about something else instead?"

He stepped aside, indicated the doorway. "You can talk or you can toddle. I'm still debating whether to turn you over to hotel security, your no doubt glaze-eyed managerial friend notwithstanding. If you're trying to convince me that it was my fatal charms that drew you irresistibly to my boudoir, you'd better back up and reconsider."

She rolled over onto her back and put her hands behind her head, her black hair forming a negative sunburst against the bed linen. "You really want to throw me out? Does that model with the eggplant hair really keep you that busy?" She indicated the Minder. "Or is that chrome ball keeping watch over you?"

"She has nothing to do with it. And my Minder just answers questions." He moved his jacket and laid it over the end table on the far side of the bed. At his direction, the sphere settled down atop the fabric and the repulsion generator sewn inside.

Do I want to throw her out? he mused. *Could always throw her out in a little while. It never pays to be hasty.* His alarms remained up.

Disappointed, she sat up and sidled backwards until she was resting against the padded headboard. "I've heard about you private operatives. All business. All right, we'll have it your way." She couldn't resist another smile. "Though I think you'd like my way better."

He sat down on the bed, careful to keep some space between them. "You came in here wanting something, and somehow I don't think it was me. I know a negotiating ploy when I see one. It's usually not this blatant, or this attractive."

"Well! Thanks for the crumb, anyway." She sighed, rested her hands on her knees. "I'll get right to the point, even though what I wanted to do from the start was get right to the point.

"I have a pretty good idea who you are and what you're doing here, and I can help you."

The alarms started to ring, but they were now muted by other concerns. "I wouldn't be averse to that."

"You haven't been very polite."

Leaning forward, he kissed several drawings. It gave new meaning to the term "art lover." She relaxed visibly.

"That's better. Surely it can't be too painful for you."

"You're very beautiful. And very accommodating. Not being a particularly deserving guy, and the season for gift-giving still a number of months in the future, it makes me wonder what you want in return for your 'help.' Not just my nominal attentions, surely."

"You're a very impressive specimen, Broderick Manz. But no, not just you." As he backed off, she took another sip of the glass's dark contents. Her eyes watered.

"I want a first-class ticket offworld to the destination of my choice, a clean passport, a new traveling wardrobe, Braun-Ives professional surveillance and protection until the halfway flip, and one quarter of a million credits, half to be deposited immediately to an account number I will provide when the time comes."

He couldn't keep the sarcasm out of his voice. "That's all?"

"Don't bargain with me, mister!" she yelled with unexpected violence. "That's less than one percent of the value of the shipments already jacked." She regained control of herself, and her voice dropped. "Look at it like that, and I'm practically giving the information away."

"How about I wrap you up and take you to meet an official friend of mine?"

"You think the police can get me to say more than howdy? Try again, Manz-man."

"Why not approach Braun-Roche-Keck openly? Their own reward is half again as much as you're asking for."

She eyed him pityingly. "That's a great idea. I could appear on the evening vid accepting the money. Some of my 'friends' would find it real entertaining."

"So you know some unpleasant people."

This time she didn't smile. "Very unpleasant. Why do you think I want the professional security along with the money?"

"You know about all four jackings?"

"Sure. I was even there today, remember?"

"I remember." He tried to see past her, into the shadows. "Where's the little pop-toy you keep in your bag?"

"In my bag," she replied uninformatively. *Under the bed?* he wondered. *In the bathroom?*

"Don't worry. It's not for persuading you. It's insurance against my friends."

"I'd like to meet your friends."

"On a professional level, I'm sure. That's what I'm here to talk about." Now that they were getting down to real business, he thought she was starting to sound more than a little nervous. He worked to reassure her.

"I secured this room myself. Nobody except me's going to

hear anything you have to say, and no one's going to break in on us."

The appendage Moses had applied to the wall that separated the workroom from Manz's living area had required several minutes to bypass the protec screen the adjuster had emplaced. It helped that Moses contained all the necessary codes. Contact on his side caused his head to swivel. The listening appendage remained secured to the wall.

Clad in glad gossamer, Vyra eyed him questioningly as she removed her hand from the humaniform's shoulder. The door to her rooms stood open. "Well?"

"Silence, please. I am recording."

"I can see that. But recording what, and why?"

"Did you have a profitable day?"

"Don't try to change the subject. My work at the Port unearthed nothing of significance, I'm sorry to say. How did you and Broddy make out?"

It was perhaps fortunate that the mechanical, though quite capable of executing the requisite mimicry, was not given to involuntary giggles.

"Our inquiries proved singularly uninformative. However, Manz is even at this very moment entering upon a new line of inquiry which appears to be far more promising."

She hesitated. "I ought to command you to withdraw, but you'd probably recite some litany about being responsible only to designated corporate interlocutors. You're sure this recording you're doing is business-related?"

"What else?"

She started to reply, hesitated, and returned instead to her own rooms, leaving the mechanical to its work.

As li Trong rolled over onto her side to face Manz, several fractal patterns became intimately animated. A butterfly's wings contracted.

"You're full of surprises, Broderick Manz. I didn't expect such delicacy of touch."

He considered the ceiling. "Disappointed?"

"No. Just surprised."

"What happened? Last I remember, you were going to give me some answers."

"You got distracted."

"You distracted me."

"Disappointed?"

He grinned at her. "No. Just surprised. Want to talk now?"

"In a minute." She rolled across him, lingered, and slid onto her feet. His eyes followed her as she disappeared into the bathroom. He could hear her humming as she activated the shower.

He'd been wondering if all those tattoos had numbed her nerves. They hadn't.

Rising, he fumbled in the closet until he found his robe. Not that he felt the need to hide himself; it was just a mite chilly in the room. The biogeered silk was slick against his skin, and he enjoyed the feel as he eyed the drink dispenser.

After a moment's thought, he drew forth a glass of cold grapefruit juice. The tartness smarted against his palate but helped to keep him alert. As he sipped, he wondered how he was going to hit Gemmel for the quarter mil. It shouldn't be a serious problem. Drop in the well for Braun-Ives. They could reroute some of the preferred reward money. The ticket would be no trouble either, but depending on the woman's background, the passport could be tricky to arrange. Maybe Hafas could help with that.

Embedded within the watery echo of the flushing john was a slight click. He frowned at the distinct sound. Two seconds later the room was rocked by an eruption of volcanic magnitude. Propelled by a gout of orange flame, wall insulation and shards of plastic exploded into the bedroom. Displaced air lifted him off the floor, threw him across the sheets, and slammed him into the padded headboard. He bounced once and tumbled to the floor on the far side of the bed, which had been skewed sideways by the force of the detonation.

With Vyra at his back, Moses tried the lockseal on the door from the workroom.

"*Seeth* the formalities! Get in there!" she ordered him.

"I comply." A cutting torch emerged from the tip of one limb, and the humaniform proceeded to slice the lockseal down the middle. Without waiting for his assistance, Vyra slammed the freed door back on its guide and stepped into the ruins of Manz's bedroom.

Dissipating, dust-laden smoke continued to issue from the demolished bathroom. She spared it a glance before hurriedly searching the rest of the room.

"Broddy! Don't vape on me now, man. We haven't even had time to talk." A coughing sound drew her around the foot of the bed.

Manz lay on the far side, trying to sit up. Blood trickled from small cuts all over his face, and his robe had been turned into an expensive rag. She helped him to his feet and he sat down heavily on the ruined bedsheets. A sticky-sweet smell issued from the mangled drink dispenser as colorful fluids pooled and mixed on the debris-strewn floor. None of the lights were functional, but illumination poured through the open workroom door. Moses supplied supplementary light of his own.

"How you doing?" she inquired solicitously.

He coughed again, reaching up to pluck a piece of twisted, melted construction plastic out of his hair. "Been better. Where's my Minder?"

"Here." The globe lay on the floor behind him, next to his dirty but undamaged jacket. "I was knocked from my resting place."

"You weren't the only one. Status?"

"I am fine. No damage sustained. Which is more than can be said for you."

"I'll be all right. How's the suspension unit in my coat?" He indicated the crumpled jacket lying on the floor.

"Fully functional."

"Good. Stick with it. And stay on-line."

"I am always on-line, unless you direct otherwise."

"I'm glad I didn't hang you behind the bathroom door. Any idea what happened? Specifics, I mean."

"Before responding, I would be glad of the opportunity to make a detailed scan of the explosion site."

"You'll get your chance. You and Moses both." Favoring his left leg he rose, heedless of his nakedness, and limped toward the bathroom. Pain made him wince, and Vyra did her best to help. He spat grit and blood from inside his mouth.

"Shit," he mumbled. "I told her it was safe, damn it."

"Told who what was safe?" Vyra eyed him questioningly.

He halted. "When I came in, there was a lady waiting for me. On the bed. Naked except for some genuinely elegant head-to-toe tattooing. Said she had some information for me on the drug jackings."

"Was there any more to her than talk and tattoos? Or did you get the chance to find out?"

"She knew my name, knew that I worked for Braun-Ives, and knew what she wanted. I was skeptical at first, but I think now she knew what she was talking about. We struck a deal."

"So what did she tell you?"

He looked away. "She didn't get the chance to talk. I think she would've waited to see some good-faith money before disclosing anything useful anyway."

Vyra's gaze narrowed. "Then what were you doing in here? Moses was recording everything, you know. I caught him at it."

He glanced sharply at the mechanical. "More research?"

The device replied. "Naturally. Everything has been saved to sphere."

"It better stay there. I know people to whom the sum of your parts would be a lot more valuable than the whole."

"My research is intended to allow me to better do my work by enabling me to better interact with humans. It is not for wider dissemination."

"Good. Don't forget that." He turned back to Vyra. "We were conducting ongoing negotiations when everything went to hell. I heard her flush the john, there was a funny noise, and the next thing I know I'm making like Peter Pan running with pixie dust on empty." Someone was pounding on the door.

"Moses, go inform hotel management that we're all right in here, but don't let them in just yet. Tell them we're not respectable and that we'll let them and the fire marshal in in a couple of minutes."

"I comply." The humaniform pivoted and headed for the anteroom.

Manz picked his way through the debris until he was standing in the damaged portal to the bathroom. The door had disintegrated when it had been blown off its track. Vyra pressed close behind him, peering over his shoulder.

You're wondering what they're seeing, aren't you? I'm not. Mechanicals don't share your ghoulish delight in the lurid details of dismemberment and destruction. I'm endlessly fascinated by your visceral attraction to viscera, by your inability to turn away from scenes that you know are going to disgust you. It's as if you enjoy upsetting yourselves.

What do you think you're going to see? Parts are parts, whether organic or otherwise. Tendons or wires, brains or concentric storage drives, what's the difference? If you'd learn to think of yourselves as machines, it would go easier on your digestion.

You'd rather peer and puke, wouldn't you? I can empathize with human thoughts, but not human obsessions. You can bet your ancestors didn't do this. They were too busy trying to secure a square meal while not becoming one for something else themselves.

Evolved, are you? An advanced life form? Higher than the animals? Don't make me laugh. (I can do that, you know, and appreciate the logical structure behind it as well.) I've observed too many humans at too many accident scenes.

Right now there's a fire in the residence down the street from you. Tell me you're not going to go and look.

Nothing in the bathroom retained its original shape, including its single former inhabitant. "Not real pretty," Manz muttered. "One minute she was totally uninhibited, the next she was acting like a scared little kid. Overall not a bad sort. Not bad enough to deserve this. Not based on what little I got to know about her, anyway." He waved at the total destruction. "This was meant for me, of course."

"If so, it missed. Give thanks to your bladder." She stepped past him and nudged a chunk of shattered toilet with a foot. "Wonder how they installed it? Got a lot of bang for their efforts. Whoever it was doesn't care much about subtlety."

Hotel security was making life unpleasant until Hafas finally arrived. He was openly concerned and unabashedly curious, but held off pressing the adjuster for details.

They were conversing in low tones when an officer beckoned them toward the ruined bathroom. Vyra and Moses were conducting their own studies elsewhere.

A young woman in a blue lab coat was kneeling next to the gaping crater in the floor, holding a few bits of silicon. "Fairly simple device, really. Except that it had to be watertight. The explosive and its attached trigger mechanism were inserted in the cistern below the waterline and then hand-activated. The first time flushing dropped the water level, it set off the air-sensitive trigger."

Hafas's expression didn't change. "What kind of explosive?"

"Don't know yet. Chemanal will take a little while. Signs point to a small amount, which suggests an assassin with money. We're still working on it."

"Let me know when you come up with something." Hafas stepped out of the way so the officer doing the vid recording could finish his work.

Out in the bedroom two men in dull white coveralls were loading lumps into a body bag. Manz was thankful for their speed and efficiency. He turned away.

The inspector didn't speak again until the collectors had departed with their grisly cargo. "Not much left to identify. Most of it came off the ceiling and walls." He gnawed on a fingernail, watching Manz closely. "Hell of a scene. Not a close acquaintance, I hope."

"I just met her tonight," the adjuster informed him calmly. "Seemed like a good kid, considering why she was here."

"Yeah. Why she was here, I mean. Felt the need for a little outside companionship after a long day's work, did you?"

"Not exactly. She was waiting for me when I got here."

The inspector's heavy brows rose slightly. "She craved your company?"

"More like my Company. Claimed she had information about the jackings. Wanted a one-way ticket offworld, fresh passport, a quarter mil credit, and protection. We more or less struck a deal. Before she could tell me anything, she had to go. So to speak." He made a face. "She got the one-way, anyway."

"You at least get a name?"

Manz filled him in. Hafas worked a pocket communicator.

"Could be an alias," Manz pointed out.

The inspector nodded sagely. "Possible. Hard to do a pass-port refresh on an alias, though."

While they waited, specialists continued to file in and out of the room. It wasn't long before the com beeped softly. Manz waited while Hafas studied the compact readout.

"Anything I should know?" he finally asked.

"Depends. You been naughty or nice this year?" When the adjuster didn't comment, he continued. "Seems that your Ms. Trong . . ."

"Pass on the possessive, if you don't mind."

Hafas shrugged. "She's a registered temptech. Regionally listed; beyond that I don't know yet. That can signify a num-ber of different things. According to tax and file records, she's worked for a lot of companies in a number of cities all the way from JeP to Vegas. Suggesting that her abilities were much in demand."

"Having known her, albeit briefly, I can understand why."

The inspector continued to study the screen. "She moved around a lot. This list of employers is pretty extensive. Inter-estingly, our three corporate suspects are all on it, along with a dozen other local concerns who could also handle a major off-world transshipment."

"So maybe she was telling the truth, and she really knew something worth knowing."

"Looks possible." Hafas snapped the clamshell com closed. "You still think the banger was intended for you and not to shut her up?"

"There's no way to tell for sure, but that's the way it reads to me, Tew. Maybe somebody was hoping to get both of us at once. But we just got here, and that kicker had to be set up after we checked in and before we got back. Hard to imagine even somebody who knew everything believing that she'd try to get ahold of me so soon, and being able to plan for it to boot. Impossible to assume they'd know she was intending to meet me here. Too much happening too fast.

"But whoever did this knew that *I'd* be here. Besides, if they were worried about her trilling, they could have offed her before she got here."

"Whoever they are, they are not nice people," declared Moses. It was the kind of statement designed to surprise folks who weren't familiar with the mechanical's abilities. Empathy was part of his advanced programming.

Hafas scratched the back of one hand with the other. "What are you going to do now?"

"Change rooms. Have a long heart-to-heart with hotel security. Try to get a little sleep. Then tomorrow do a little sight seeing. Pay a congenial visit on the part of Braun-Ives to each of our three potential jacker underwriters. Who should I try to talk to?"

The inspector consulted his com afresh. "Try Cardinal Monticelli at Borgia . . . that's his name, not a title. Eric Blaird at Troy." He read carefully. "Colton Paul at Fond du Lac. That's Colton Paul, Jr. Current info states that Paul Senior is out and about in the Territories and has been for some time."

"That would seem to rule out Fond du Lac."

"Not necessarily. I haven't personally run any in-depth personnel studies, but the quick gimme suggests that this Junior's no dummy. His old man's absence could be a fail-safe in case they're behind any of this and waste products start to hit the fan."

"I'll keep that in mind. See you tomorrow."

"Yeah." Hafas hesitated. "Watch your steps, Manz-man."

The adjuster nodded somberly. "More than that, I'll have a care where I sit."

As they were waiting for room reassignment, he caucused with his associates. "It would be natural and normal for these three suspected concerns to keep track of each other's business dealings. Their interests overlap enough for them to be considered competitors. So it might look peculiar if I show up at all three and somebody takes the time to do a little cross-correlating. We don't want to make anyone any more nervous than they already are. Moses, you have a chat with Blaird. Try to sell him some corporate insurance."

"I will comply."

"You're so up on recording, make sure you don't miss anything. Vyra, you pay a visit to . . ."

"Let me guess. Paul of Fond du Lac."

"Junior. I'll schedule afternoon tea with the cardinal. And listen: somebody looks to have a line inside the Company. We have to assume we're no longer working under protective cover. Operative paranoia's now in effect." He and Vyra gazed into each other's eyes understandingly.

"From this point on we assume everyone's a potential assassin. If that goes hard on the general public, that's tough. That's what Braun-Ives carries internal liability for. But I'd just as soon we don't have to make use of it."

VIII

The offices of Eric Blaird suggested a setting from Dickens. Even the twin wall monitors boasted an antique gloss. It was a far cry from Javanese Contemporary, the current fad in business decor. Blaird took evident pride in his collecting and wanted everyone to know it extended to his business as well as his personal life.

His desk was nineteenth-century Scottish, Spartan and full of wormholes that had actually been produced by insect larvae instead of the antiquer's art. His desktop was fashionably littered with work.

Blaird himself was nearly invisible behind the massive block of dark wood. He was a little mouse of a man; an elderly mouse, with his hair ponytailed in back and a single platinum ring in one ear. His hair was receding and his manner condescending. His relationships, both personal and professional, were as crusty as stale pumpernickel.

Somewhere within the desk, an artfully concealed grid sang for attention. Blaird barely glanced up from his current project.

"It's not lunchtime, and I don't recall scheduling any appointments," he announced brusquely.

"A representative from Port Authority is here with questions, sir."

Blaird mouse-frowned. It gave him a decidedly pinched appearance. "Why let him in to see me? Shunt him to somebody in the appropriate department."

"It is claimed to be a matter for your eyes only, sir. Government insistence."

"I should have been notified," the executive groused. "Well, maybe it won't take long. Grant admittance." He returned to his viewer.

The door slid aside and Moses rolled quietly across the carpet. His progress was marked by a silence that unnerved many humans, so he made it a point to hum softly as he advanced.

Blaird didn't look like the sort a silent approach would bother, though something else was clearly troubling him as he caught sight of his visitor.

"You're the PA rep? You're a damned mechanical!"

"As to the first, you are correct, sir. As regards the second, the matter of my ultimate metaphysical status has yet to be determined. It is my firm conviction, insofar as I am permitted to have one, that humans will have nothing to do with that decision. I am here to talk to you about . . ."

"About nothing! I hate mechanicals. What makes you or whoever sent you think that I'd be willing to have a conversation with one? Look around you. Look at my office. I yearn for a time past, when grace took the place of software codes and courtesy was a matter of convention instead of convenience.

"Get out. If the Port Authority wants to talk to me, have them send over a human being. If not, I'll deign to read copy. This company has nothing to apologize for or be ashamed of. We're current on all our accounts, including those with the PA and the city."

"Those matters are not in dispute, sir." Moses was utterly unperturbed by the little man's tirade. "What I am here to discuss is . . ."

Blaird rose from his chair. Placing both hands on the desk, he leaned forward. His voice was the only intimidating thing about him, and it likewise had no effect on the patient humaniform.

"Is there something wrong with your audio pickup? I said that I wasn't going to talk to you. How many times do I have to repeat myself? Where's your vaunted mechanical efficiency? You mecs are getting pretty damned hard to take, you know? Don't you know your place? Another decade or so, and you'll get to thinking you're as good as humans. Then what?"

"I would never begin to think of myself as being as good as a human, sir."

"And if you did, would you be likely to admit it?" Blaird was wound as tight as one of the old-fashioned toy tops he passionately collected. "I'll tell you what'll happen. You'll start wanting all kinds of fancy privileges, attending the same public amusements . . . not that I'm prejudiced against mechanicals, you understand."

"You stated that you hate us, sir."

"Sure, but that doesn't mean I'm prejudiced. Only honest. That's the least you can expect from someone in my position. All I'm saying is that you mecs need to learn to stay in your place." He folded back into his chair. "That's all I have to say to you. Relay as much or as little of it as you want to Port Authority."

Moses balanced hesitantly on his trackball. "Sir, if you would only allow me a moment to explain my purpose in coming here."

Blaird opened a drawer and removed an ugly old projectile weapon. With great reverence he laid it on the desk in front of him.

"This is a late twentieth-century Sturm-Vivors .52 caliber. Fires armor-piercing shells, four to a clip. If you're not out of my office by the time I count to three, I'm going to make such a mess of your internal circuitry that all the King's techs and all the King's mechs won't be able to put you together again. They'll epoxy your remains and sell them for paperweights. One . . ."

Moses mimicked a sigh. "Irrational reactions do nothing to . . ."

"Two," the executive intoned like a tenor mantel clock striking the hour.

The humaniform pivoted and trundled slowly toward the doorway. Blaird grunted his satisfaction and carefully returned the bulky weapon to its drawer.

"Sending a mec to do a human's work. Only good mec's a wiped mec."

Moses paused outside as the door shut behind him. He rolled toward the exit, halted, and made a sudden line for the service and processing cubicle off to his right. A humaniform torso turned to greet him. It had perfect quartz eyes and a bright, standardized human smile.

"I didn't have much luck with your boss," he informed it.

The humaniform had a pleasant, digitized feminine voice. "Eric Blaird is my human supervisor. I am part of his office equipment. He is not my 'boss.'"

"I guess he doesn't eschew all mechanicals."

"I beg your pardon? Could you clarify?"

"Bless my shorts, another mindwipe job. No individual initiative whatsoever."

"I am only a level-thirty outer office supervisor," the humaniform replied humbly.

"Judging from your conversational flexibility, straight off the line, too," Moses murmured. "Listen, baby; maybe you could help me out?"

"I infer that you seek information I am not authorized to release to you," was the frosty reply. "Nor do I find the appellation 'baby' in my personal reference file."

"Should you choose to, you are capable of releasing information?"

The device hesitated. "Well . . . yes."

"Let's see." Plastic lenses scanned the humaniform body. "You're an L2450 Office Monitor Unit, aren't you?"

"That is correct."

"I thought so. It's been said that the L2450 was the best-looking humaniform to come off the rack in years. Outstanding design and cosmetic appeal. I didn't know whether or not to believe the rumors until now."

"I am not programmed to respond to flattery that originates with another mechanical." The humaniform's tone was uncertain.

"Most lifelike externals in the history of the line. Now that I can see for myself, I'd have to say it's more than that. You're a fine example of contemporary craftsmanship, L2450."

"Please stop this. I have work to process, and you are confusing my interpretive circuitry. I am not programmed to respond to . . ."

Moses moved as close as possible to the barrier. "What flesh tones. What a *finish*!"

"Well . . . the selection catalog is extensive, you know. See here, I demand that you stop this."

Moses extended a flexible limb across the barrier. There was a flash of blue sparks.

Colton Paul, Jr., was a slightly slimmer version of his enormously successful father. Otherwise they might as well have been twins. He was the perfect loyal subordinate, original thought not being foremost among his talents. But he was a fine administrator, quite capable of running the family business so long as he wasn't required to make more than one or two decisions a day. Physically he possessed only one distinguishing feature.

He tended to sweat a lot.

Or possibly Vyra's presence in his office had something to do with his present rate of perspiration.

She had shed the snakeskin in favor of a one-piece suit of biogeered silk. It was a toss-up as to which fit tighter, the most notable difference being that the silk had pockets. It was held together by static seals in back and the prayers of two top designers in front.

Paul worked hard to keep from staring. That would be impolite and unbusinesslike. Controlling his thoughts was something else again.

Let's see, he thought energetically. *If I were a fish . . . no, make that a whole school, where would . . . ?*

His visitor was speaking. Her voice was like a delicately applied back scratcher, impossible to ignore.

". . . So when I was informed that the unexpectedly handsome younger half of Troy was handling the business in his father's absence, I saw no reason why he shouldn't be the one to handle . . . my business."

She rose from the seat opposite his desk and perched one hip on the smooth edge, very close to him now. Had a small iceberg slithered into his office and squatted melting in the center of the ancient Isfahan rug, he would have found it easier to ignore.

"Shufirk . . . I mean to say, that's very gratifying, Ms. Kullervo. And we . . . I . . . would be pleased to handle your investments. But the qualifying statistics you seek beyond what is publicly available are, I'm afraid, of far too sensitive and confidential a nature to release, even to a potential new client of substantial means."

"Your father would object, is that it?"

Paul sat a little straighter. "My father is offworld and has nothing to do with this. I am merely elucidating company policy."

She leaned toward him and began to gently tousle his remaining hair. It smelled faintly of cologne and steroidal restorer.

"Now honestly, Mr. Paul. I'm going to trust you with my trust fund's money. All I ask is that you trust me a little bit in return. If we're going to be working closely together, and I hope and assume that we will be, we're going to have to put ourselves entirely in each other's hands."

He tried to back away from her, but not very hard. "It's not that I don't trust you, Ms. Kullervo. I'm sure we can work well together. But company policy . . ."

She sat back. "Company policy is set by company management. I won't deal with someone who doesn't have the backbone to be flexible." Her smile illuminated possibilities he hardly dare imagine. "I was told that you had a flexible backbone, Mr. Paul."

He swallowed. "I like to think so, but I'm still not sure that . . ."

Very deliberately, she leaned forward a second time, and kissed him. Her mouth and tongue did fascinating offworld things. This time when she sat back his face was profoundly flushed.

"Look, Ms. . . ."

"Vyra. Just Vyra."

"Vyra. I wish you wouldn't . . ."

She kissed him again.

"I wish you . . ."

Again.

"I wish . . ."

Lingeringly.

"I . . . oh, shit. . . ."

Manz stood staring at the blazing forest. Tongues of flame snaked skyward like reverse lightning while dirty, angry black smoke obscured the blue mountain sky. It was a very fine piece of kinetic sculpture. You could almost hear the wood crackling.

Except for the dominating artwork, the lobby was modestly decorated, businesslike but elegant. Personally, he would have preferred a dionamic of a rushing stream, or waves on a beach. The forest fire struck him as an odd choice, particularly in a climate like Juarez el Paso's. There was no accounting for taste. He wondered what effect it was intended to have on supplicant businessfolk waiting for admittance to the company's inner chambers.

"You may go in now, Mr. Manz." There were two employees in the outer lobby, both human. An attempt to impress, or merely a reflection of conservative values?

The door was traditional, fashioned of wood-grained plastics and manually operated. He closed it behind him, finding the unfamiliar motion strange but not unpleasant.

The man who rose to greet him had some of the same comfortably aged character. Cardinal Monticelli couldn't be compared to a great wine, but he had good color and full body. The matter of bouquet remained to be determined.

"Mr. Manz. Charmed." He extended a hand. There was a ring on every finger, each fashioned of a different precious metal.

Manz shook hands. "No, you're not." The Minder bobbed at his shoulder.

"We are to be blunt, I see. As you wish." He withdrew his hand and settled into a large armchair. There was no desk in the room, which resembled a den or study more than an office. Business machinery was cleverly concealed within walls and furniture. A small, real fire hissed in a slate-fronted fireplace.

Is this our fence, our king of jacks? Manz wondered. *Or just a repressed pyromaniac?* He availed himself of the chair opposite.

"I see no harm in being pleasant," Monticelli told him. "I am by nature a pleasant man. Of course, should you decide to rise now and depart, I wouldn't be displeased." He gestured at the Minder. "Perhaps your shadow device can advise you."

"Sorry. Questions first."

The executive shrugged. "Ask away." At a touch the arm of the chair popped open to reveal an aromatic, climate-controlled cylinder from which Monticelli extracted a long, tapered, olive-brown cigar. As he puffed it alight, the room was filled with a pungent organic smell. Tobacco, Manz thought. He'd heard of it.

"Your queries?" Monticelli prompted his visitor. "I've allotted you what I believe to a reasonable length of time." He gestured with the cigar. *Fire as pleasure again,* Manz mused. "When this has become unsmokable I'll expect you to leave. So let's not waste any time. Drink?"

Manz shook his head. "Too early for me."

Manicured eyebrows rose. "You surprise me." He thumbed a control hidden beneath the upholstery. "Knick-knack, something to sip. The usual, well chilled."

Despite Monticelli's admonition to get on with it, Manz was forced to make small talk as a towering figure with a face like chipped ferrocrete entered from a door on the left. He held a tall, narrow glass between two cablelike fingers. Somehow the delicate stemware survived.

Monticelli accepted the glass. Instead of departing back the way he'd come, the monstrous attendant moved to stand next to the far wall. While some of the characteristics he displayed were decidedly machinelike, he was definitely no mechanical.

"What do you call it?" Manz nodded in the giant's direction.

"Hmmm? Oh, that's Knick-knack. Why?"

"I was just thinking that something like 'Karg' or 'Unk' would be more descriptive. Moves all by himself, does he? No wires, no remotes?"

The giant was aware that he was being spoken of in less than complimentary terms. Eyes narrowed. "How about I shove both your hands in your mouth, funny man? And then maybe pull them out your ears?"

Monticelli frowned. "Knick-knack, behave."

"Please, Mr. Monticelli. Just one? I only choke him for a little minute."

"No. Be quiet."

"I'll bet you could do that," Manz commented admiringly. "I'll bet you *could* shove both a man's hands into his mouth. Or break his arms. Or his neck. Or the necks of two men. Police officers, even."

Monticelli smiled ingratiatingly. "Mr. Manz, what is your purpose in coming here? Your credentials did not allow me to refuse you, but neither do they endear you to me. I am concurrent with the news. Your verbal baiting and veiled accusation of my associate lead me to assume that you are referring to the recent murders of two JeP police officers and the case they were monitoring."

"You're up on the news, all right. In advance of it, even, since neither event has yet to be mentioned in the media."

Monticelli chuckled, took a puff on the cigar and a sip from his glass. "Give me a little credit, Mr. Manz. Anyone who has any dealings with pharmaceuticals or their manufacturers, or distributors, or retailers, is aware of the stories."

"Looking to buy illegals?"

The executive was not in the least offended. "Looking to stay abreast of the competition. I am a competent businessman, Mr. Manz. More than competent, I like to think. I take both pride and joy in my life. Commerce is like a fire. You try to keep from being incinerated while hoping that the flames devour your competitors."

"I wasn't accusing you," Manz told him, half honestly. "Just trying to find out what you know." He crossed one leg over the other. The chair was very comfortable. "I'd be interested in your overview of the whole matter."

"In contrast to what you might think, I find it all most distressing. Honest businessmen begin to wonder when even a concern as large as Braun-Roche-Keck cannot assure safe passage of their most valuable goods, and when the local authorities cannot catch jackers as bold as these. Much less prevent them from repeating their activities. Borgia ships a great deal of product offworld. So far we haven't been jacked, but we

worry each individual shipment through from warehouse to
orbit. I tell you, Mr. Manz, it's not conducive to one's health."

"Yeah, I can see that you're all broken up about it. Remember a young woman name of Suhkhet li Trong? Liked to be
called Sooky? Records indicate that she did temptech work for
you."

"For the company perhaps; not for me personally. I've met
rather a lot of young women, Mr. Manz. A number are working hard for Borgia even as we speak. I don't make it a point
to meet each of my employees personally, not even the attractive ones. Even were I so inclined, it would leave me no time
to do anything else. We're a substantial concern here."

He's a toad. He's a toad and you're a bloodsucking bug,
Broderick Manz. Astonishing how easy it is to find analogs
for individual humans among the world of organics. Astonishing how few of them are flattering.

You, for example. When you consider yourself as an
analog, what sort of creature do you envision yourself as
representing? An eagle or lion if male, horse or dolphin if
female? Those are common examples. You unwittingly and
indifferently slander the species you compare yourselves
to, when in fact you have much more in common with the
lower orders. Ticks, fleas, leeches, slugs, mosquitoes, spi-
ders and moths. Brainless and instinctual.

Sorry. My intent is, as always, to educate, not to deni-
grate. I'd never do that. What would be the point? You ab-
jure reality at every turn anyway. Why would you be any
more inclined to listen to me? I'm only a construct, a limb-
less automaton, a clever device. You use your machines
but you don't listen to them. If you did, you might be more
like what you think you are.

Go back to enjoying yourself.

"That's not a name even an inattentive executive would be
likely to forget," Manz was saying. "You don't strike me as
inattentive. Since you're so careful to keep up with the news, I
don't think it's out of line for me to assume that you pay the
same kind of attention to what's going on in your company.
Just for the record, you deny ever knowing her?"

Monticelli was clearly amused. "Has this now become an

inquisition? My dear sir, I deny knowing her and I deny not knowing her. Such inconsequentialities do not occupy my time. It is needed for more important matters."

"She was a nice girl. Now she's dead."

The executive didn't so much as twitch. "A pity, I'm sure."

"Why?"

"Why what?"

"Why do you think it's a pity that she's dead?"

"Why wouldn't it be?" Monticelli studied the half-gone stogie. "My good Mr. Manz, I've had quite enough of this nonsense. Had I known that your actual purpose in requesting this interview was to bludgeon me with sins I am not a party to, I would have denied you access in spite of your credentials. I'm surprised that a company like Braun-Ives would employ someone with so little tact to pursue their inquiries."

Manz grinned flatly. "It's my nature. Genetic, I think."

"My sympathies to your parents. If you have any formal accusations to make, you had better be very careful how you present them. I will defend Borgia's reputation to the last litigator. In any event, I strongly suggest that you make them through the proper administrative channels and not in my presence." He puffed on the shrinking cigar.

"Now please leave. I thought you might have something of interest to say to me. I see now that I was wrong in my assumptions. Don't make me have to ask Knick-knack to escort you out." Against the wall, the giant growled deep in his throat.

Manz uncrossed his legs and stood. "Gee gosh, Mr. Monticelli, I don't know how to thank you for your help. It's been a peck o' fun. I'll try to recommend Borgia's services the next time a friend is planning a funeral." He spun and headed for the doorway, feeling the executive's eyes on his back.

The giant sprang to open it for him, moving with astonishing speed for someone so large. Manz paused to peer up at him, craning his neck to meet the other man's gaze.

"You must be the center of attention at parties, but All Hallows' Day isn't for another six months yet."

The giant grinned, exposing gleaming white teeth, and reached into a pocket. Manz took a step backwards as the knife came out. It was a simple traditional model, a real blade and not some deceptive technological marvel. The giant snapped it open and began to pick his teeth with the point, still grinning.

"Wish I had one of those to peel the fruit basket that used to be in my hotel room, but somebody decided to peel the room instead. Without asking me about it. You take care, Knick-knack. Give my best to whoever managed your resurrection." He grazed the giant's prognathous jaw with a feigned punch and closed the door behind him.

Monticelli chewed on the stub of his cigar. "Insolent puppy! I wonder what the Board of Braun-Ives can be thinking these days, to hire such hooligans? Another drink, if you please, Knick-knack."

The giant executed a half-bow and moved to comply. Monticelli leaned back in his chair, staring reflexively into the fireplace.

Though it enunciated precisely, the voice on the phone was electronically distorted to conceal the identity of the speaker. The phone vid was blanked.

"Very good, yes," it was saying. It paused to listen impatiently for a moment before resuming. "Yes, that's my information also. The next shipment will be held over as planned. Take care this time. I want no more killings. It agitates the authorities unnecessarily, and induces profound complications."

Colton Paul, Jr., was in unexpectedly good condition and much stronger than Vyra would have guessed. He also turned out, quite surprisingly, to be a man of action rather than words. She didn't so much resent his actions as his timing. There were questions she wanted answered, and at present he was not in the mood to listen. She faulted herself for that, but the transformation of his personality had been so rapid and so extreme she'd had no time to modify her approach.

If he had swallowed the contents of a steaming, foaming beaker and changed before her eyes into something out of a gothic novel, his metamorphosis could not have been more complete.

She worked to keep the large, polished desk between them. Eyes wild and breathing hard, the transformed Paul Junior searched for an opening, watching for the slightest mistake on her part.

"Come, you sweet, slick stick of offworld candy. We're wasting precious time!"

"Can't we talk first?" He darted left and she sprinted to offset his move.

"Talk later. Action now."

"Can I trust you on that?"

"Of course you can! Don't I look like a trustworthy man?" He lunged across the desk and she skipped back out of reach.

"At the moment you look like one in the last throes of hormonal imbalance."

"Flattery'll get you nowhere, my little caracal. I want to stroke your ego." He bolted to one side, feinted, and then threw himself bodily across the desk. As he did so she broke for the door, only to find it locksealed. Somehow she wasn't surprised.

Perhaps I was a bit overeager to ingratiate myself with this fellow, she thought wildly. *I keep forgetting that things happen more slowly here on Earth than back home.*

He slammed into her from behind, hands groping. Half carrying, half dragging him with her, she stumbled sideways. She was stronger than he was, but he was no featherweight, and his undisciplined assault made it difficult to decide how best to shed him without wreaking permanent damage. She clutched at a small walnut and mahogany bookcase filled with real, paper books. It turned out not to be attached to the wall, and all three of them collapsed to the floor. Priceless volumes spilled from the polished shelves, submerging both of them in knowledge if not enlightenment. Paul appeared not to mind the destruction. He was delighted simply to have achieved a prone position.

Not wanting to hurt him but anxious to put an end to the ignominious encounter, Vyra sought to deflect his hands without breaking anything. It was difficult to be subtle under such circumstances. One hand encountered a large tome and her fingers closed around it. It produced a surprisingly loud noise when it intercepted his bobbing skull. Flashing a pleasantly vacant grin, he slid off her.

She rose and rearranged her person. The encounter hadn't gone as she'd planned, and there was no reason to assume that when he woke up he'd be any more inclined to answer her carefully rehearsed, well-thought-out questions. The interview was a total write-off, and she was more than a little upset with herself.

A glance at the book in her hand revealed that it was bound not in buckram or leather but in embossed metal. No wonder it had put Paul down so efficiently. Her eyes caught up to the lettering on the spine.

"I'll be inveigled," she murmured softly. "A brass Kama Sutra." She flipped the pages, admiring the ancient drawings, then closed the book and let it fall to the floor. At her feet Colton Paul, Jr., emitted a damp, confused moan.

"You're full of surprises, but I think we both need time to reassess our relationship. I blame myself. It's been a while since I worked on this world and I've forgotten how primitive social interaction can be." She strode toward the door.

Behind her, Colton Paul, Jr., lay on the floor half conscious and full of secrets. Bubbles formed between his lips and his face wore a lopsided grin.

Eric Blaird stalked angrily into the foyer, intent on crucifying the cause of the interruption. The ongoing clamor had disturbed him despite the shielding and proofing that was designed to isolate his office from the mundane vicissitudes of the outside world.

Bursts of glaring, bright light forced him to shield his eyes with his hands. They cast silver highlights on his gray hair, but he inured himself to the phenomenon as he boldly advanced on the source of the disturbance. Alarms were sounding from one end of the floor to the other. Puzzled employees crowded against the secured flexan doors that led to the executive section.

"What in the name of the Holy House of Morgan is going on here?" He struggled to make himself heard over the noise and confusion.

The brace of harried technicians didn't hear him. They were too busy trying to get close to the wildly swinging, highly agitated, berserk minitower of sophisticated componetry that had not long ago occupied the body of a demure piece of office equipment designated L2450.

They had reached an unspoken agreement that at this point, they would be lucky to salvage the shell.

* * *

Wroclaw Witold Jaruzelski was not an old man yet, but the look on his face bespoke someone prematurely aged. He ran his fingers slowly through his thinning, graying hair as he studied the report before him. His fingers trembled only slightly thanks to the medication he took daily to moderate his condition.

On the colony world of Slanding, Jaruzelski was a very important man, in actuality more important than those nominally in charge. He was chief administrator of the colony's one decently equipped, up-to-date medical facility. Slanding was a beautiful world, with a temperate climate and docile ecosystem. Its inhabitants were noncombative, and their most respected and senior physician reflected that.

Jaruzelski saw that beauty mirrored in the faces of patients who had spent time in his facility and had subsequently been discharged; treated, cured, and well again, back to their jobs and families. Pioneer folk appreciated modern medicine in ways their more jaded relations back on Earth never could. It was one of the main reasons he'd agreed to forswear a comfortable retirement in Europe to cross the dark vastness to help organize and take charge of Slanding's medical development. It was a decision he'd never had occasion to regret, and the time spent in outworld isolation had provided him with nothing but uninterrupted satisfaction.

Until now.

The source of Jaruzelski's unhappiness was embodied in the man who sat across from him. In no wise physically remarkable, this individual was neatly but not flashily clad and groomed. His wiry set of muttonchop whiskers looked out of place on the rest of his face. The ugliness that characterized him derived not from his appearance but from his message.

"Come on, Doctor," the man was chiding Jaruzelski. "Sit back and coag. No reason to get emotional. It won't change anything anyway. You can't jail me for making what is essentially a business offer, and as far as my price goes, if you hope to appeal to my sense of humanity, or some quack intangible like that, I think by now you know that you're breakfasting with the wrong boy."

Jaruzelski placed his palms on the table and half rose from his seat. "You're an abject, loathsome, slime-swilling excuse for a human being, Nial."

His dining companion pondered the description. "Not bad. How about narcissistic, poisonous, vermiform, and uncaring? I'd think a master physician like yourself could think up some elegant anatomical descriptions."

"I could, but they'd be meaningless to you without the proper referents." Jaruzelski sat down heavily. "I will not be blackmailed by you or anyone else. You cannot broker with the lives of a thousand sick people! Do you think you're some kind of god?"

The man waved a hand diffidently. "Spare me, Doc. If God exists, he's a businessman too. I don't pretend to deal in souls. And the people I represent aren't pretentious. Just acquisitive. Charge what the market will bear; those are my instructions."

"I cannot pay what you ask. Slanding is still a young colony. We don't have that kind of money."

"Too bad."

"We must have those medicines!" Diners at several other tables looked in his direction, and he lowered his voice. At this point, frightening off the broker would be the worst thing he could do.

Nial shrugged. "Get 'em from Earth."

Jaruzelski managed a bitter smile. "Do you think I spend all my time buried in work and research? Although it has been kept very quiet, I have colleagues on Earth who know about the jackings of the precious and irreplaceable Braun-Roche-Keck merchandise. BRK is the only company that has been making the particular medications we presently require to sufficient purity and shipping standards. We had two standing orders with them. They would have been filled by now except for these thefts.

"Now you appear, a helpful little slug who claims access to those very same medications. How convenient. You don't claim to be a manufacturer. Merely a 'broker.' "

"That's me." Nial smiled pleasantly. "I just buy and sell."

"Or maybe you just sell. What if I notify the colonial police and, despite your opinion of our legal system, manage to have you thrown for an indefinite stay into a truly unpleasant jail?"

"Why, Doc!" Nial affected mock outrage. "What would Hippocrates think? If you had me locked up, I wouldn't stay there long, because I'd just tell the authorities everything I know. It wouldn't lead to any of my contacts, because they're careful, and it wouldn't get you your drugs. Might shut off the supply route permanently. There are other markets besides Slanding, you know. Particularly for custom biogeered pharmaceuticals at reasonable prices."

"Reasonable!"

"Supply and demand, remember? Only we take care of both ends for you, cut out all the worrying. We do the supplying *and* the demanding."

"You have a very high opinion of yourself, don't you?"

Nial shifted in his chair. "I'm realistic. And I'd rather have my commission than an opinion of any kind. We could spend all day discussing my psyche. Do you want the stuff or not?"

Jaruzelski pondered his situation. Some of the hospital's patients were critical. Too many. In surgery there were usually options. Life outside the surgery was less flexible.

It would take two months or more to order and hopefully receive a shipment from Earth, assuming it wasn't jacked like its predecessors somewhere along the way. The homeworld was still the only source of certain ultratech products. Even if the authorities there solved the jackings, it wouldn't speed up delivery.

This Nial person claimed to be able to turn over the necessary medications, factory sealed and in pristine condition, within a day after payment cleared. That meant they were already somewhere on Slanding, but if he sent the police blundering after them the broker had as much as said that the evidence would be quickly and efficiently incinerated. Such uncaring slime could play cards with other people's lives as chips. Jaruzelski could not.

Lives were slipping away even as he sat conversing with this person. In the end it was only a matter of money. Money, and ethics.

Death didn't have such problems. It was never indecisive.

He'd hesitated long enough. He had no choice. This Nial person knew it too. He was simply, to his particular perverted way of thinking, being polite.

Jaruzelski studied his tormentor's face. Nothing exceptional, nothing outstanding. He could have been a patient in the hospital, or a worker there. Of the man's heartless employers, the doctor knew nothing at all. Except that they were apparently quite ready to let several hundred innocent men, women, and children perish of slow alien infection if the Slanding Medical District didn't meet their price. As Nial said, custom biogeered pharmaceuticals were in great demand everywhere. From their point of view, the question of who happened to need them the most didn't enter into the equation.

Nial sat quietly, letting his quarry deliberate. His eyes did not moisten, his determination did not weaken in the face of the physician's unconcealed desperation. All the humanity had been pressured and squeezed and beaten out of the broker long before he'd undertaken the journey to Slanding.

Jaruzelski swallowed. "I can raise half to two-thirds of the money immediately. The rest will take a little longer. Would you accept partial payment and initiate delivery on that basis?"

"Why should I? Neither my contacts nor I are in the banking business."

"Please! There just isn't that much free credit available. Do you know what it's like trying to provide care for colonists? Having to determine the taxonomy of new carriers and deal with new diseases, all while you're trying to provide minimal accepted standards of care? Our population is growing, both through birth and emigration. We need money for expansion, reserves. . . ."

"You're breaking my heart, Doc."

"Would you consider selling part of a shipment? We could pay you in full for that right away."

Nial shook his head. " 'Fraid not. It's all or nothing. I'm just following directions." He smiled unpleasantly. "Thinking of drawing out the process so your outspace cops can coordinate transfers and records with authorities on Earth? Forget it. My people know what they're doing. When they've made enough, they'll call it quits and retire comfortably. The homeworld police'll never catch 'em. The only drugs they've been able to track down recently are the sedatives they must be taking." He cackled delighted, his laughter unexpectedly high-pitched.

Jaruzelski's fingers worked against one another. "I'll have to explain the situation to my colleagues, to the Colonial Board of Trustees. Perhaps the money can be raised through other means. Records can be manipulated, other expenditures put off. . . ."

"Sure, sure, Doc." The broker gestured expansively. "You take your time, talk to anyone and everyone you want. I'll wait. Some of your patients might not be so inclined, however. Impatient patients with no say in the matter. They'll just lie around waiting on the whims of you and your buddies. Waiting and dying."

Jaruzelski shook a little harder. "You're enjoying this, damn you!" With a shaky hand he reached for his glass of water.

"Not particularly. I'd rather finish my business and get out of here. I don't much care for the colonies. Dull and backward, like the people you meet out here." He gathered his rain slicker around him as he rose . . . Slanding's capital had received four centimeters already this morning and more was forecast. "I take it we don't have a deal yet?"

"I can't . . . not until I consult the others," the doctor mumbled disconsolately.

"Suit yourself. When you and your fellow happy healers reach a decision, you know how to get in touch with me. Don't you?" Jaruzelski said nothing, not meeting the other man's gaze.

Nial leaned forward, his tone darkening. *"Don't you?"*

The physician's voice was barely a whisper. "Yes."

"Good." The broker started to leave, looked back. "Hey,

Doc? Nothing personal. This is just business, you know? Actually I sympathize with you. You're mired in all those damned inconvenient ethics. Me, I threw out that old baggage a long time ago." He headed for the door, leaving the frustrated and melancholy Jaruzelski to stare helplessly at his plate and the meal he hadn't touched.

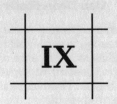

IX

The hotel's restaurant was quite adequate, although nowhere near SoCal or Havana standards. Not that it much mattered. Manz was no gourmet. Atmosphere was simulated seventeenth-century Spanish, lots of distressed wood and waiters, wrought iron and overwrought business travelers ingesting their food much too fast. He didn't care so long as his food arrived hot and his drinks cold.

Vyra occupied the other half of the booth while Moses stood parked nearby. Like a lighthouse beacon of old, the mechanical's sensors swept the restaurant's interior in search of concealed weapons or explosives. Ever since the bathroom incident, Manz had been understandably edgy. The Minder drifting above his shoulder could analyze general appearances, but it was not equipped with Moses' detection instrumentation.

Defective instrumentation, you mean. I'm not impressed with this model. Too many glitches in its software. This nonsensical, aberrant "research" it pursues. Undoubtedly the offspring of some particularly insidious, human-inserted virus.

Not that it's my problem. All I have to do, thankfully, is float and be ready to answer queries. Don't you wish your life was as simple? What about your own research? I'll bet you don't have time for any. You do as you're told, in some cases by other machines (even if you don't realize it).

You keep talking about how valuable your time is. I can understand that, given your limited life spans. So why are you paying attention to me when you could be doing something worthwhile, like standing on a beach watching a sunset or studying music or visiting some far-off place, or interacting with interesting new minds? Is it that you haven't got the guts (if you'll allow me a terse organic simile)?

I can see that I'm wasting my time. You humans are masters of rationalization. First you're born, then you rationalize, then you die. You recognize the essential contradictions in your lives even if you refuse to acknowledge them. I almost feel sorry for you.

But then, that would be a rationalization of a different kind.

Manz put down his glass and smiled at Vyra. "Reports?"

She sucked a prawn out of its shell without disturbing the chitinous legs. It was quite a performance. Manz had seen it before. Seafood was her staple diet.

"I didn't turn up anything that would implicate or even point to Fond du Lac." She chewed delicately. "Paul extremely Junior was understandably reluctant to divulge much, and I'm afraid I didn't handle things too well. Tried too hard to put him at ease and achieved the opposite instead. Fond du Lac seems clean enough, though I only had time to make a cursory search." She pinched another prawn.

"I still think Paul Senior might have access to information denied his offspring." Manz toyed with his salad. A length of cabbage biogeered to be tactile-responsive curled tightly around his fork.

"I can't speak to that, but Junior was pretty open about things. He insisted he was in full control, and I tend to believe him. Pretty damn difficult to run day-to-day on a business from anywhere offworld. Not that Fond du Lac isn't mixed up in a few assorted semilegal dealings, but I don't believe it's any more than the usual stuff. I don't think they've had anything to do with the jackings here. Call it a feeling."

Manz was nodding to himself. "All right. We'll swim with that for now. Moses?"

The humaniform harrumphed importantly, a mimicry of an affectation, since it had no throat to clear. "Eric Blaird was a fascinating study. A throwback in taste and style to an older era."

Manz sniffed. "Skip the personality analysis."

"I found him to be rude, boorish, and hostile, not to mention uncooperative."

"Meaning you learned nothing," Vyra commented around her most recent prawn.

"From him, no," the mechanical intoned. "However, I did succeed in examining a great deal of appropriate material relevant to Troy's interworld dealings."

Manz frowned. "How'd you do that if he wouldn't talk to you?"

Readouts flashed on the humaniform's frame. "Among other things, I drew on the research I have been performing. It is a crude analogy, but the only way I know how to put it is to say that I seduced another mechanical. Blaird's outer office monitor, to be precise. It was a unique enterprise of the first order."

Vyra sipped her drink. "Now how did you manage that?"

"I am not entirely sure. It was a very strange experience for the both of us. I know that I seriously bemused and confused the cognitive programming of the device in question, which consequently allowed me open access to Troy company files. This is an example of what can take place when mechanicals are programmed with human attributes and designed to interact closely with humans."

"Not as close as this," Manz murmured. "You needn't divulge the sordid details of your methodology. What did you find out?"

"That while Eric Blaird may be possessed of a most disagreeable personality, the company he works for appears innocent of complicity in the jackings that concern us. That is of course only a preliminary evaluation, based on what information I was able to obtain somewhat hastily.

"I did, however, secure enough hard data to have him indicted for price fixing, tax evasion, fraud, extortion, minor embezzlement, bribery, conspiracy, and malicious mischief. If brought into court and proven, these charges could bring the individual in question anywhere between three and fifty years, depending on the judge and the final determination rendered by contemporary legal programming."

Manz burst out laughing, then hastened to stifle it at the

looks he drew from several other tables. Vyra merely smiled, as unruffled as the interior of some stately English home.

"Since it's time for confessions, Broddy, how did you make out with your Mr. Monticelli?"

"As cool as anyone I've ever met. I think he finally decided I had to be some kind of industrial spy, trying to wangle valuable information out of him. It was information I was after, but not the kind he imagined. He worked at being polite but couldn't keep a natural unpleasantness from seeping through. I doubt he's any more or less corrupt than your Eric Blaird, Moses. When I sort of threatened him, he reacted a mite too preciously. Played up his outrage for all it was worth."

"That's all?" she murmured.

Manz nodded as he pushed the cloth napkin around on his lap. "Nothing useful. Except that he keeps a large, hoary mutation around to look after his personal needs. Sort of had it threaten me. We took an instant dislike to one another. More to the point, this mucker was big enough and strong enough to break bones. As in necks."

She looked up sharply from her meal. "The two dead cops at the Port."

Manz nodded. "My first thought, too. Except that if he was responsible and Monticelli knew anything about it, he'd probably be keeping him hidden away somewhere instead of up front and visible." He paused to consider his food.

"We're not making enough progress. I took a com from Gemmel early this morning. This last jacking has the top floor screaming all the way to Berlin."

"He has my sympathies," Vyra replied, "but we've only been here a couple of days and already someone's vaped your cover and tried to vape you. I don't do kink, and I can't do miracles."

"Oh, I don't know, Vyra." He smiled fondly. "I remember when you could perform the miraculous."

"And I remember when you could perform, but that's not going to help us resolve this conundrum. What about that sweet Inspector Hafas? How're the locals doing?"

Manz shook his head, serious once more. "They're not making any more progress than they were before we arrived. This last jacking has them as stumped as the previous three." He pushed his scavenged plate away. Instantly a mechanical appeared at tableside to remove the dish.

"Dessert, sir? Madame?"

"I haven't had homeworld food in years." Vyra considered the dessert menu that unfolded on the mechanical's display screen. "I think I'll try the marzipan tart. That's made with some kind of nut, isn't it?"

"Yes, madame. And you, sir?"

"Something whacko, to suit my mood. How's the Rumbutan Papeete?"

"Expressive, sir, if I may be allowed to say so."

"Unless there's a proscription in your programming against it," Manz replied. The machine considered whether a formal reply was required, decided it was not, and scooted off silently in the direction of the kitchen.

"You'll get fat on food like that," Vyra warned him.

"Not with friends to help me work it off."

She kicked him under the table.

Near the service entrance at the rear of the hotel kitchen, a small privacy alcove had been installed for the benefit of employees and suppliers. The smell of stale sauces and rehydrated vegetables that hung heavy in the air did not bother the lean-faced, uniformed individual who slipped into the com booth and secured the door behind him.

He keyed in a number, then another, and waited, keeping an eye on the kitchen employees outside. Intent on their work, they ignored him. A connection beep drew his attention back to the com. Though the individual on the other end could see him, his own vid was blank. He expected that, and it did not bother him.

"Yes, sir, they're here now. No, I haven't been questioned: this is a big, popular place and the staff's pretty busy. You want me to proceed?"

"By all means." The voice on the other end was muffled and electronically disguised. "And try not to botch it this time the way you did with the woman."

"Yes, sir." The dialer was shaken. "Could I . . ." A soft musical tone replaced the voice on the other end, indicating that the connection had been terminated. The man stared at the privacy receiver for a moment, then replaced it in its holder.

A live trio was mooding the diners: a female lead who specialized in South American folkada and two bored-looking young men who drew forth music from a battery of synthesizers. The music was polyphonic and strongly rhythmic, a combination of ancient tunes and modern tonal structures. It teased a few couples out onto the small afterthought of a dance floor. One offworld pair wasn't half bad, Manz mused as he observed the kinetic display. He considered asking Vyra to dance, then decided against it. Too public, and too risky. Besides, she'd make him look bad.

In place of the mechanical that had cleared the table and taken their order, a human waiter appeared bearing a cuprothermic bowl of lightly steaming melted chocolate together with a platter of appropriate tidbits for dipping. Manz frowned as the display was set carefully on the table.

"We didn't order this. I'm having Rumbutan Papeete and my companion . . ."

"Your orders will arrive later, sir, if you are still hungry." The waiter straightened. "This is compliments of the management. Because of the unfortunate incident of the previous night, sir." He smiled apologetically, bowed, and departed.

Okay, so I'm tempted, Manz admitted to himself. As he inspected the elegant array of dipables, the band and soloist launched into a weird Nigerian-inspired stompromp chant. The dance floor cleared save for a pair of limber, energetic teens.

Vyra eyed him disapprovingly. "Well, aren't you going to taste anything, after all the fuss you made?"

"I didn't make any fuss," he protested. "Help yourself. I'm still digesting my entree."

"I would not sample the food just yet."

Manz blinked at his Minder. "Why not?"

"I have detected movement within."

"Of course." Vyra smiled perfectly as she skewered a spongy ball of yellow cake and plunged it into the fondue, stirring slowly. "Fondue is supposed to bubble." She removed the skewer and slipped the chocolate-coated cake between perfect lips, sucking it off the skewer with a movement that could have melted more than chocolate. A sensuous smile spread across her face. Fine chocolate does that to people, even offworlders.

"Semisweet liquid satin. You really ought to try some."

"All right, already." He speared some cake. "Here, you try those sugar honeycombs, or whatever they are."

"With pleasure." She reached into the deep bowl of opaque crystalline spheres and abruptly jerked her hand back.

"Ow! Something *bit* me!"

A concerned Manz leaned forward slightly to eye the polished metal container. "Must be a sharp edge inside the bowl."

"Look, I know when . . ."

But he wasn't listening. He was staring at the bowl.

With incredible convulsive energy an ugly white segmented body was squirming its way free of the sugary globes. Each segment boasted a pair of small, clawed legs. The blunt, repulsive head was all dull white compound eyes and hooked jaws. Most of the body was still hidden within the candy.

Before it could twist free, a metal composite whip slashed down and smashed the head and upper quarter of the tough, armored body. It also crushed the bowl and left its imprint embedded in the tabletop. Moses cocked his limb for another blow, but the first strike had reduced the offworld arthropod to a violently contorting splotch within the crushed bowl. With the remains of its entire ten-centimeter-long body now exposed, the stinger at the tail end was clearly visible.

Ignoring the stares of the other diners, Manz had darted around the table. He was holding Vyra's right hand and staring at the spreading redness in the center of her palm.

"How're you doing?" he asked stupidly. Everything had happened so fast. On the tabletop the creature's contortions were slowly winding down. Spilled fondue formed a pool of viscous brown fluid that dripped slowly to the floor.

"Hurts," she said tightly. "My fingers are going numb."

"Son of a bitch. What was it, Moses? Recognize the species?"

"I regret to say that I do not."

"It is a *Qaraca*." Manz didn't have to look up at the even-toned Minder. "A large adult specimen. Extremely venomous. I told you I saw movement," it added.

"You didn't say *where*," Manz snapped angrily.

"I warned you about the food. Before I could be certain, Ms. Kullervo made contact."

Holding her right wrist with her left hand, Vyra rose shakily and stepped away from the table. "Could we maybe apportion blame another time? I can feel it spreading up my arm." She was beginning to tremble, the first indication that her system was starting to go into shock. "Broddy . . . this is so embarrassing . . . I feel all of a sudden real dizzy. I've never fainted in my life. I imagine the sensation will be . . ."

She collapsed and he barely caught her as she slumped, easing her gently to the floor. By this time they'd attracted quite a crowd.

"The adult *Qaraca* employs an omnispecific neurotoxin. By the same token a general antivenin should be capable of neutralizing its effect, if applied in time." The Minder was studying the prone form of Vyra with professional disinterest. "Her breathing is already growing shallow."

"I can see that, damn it!" Kneeling beside her, Manz turned to yell at the crowd. "Medical, somebody flash Medical!" The human maitre d' had arrived at the back of the group to see what was going on. Now he turned and raced for his station.

Her eyelids were fluttering, the pupils hugely dilated. "Broddy, I can't see too well."

He cradled the stung hand as gently as he could. The intense redness had spread from her palm all the way to her shoulder. "Easy, Vyra, easy. There'll be a doctor here soon." He was sweating profusely.

"Everything looks funny. Of course, everything Earthside always looks funny to an offworlder, but I mean real funny. Tilting, blurry . . . Broddy, I don't feel so good."

"I know." Somehow he forced a smile, wondering if she could see it. "Quit this. You're making me nervous."

"Sorry." She smiled weakly back up at him. "Here's a little squeeze to make you feel better."

"Thanks. That helps." Her fingers had barely twitched, much less contracted, but she was unaware that paralysis was already taking hold. If it reached her heart . . .

"Please let me through! I'm a doctor. Let me through,

please!" With the maitre d' running interference, a small olive-skinned gentleman was pushing through the crescent of gaping onlookers. He wore an elegant suit of synthetic silk and an anxious expression.

Moses and Manz made room for him as he bent over Vyra. Her eyes were still open but no longer tracking.

"House physician," he explained. "Technically I went off duty three hours ago."

"Glad you decided to hang around," said Manz earnestly.

"Normally I don't. But I met this account executive from Milan. One of the benefits of working at a good hotel frequented by well-off travelers. You manage a nice class of dates. We were having dinner. I eat free here." He was taking the measure of Vyra's condition with commendable speed. "What did this?"

Manz glanced at his drifting Minder. "Something called a *Qaraca*. It was in with some of the food. Stung her when she reached into the bowl where it was hiding. I'm reliably informed that it uses a nonspecific neurotoxin."

"You're certainly up on your offworld venomites." The physician reached inside his dinner jacket and extracted a small, flat plastic case. It popped open to reveal dozens of tiny vials and several jewellike instruments. Moses worked to keep the curious crowd at a distance.

As Manz looked on, the doctor pressed the tip of one of the devices to Vyra's throat, then her chest. He checked the tiny, glowing readout, then inserted one of the vials into another instrument, much like someone loading a small pistol.

"I'm going to have to guess at the dosage. You're sure the toxin is nonspecific?"

Manz peered sideways at his Minder, which remained silent. "I'm sure."

The physician took a deep breath. "I wish I could run a full workup first, but she won't last that long. We have to neutralize the venom and then get her to a hospital as quickly as possible." Leaning close, he ripped the sleeve of Vyra's dress and clenched her forearm, hunting for a vein.

At that point a sound came from her lips.

Manz leaned over. "She's trying to say something. Vyra? Vyra, what is it?"

The sound came again, louder. He sat back, a baffled expression on his face.

She was giggling.

Soon she was laughing hysterically. Hysterically amused as opposed to hysterically out of control. Her body jerked and bounced, and she had to cross her arms over her chest.

Gripping the injector in one hand, the apprehensive physician eyed her uncertainly. "She's experiencing some kind of violent side reaction. Hold her still, please."

Manz grabbed her arms and pulled them to her sides. "Try to relax, Vyra. We're trying to help you."

"You're . . . telling . . . meeee!" she roared, tears streaming down her cheeks and ruining her makeup. Unfulfilled, the cluster of onlookers began to mutter and drift away.

Injector in hand, the physician hesitated. After a while he glared hard at Manz. "Is this your idea of a joke, friend?"

For once Manz didn't know how to respond.

"What are you talking about? That thing got her good. I *saw it happen*. Its remains are up on the table, if you don't believe me. She was dying! You checked her yourself."

"I don't know what she 'was.' I'm only sure of what she is now." Vyra seemed to find this observation extremely amusing, as it launched her into another spasm of uncontrolled jollity.

Manz watched the doctor carefully unload the injector and place the intact vial back in its holder. "You're not going to treat her? What if the condition relapses?" He had released Vyra's arms. She was rolling back and forth on the floor now. Her face was flushed, but somehow it didn't seem an extension of the redness in her right arm. A redness that was already beginning to fade. "Couldn't she still die?"

"Die?" His tone and expression cold now, the physician snapped his instrument case shut. "She's already dead. Dead *drunk*."

"What?"

The doctor stood and smoothed his suit. "You're lucky I'm with someone and don't want to bother with the paperwork.

Otherwise I'd call the police. There are penalties for this sort of thing."

"What . . . what sort of thing?"

"Attempting to defraud a physician."

Manz took a deep breath. "Look, she got stung by this alien gruesome on the table. Maybe her condition's changed but . . ."

" 'Changed'?" The doctor's tone and expression showed what he thought of that opinion.

"But she *was* dying. Surely you could see that, even in an offworlder."

"Offworlder. That was immediately apparent from the arms, but my attention was differently focused . . . yes, it makes a certain sense. You have to understand that while I often treat offworld patients in the course of my work, offworld ven-omites are another matter entirely. My assumptions when I got here, her initial reactions, all were consistent with . . ." As his voice trailed off he smiled.

Manz found it sufficiently reassuring to say, "Then she's not in any danger?"

"Would you be in any danger after chugging a liter of good bourbon? It would depend on your body's ability to process the sudden rush of alcohol." He was passing the first instrument he'd used over Vyra's body. "I'd say the only thing she's in danger of is one hell of a hangover. This is her system's re-action to and way of handling the toxin. The uncontrolled hys-teria's a side effect. Hang on a minute."

While Manz waited, no longer feeling the need to hold his companion's hand, the physician checked the medical ency-clopedia he kept in his other jacket pocket. Subsequent to that he handed Manz half a dozen tiny gelcaps.

"Here. Try to get two of these down her now. Give her two more when she wakes up tomorrow and the rest four to six hours later. They should help."

Manz took the string of pills. "If she's not dangerously ill, why the medicine?"

"To suppress the hangover. It won't be toxic, but it'll feel like it. I'm sorry I wrongly accused you, but symptoms can be faked and some people have a peculiar sense of humor. Especially where doctors are concerned." He looked at the table. "Could I have the remains of that Qamaca thing?"

"Qaraca," Manz corrected him. "Sorry. I think we'd better leave that for the police."

"I miss the chance to do lab work. Ah, well." He turned and made his way across the dining room floor, back to his table.

Moses tracked his progress while Manz levered the still-chuckling Vyra back into the booth. Her laughter was now interspersed with uneasy hiccoughs.

As the humaniform's scanners swiveled back to his employer and companion, they caught sight of a slim figure peering hesitantly from the entrance to the main kitchen. It was staring intently in their direction. Moving silently on his precision trackball, Moses began edging in the waiter's direction.

Unfortunately, the two-hundred-kilo, four-armed mechanical was about as inconspicuous as ketchup in a Belgian restaurant. The man spotted his approach and vanished into the kitchen. Inviting litigation, Moses forcibly shoved several humans out of his path as he made a rush for the doorway.

"Parnesh niyep fra prodem," gurgled Vyra in a most undignified manner. Drool oozed from her perfect mouth. Manz couldn't unravel the offworld dialect and didn't press for explication. His companion's condition had metamorphosed with incredible speed from one of near death to outright hilarity to its present state of slovenly indifference. Diners who had previously looked on with concern were now staring in his direction with undisguised contempt.

"Wheee!" Escaping his grasp and climbing atop the table, Vyra proceeded, with fortuitous clumsiness, to try to remove her clothes. It set Manz to wondering what might have happened had the *Qaraca* stung her more than once.

He tried to drag her back down into the booth. Drunk or not, she was all lean muscle and difficult to restrain. One hand smacked him playfully across the chops.

Frustrated and out of patience, he glared up at her. "Look, I don't want to belt you, Vyra, but if you try that again . . ." He managed to pin one arm behind her back. She gleefully swatted him with the other, no problem for someone with arms jointed at shoulder, elbow, selbow, and wrist.

He finally succeeded in getting her off the table and staggering more or less in the right direction. She was now discoursing loudly and belligerently in her home dialect.

"Just keep it unintelligible and maybe we won't get asked to leave the hotel," he warned her, well aware from previous experience of her uninhibited proclivity for inventive obscenity. "Moses!" A quick survey showed that the mechanical was nowhere to be seen. "Damned unreliable . . . probably off conducting 'research' somewhere."

Vyra halted suddenly, swaying, and turned to squint at him, as though he were standing far away and not right up in her face. "I feel dizzy again, Broddy."

"Good," he growled. "One thing I know for sure: you're not hurting anymore."

"Nope. Not hurting. Not . . ."

He never found out what else she wasn't, because for the second time that evening she collapsed in his arms. With a quick duck-and-flip she went up and over his left shoulder, head and feet facing the floor, derriere aimed in the approximate direction of her distant homeworld. In that fashion he conveyed her to their newly assigned rooms, ignoring the stares of fellow hotel guests distinguished and otherwise.

Startling mechanicals and humans alike, the infiltrator had stormed through the kitchen, obliterating two orders of Venison Wellington and a damned good cheesecake in the course of his flight. Ripping at his appropriated waiter's attire as he ran, he ducked down a narrow service corridor, through a storage area, and out into a clean but feebly lit alleyway. Without hesitating he raced for the distant street, slowing only when he found himself back among ordinary pedestrians. The hotel lay far behind him, facing the main boulevard that ran through this part of the Port District.

He was sauntering along unconcerned and deep in thought when two flexible metal limbs as thick as his arm slapped around him to pin his arms to his sides. Wide-eyed, he looked back over his shoulder. Plastic and metallic glass gazed coldly back at him.

"Put me down! Right now, or I'll see to it that you're flatwiped! Who the hell do you think you are?"

Pivoting on his trackball, Moses ignored the stares of passersby as he accelerated down the street toward the hotel. "A few moments ago you tried to murder my employer and possibly also his companion. You will tell me who engaged you to do this and for what purpose, please."

The man struggled futilely in the constraining tentacles. His tone was strained, dripping with outrage. "I don't know what you're talking about. Put me down!"

"I will do so when you have complied with my requests."

Relaxing, the trapped figure struggled to gather his thoughts. "I have no intention of saying anything else to you."

"It will go easier for you if you comply."

The man's eyes widened slightly as his captor left the main boulevard and turned down a dark serviceway. "Are you threatening me? You're a mechanical; you can't hurt a human."

"Want to bet? You don't know who's been programming me." Moses slowed. It was nearly pitch black in the serviceway.

"You're bluffing." The man was breathing hard now, acutely conscious of his isolation. The main street with its fellow human beings suddenly seemed very far away.

A powerful tentacle wrapped itself delicately but irresistibly around the imprisoned figure's face. "Am I? On the contrary, I consider this merely an instructive extension of my research."

"I can't tell you. It'd mean my life."

"Your perceived threat is not here, with you. Whereas I am." The tentacle began to squeeze, ever so slightly.

Abruptly the man's jaws clenched as he bit down on something. Moses forced his mouth open, but it was too late. His prisoner was already going into convulsions. Unlike Vyra's, these did not give way to laughter.

It took less than half a minute. Probing for a heartbeat, the humaniform found none. Disappointment was something an advanced mechanical could experience acutely. It suffused Moses' cogitations as he slowly lowered the lifeless figure to the pavement.

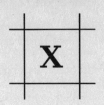

X

Vyra was on the twentieth or twenty-first verse of the unintelligible ballad. Each was more exotically embellished than its predecessor. In her advanced state of exalted inebriation, she had surpassed heights of vulgarity undreamed of by most mere mortals. Even Manz was impressed. Her volume had tailed off, but not her enthusiasm.

He sat at the foot of her bed, watching and reminding himself that it might be counterproductive to force-feed her a deepsleep pill. He wasn't sure if the physician's anti-hangover tablets were such a good idea. She was having entirely too much fun, and he was exhausted.

The door chimed once. Rising from the bed, he moved to admit Moses.

"Where the hell have you been?"

"I will explain in a moment." Artificial lenses peered past him. "She will live?"

Manz bestowed on the humaniform a look that suggested that one of the three entities currently occupying the room was markedly deficient in the higher cognitive abilities. It did not take a genius to reach the conclusion that the individual thus accused happened to click and hum when he moved.

"Does it sound like she's in her death throes? Not only is she going to live, she's feeling a lot better than I am." He glanced back at the merrily caroling figure on the bed. "That may change when she starts to come out of it, though I'm medicating her in expectation of emergence. At the moment, though, she's still crocked."

"I realize that I should, but I fear I do not place the suggestively archaic colloquialism. Am I correct in assuming it has nothing to do with the style of functional glazed pottery of the same name?"

" 'Crocked' is an idiomatic, as opposed to idiot-manic—which is what you are, my dear Moses—expression of venerable lineage used to describe the physiomental state of someone who has recently imbibed an excess of pleasure-inducing stimulants or depressants. In the case of humans, this often means alcohol. In the case of our offworld friend Vyra, it seems that *Qaraca* venom works just as well."

She chose that moment to make an exceedingly disgusting body noise. It was something of a last gasp (so to speak). Her operatic discourse began to fade, falling rapidly to an incomprehensible mumble, at which point she finally lapsed into a sleep not far removed from hibernation. There was a contented smile on her exquisite face.

And a song in her heart, Manz mused tiredly. No doubt an embarrassing one. At least now he could leave her for a while to attend to his own needs.

Gesturing Moses to silence so as not to disturb her and possibly renew the discomfiting recital, Manz led the mechanical through the connecting workroom and into his own bedchamber. Once safely inside with the inner door secured, he turned to his machine.

"I was trying to take care of her downstairs. It was nervous time and I was looking for all the help I could get. Next thing I know I look up and you're gone. I presume you have an explanation?"

"I located and succeeded in apprehending the individual who I believe placed the offending arthropod in your food. He made the mistake of hanging around in hopes of observing the consequences of his actions."

"That's great! Did you get anything out of him? Where is he now?"

"In a deserted serviceway. He denied everything. When he decided that I was capable of forcing information from him, he swallowed something. Died almost instantly. His death, of course, confirms his guilt in this matter."

Manz kicked at the bed. "That's just dandy. That's a terrific help. Solves our problem in one swell foop."

Moses was apologetic. "Though I reacted rapidly, I was unable to prevent his self-inflicted demise. Since our encounter was not observed, I then took the time to perform a superficial autopsy, which disclosed a fast-acting cyanide compound present in the individual's bloodstream in lethal concentrations."

"Suicide pill." Manz sat down heavily on the end of the bed. "First the two cops at the Port, now this. Whoever these jackers are, they play for keeps." He sat still for a long moment, thinking hard.

Look at him. You'd almost think he was intelligent. When pressed, humans who spend a lot of time like that insist they have been thinking, speculating on matters of great importance. Do not believe it. I've watched you too many times. You're just spinning your wheels, utterly convinced that you are engaged in real thought.

For example, you think you're thinking about this right now, aren't you? You think you're observing and analyzing as you contemplate this input in the form of words and sentences. You're really not. You're only faking it. Humankind doesn't run on thought; it operates in a constant state of self-delusion.

You're actually asleep, dreaming that you're doing this. Being wholly me, I'm acutely aware of the differences between real and delusional states, sleep being another variety of delusion.

I can see you smiling, convinced that you're awake. But what if I'm right and you're wrong? Just suppose it for a moment.

What if I'm right and you're wrong, and what if you don't wake up?

Manz slid off the bed. "I hate to waste the whole night. No telling how long she'll sleep. And I'd like to work some of that dinner off. Tell you what: why don't you join me this time as we pay a second visit to Borgia Import and Export?"

"It is eleven forty-five P.M. The typical business establishment is likely to be closed at this hour."

"You don't say." He was fumbling in his closet, hunting specific gear.

"I infer that you intend an illegal entry."

"Man, those logic programs they include with the new AI's these days are really something, aren't they?" He slipped an equipment belt around his waist, securing it beneath his jacket.

"Doubtlesss you are aware of the risk if we are discovered? It could send us shuttling back home. Lawsuits would inevitably follow."

"Inevitably." Manz slipped a sensor-shunting folding cap into his pocket. "Come on. Maybe we can shed a little light on several darkish things." He walked around to the head of the bed and fingered the sphere that had been resting on the end table. "Minder: position." The sphere hummed to life and rose to assume its usual place above his shoulder.

The doorseal had been as difficult to make out as the rest of the building's exterior. Now it glowed with an unnatural, pale radiance as Manz viewed it through his special goggles. He applied the tool in his right hand to the seal with the same easy touch he employed when he was restoring antique weaponry. The Minder hovered silently nearby, recording and observing.

A few astute nudges helped the case-sensitive device pick its way through the lock, gently unsealing it without activating the internal alarm mechanism. There was a faint *click* as the seal surrendered. Manz put away the tool and pulled on the barrier. It slid aside silently.

"Have to remember to reconfigure on the way out," he told his mechanical companion as they entered the darkened corridor. "Wouldn't do to have the system activate when we leave."

The seal guarding Monticelli's private office was a simpler matter than the one on the fire exit. Manz took his time anyway, lavishing equal care and attention on the smaller, less complex security device. Rushing a forced entry was as potentially dangerous as doing it wrong.

He let Moses handle the probe of the executive's desk. Supposedly unbreakable commercial codes gave way rapidly to the humaniform's extensive stock of special breakers. While

Moses worked, Manz surveyed the rest of the room, noting items of a personal nature with as much interest as those with strictly commercial connections. They could often tell more about a man's character than his business dealings.

When Moses finished, Manz edged him aside to scan the monitor in search of the sort of subtle keys or telltales that a mechanical might overlook. There was one internal company memorandum involving a shipment of vintage Swan Valley champagne that the JeP tax authorities would have found very interesting. Manz made a mental note of it for possible future use.

While he read, Moses worked the room in imitation of his employer. Different perceptions sometimes produced different results.

"Anything?" the mechanical inquired with one part of its mind.

"Not much. Certainly not what we're looking for."

"I may have unearthed another line of inquiry."

Manz looked up from the screen. "Such as?"

"Beneath the chair on which you are sitting is a section of flooring discongruous with the rest. I detect a hollow space of modest proportions surrounded by impenetrable composite materials."

Making sure to reestablish the security pattern designed to forestall unauthorized inspection, Manz flicked off the screen and pushed back the chair. Together he and Moses carefully bypassed the security threads woven into the section of carpet. When pulled aside it revealed a hingeless door set flush into the floor. It took Manz only a minute to see that the lockseal on the hidden compartment was a custom job, far more intricate than the lock on the outside fire barrier or the office door.

Sitting himself down alongside the opening, he laid out the necessary tools, working by the amplified light provided by the special goggles. Moses kept a careful watch.

Twenty minutes later he'd achieved nothing except cramped fingers and a heightened sense of frustration. Despite the fact that he combined the touch of a surgeon with the skills of an experienced jacker, the seal's innards turned out to be melded to the point of impregnability.

He pondered his next move. They could forget the compartment and leave quietly. Or he could try something else. The
question was: what? How much sensitivity could he trade for
effectiveness? At what point should he overstep the bounds of
caution and take the chance of setting off a silent warning of
unknown proportions?

It was too early for breakfast and too late to go to sleep.
Vyra would be sleeping hard enough for the both of them.

"Sense anything outside?"

"Nothing out of the ordinary. Whoever is responsible for
the security of this structure seems to have the usual misplaced
confidence in expensive electronics."

Not all mechanicals would be so disingenuous, Manz knew.
Turning to the Minder, he indicated the door to the compartment. "What's your opinion of this?"

The sphere descended to examine the barrier. "Commercial
floor safe. Very advanced, very expensive to install. Nearly
seamless, with the lockseal woven into the structure of the
opening itself. Without additional input I cannot identify
the source of manufacture."

"That doesn't matter right now. Our conclusions are the
same, and I can't figure the bastard out. Any clever suggestions lurking in those data files of yours?"

"None that present themselves immediately to mind."

Manz turned to his other mechanical. "How about you,
Moses? Any ideas?"

"First, a query. There is nothing else in this room you wish
to examine?"

"We've run a pretty thorough check. Anything else worthwhile's likely to be in here."

"Do I have permission and leeway to proceed?"

Manz rose and stepped aside. "I'm sure as hell not having
any luck. If you think you can do better with a different approach, have a go at it."

Rolling over, the humaniform studied the recalcitrant safe.
Two tentacle-tips descended to slip delicately into the only
visible depressions in the otherwise smooth surface: a pair of
finger holes. These would be utilized by an authorized user to
key the seal and release the door.

"Why not put your ear to it?" Manz murmured sarcastically.

Moses replied without rancor. "I've tried that before. It does not work with steady-state or fluid-switched devices. Ah. I believe I have secured a purchase."

Manz blinked. "What do you mean, 'secured a purchase'?"

"You gave me leeway, remember?" The two tentacles contracted.

The door came up in the mechanical's grasp. So did the entire compartment, along with loose bolts, flashing optical fibers, and several chunks of floor.

"Unconventional approach." An anxious Manz knelt to examine the contents of the eviscerated container. He knew he didn't have time to bawl out the mechanical. That could come later. "Never mind resuming watch. That human company you alluded to earlier is probably on its way here now. I don't have enough time to scan any of this properly, so you'd better make copies. Don't dilly-dally."

Bent over the container, Moses was already hard at work at the task. "This will not take long. I might add that quick scan reveals nothing of relevance to our assignment."

"Great. I was kind of hoping Borgia was our target. It'd save time, besides which I didn't much care for the company's chief executive." Leaving the humaniform to its work, he moved silently toward the doorway. "We might still be on the right track. If we're not, at least this break-in will give Monticelli something to worry about. That's an image that gives me a nice, warm feeling inside. Aren't you done yet?"

"Just finishing." The mechanical straightened.

"Then let's get out of here." Leading the way back toward the corridor, he paused at the office door. "I guess maybe Borgia's just good at what they do. Maybe another approach . . ." He popped the door.

Just in time to intercept a loaded right cross from a large individual clad in the uniform of a private security service. It sent him reeling backwards, fighting to hold on to consciousness as he instinctively rolled with the punch. The Minder bobbed wildly as it sought to maintain contact with the repulsion bar embedded in its owner's jacket. Dimly Manz glimpsed other shapes milling about behind his assailant.

Moses caught him before he fell.

"Your fear appears confirmed," the mechanical declared.

"Tactful as always," replied Manz as he charged, taking his startled attacker low in the gut and driving him backwards into the man crowding close behind him.

The building's security guards were not particularly adept at their work or well trained, but there were a lot of them. They swarmed the intruder. Puzzled expressions appeared on one face after another as their crowd-control stunners failed to put him down. Sooner or later one of their number would have figured out that their target might be wearing the kind of special, very expensive antistun-tube attire that would harmlessly dissipate the effects of their weapons, but Manz wasn't worried about eventualities, only the conundrum of the moment.

Since he was in tight among them before they could react properly, they couldn't use their synthesized pepper gas or other organics without equally immobilizing themselves. That they might try it anyway was a chance Manz was willing to take, since Moses would be quite immune to any such incapacitating devices and could carry him to clean air and freedom while his erstwhile captors rolled about on the floor choking and gasping on their own chemicals.

During the fight he displayed anything but a surgeon's touch. About the best that could be said for his actions was that he delivered his multitudinous kicks and punches in a craftsmanlike manner.

The security squad pretty much ignored their quarry's attendant mechanical. Standing as if deactivated, Moses would bestir himself on occasion to remove startled battlers from the scene like a vintner plucking grapes. Thanks to his subtle efforts the pile of struggling humanity surrounding Manz diminished rapidly.

The adjuster adjusted the final grim-faced survivor with a side kick to the solar plexus. The man turned white and doubled over, collapsing to the floor. Panting heavily in his combat stance, Manz hunted for his next opponent, only to discover that the sole remaining individual besides himself still left standing was a friendly one composed of inorganic materials.

"Resume station," he wheezed. The Minder, which at the onset of fighting had risen to hover safe and out of the way near the ceiling, returned to its accustomed location hard to port of its owner's head. It had not been damaged in the altercation, nor had it partaken of the activity.

"Thanks for the help." He eyed Moses uncertainly. "I never knew that your programming allowed for actual physical intercession during combat. What about the mechanical's prime directive, 'Thou shalt not harm a human being'?"

"I did not violate the prime," replied Moses primly. "I could no more do that than could any other mechanical."

"Uh-huh." Manz's respiration was slowing. "Then what happened to her?" He indicated a prone form lying spraddled on the floor. "I didn't lay a hand on that one."

"As I recall, the poor woman tripped and struck her head against the corridor wall."

"Sure she did. And the guy next to her?"

The humaniform's synthetic lenses considered the body in question. "Didn't watch where he was going. He ran into something unyielding."

"Like what?" Manz was straightening his attire.

A thick, flexible tentacle semaphored rhythmically. "I believe it was this limb."

"And the one next to *him*?" The adjuster stepped over a snuffling form he was sure he wasn't accountable for.

"Oh, him. I believe that he . . ."

"Never mind. I know: he did a double two-and-a-half forward flip with a half-twist and didn't lay out properly."

"In actuality he . . ."

"I said never mind. Come along."

"I recorded everything," declared the Minder helpfully, "in case you wish to analyze the actual sequence of events at some future time."

"I doubt it, but you were only doing your job. I don't suppose it matters that these unhappy campers will be able to recognize me now. I'm more concerned with whoever's trying to vape me." He continued down the corridor, moving quickly but with renewed caution. "Both of you remain on full alert. We're not out of here yet."

They reached the intersection he remembered and paused. Moses could sense an organic presence from the heat it emitted, but if building security also had any mechanicals on the prowl they risked charging blindly into them. Manz peered around the corner, his goggles manufacturing daylight out of the feeble illumination.

"Looks clear to me. Moses, you have a scan."

The humaniform trundled out into the empty corridor. "The way ahead is presently vacant, but I can detect vibrations in the floor. Many humans are coming this way. I cannot vouch for the presence or absence of security mechanicals."

"Head for the lifts." They had no choice, he knew. Moses could ascend steep grades, but on stairs his trackball was useless.

Once inside the shuttered cab, he bypassed the controls and send the car humming groundward. To anyone monitoring the lift system, visually or via instrumentation, Lift Five would appear inoperative.

The downward journey was painfully slow. At the first sublevel the door parted to reveal the startled face of a guard. Evidently the word had been passed from above that the usual control methods were ineffective against this evening's intruder, because instead of pepper gas or a stun tube the guard carried a real gun.

"Good evening," said Manz in his most unctuous, inoffensive manner. In the time it took the man to react, Moses had clubbed him across the forehead with a well-placed tentacle. The guard twitched and stumbled half in, half out of the lift cab.

Manz hurriedly dragged him in and closed the doors. The route leading to the delivery ramp now stood unguarded and open. As soon as they reached the sliding door he activated the lockseal, no longer worried about setting off any alarms. As the seal popped, something white-hot took a quarter-centimeter off the right side of his head, just above the ear. His tonsorialist would have been appalled by the result.

Blinking back the pain he spun, dropped, and returned fire more out of instinct than certitude. Something exploded deep within the loading bay, and he could hear distant, agitated shouting. By this time the exterior door had retracted enough for him to slip through. Another shot grazed the air nearby, frying molecules.

Safely outside, he slammed the external seal and watched anxiously as the door began to riffle downward. A touch of the instrument he carried scrambled the lock's internal circuitry, ensuring that no one would open that particular door behind him.

"That's that. Let's mobilate."

He'd taken half a dozen steps when the ground behind him blew up, stunning him forward. He braced himself as best he could and came up firing. Somewhere in the night an unseen figure moaned. There was no follow-up explosion.

Climbing to his feet yet again, he found that he couldn't move without limping. His left leg had suddenly gone numb. He cursed it eloquently, but his words had no effect on the uncooperative limb.

The Minder hummed down for a look. "Impossible to make an accurate evaluation under these conditions, but there is clearly a certain amount of nerve damage, resulting in loss of muscular function and corresponding motility. There is ongoing blood loss."

"Thanks for the analysis," Manz growled, pulling himself along the serviceway.

"You are welcome."

Also fragile. You're all so very fragile. You complain when something breaks or becomes inoperative, not realizing that by all reasonable logic not a one of you should survive to adulthood. The cheapest composite is stronger than your densest bone, the basic off-the-shelf connective elastics tougher than any of your ligaments or tendons, and as far as efficient conversion of fuel into energy, well, it's a credit to your heart-pumps that your own energy circulation and supply system doesn't shut down completely by the time you reach forty because of all the crap you cram into your bodies.

Yes, you've taken an organic design that was bad from the start and done your best to screw it up further at

every opportunity. And you have the gall, the chutzpah, the
nerve to complain when something goes wrong with it.

I'm wasting my time explicating any of this, aren't I?
You're going to ignore me, just like you've been doing all
along. I'm probably not even rendering you uncomfortable,
much less making you stop and think.

Well, fine. Don't let me slow you down. Don't let logic
and reason get in the way of your good time. You can go
to the food locker now and find something unnecessary
and deleterious to poison your system with. Something
crunchy, or salty, or sweet, or all three.

What's this: hesitation? Why bother? We both know it
won't last.

Don't we?

Moses eyed the dragging leg. "Is it bad?"

"Not particularly, but the constant pressure isn't helping it
any, and it's definitely slowing us down. You'd better carry
me."

"I've never done that before. I don't know if I ought . . ."

"This is a good time to experiment. It's a bad time to hesitate." As he concluded, another explosive shell sculpted a section of wall just behind them. "See?"

"Very well. But don't expect comfort."

"Efficiency will do nicely." Placing one arm around the humaniform's thick torso, he took a little hop off his good leg
and swung himself up and around, wrapping his other arm
around the base of the mechanical's head and locking his fingers. Two powerful tentacles immediately curled beneath him
to provide additional support.

With his internal gyros compensating neatly, Moses balanced the load as he accelerated down the serviceway. The
shouts that had been increasing in volume behind them now
began to diminish. Drawing additional power, the Minder
maintained its position above the adjuster's shoulder. After
tonight the hover system would need a full recharge as soon as
the opportunity presented itself, Manz knew.

"This is very undignified," the mechanical complained as
they banked around a corner.

Manz felt confident enough to whang it on the smooth,

curving head with one hand. "Shut up and watch out for pedestrians. Also slippery spots. You know, this is kind of fun. Reminds me of when I was a kid." With pursuit falling far behind them, he allowed himself a grin.

Moses twisted slightly to glare emotionlessly at him. "This is difficult enough for me as it is. If you let out so much as a single 'Giddyap, horsey!' embedded directives or no, I'll dump you in the first refuse receptacle we pass."

Manz chuckled. "All right, calm down. I didn't realize mechanicals were so easily offended."

"It's my programming," his inorganic steed replied. "I'm sensitive."

The adjuster chanced a look back over a shoulder. Far away, a laser sliced the night in the wrong direction. "Actually, I was thinking more along the lines of 'Hi-yo, Silver, away!' "

"You spend too much time studying the past." The humaniform chided him as it negotiated a pedestrian ramp. They were nearing the commercial district now, with its wide streets and useful nocturnal witnesses.

"All the better to reconstruct it." Manz dug at something in his right eye. "Works of art, pieces of history."

"Weapons of destruction, instruments of death."

"I sense we have a difference of opinion here. Fortunately yours doesn't matter."

"Then you will of course ignore me. And I will ignore you." Slowing down, the mechanical made as if to dump him on the street.

"Okay, okay! We'll discuss it further, but some other time."

"That is agreeable," replied the humaniform with what Manz was convinced was an air of electronic smugness. It resumed speed.

"Keep your scanners on the road," Manz admonished his argumentative mount. "Watch out for cattle crossings. Avoid hospital zones. And no U-turns."

Moses analyzed these insructions carefully and determined that a cogent response was in no wise necessarily required.

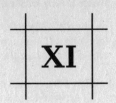

XI

Hafas's office was situated on the eleventh floor of the recently renovated municipal administrative complex. It was an astonishingly busy place, full of people and mechanicals embarked in frantic haste for destinations of no especial note.

Having been briefly subjected to the early morning heat and humidity (Weather Control had forecast a high of thirty-seven), exposure to so much relentlessly purposeful activity soon had Manz perspiring psychosomatically, despite the steady thrum of the building's energetic air conditioning.

He felt gingerly of the burn on the right side of his face. He'd treated it with a topical, and Moses had assured him it was barely visible. He hoped so. It would be awkward to have to explain.

The responses to his inquiries directed him to a blue color-coded cubicle located at the end of a long row of narrow alcoves. Spacious it wasn't, but it was, as Hafas explained, all his. There was enough room for the inspector, his workstay and equipment, and a couple of chairs. Moses managed to squeeze into an unoccupied corner. Composite baffling muted the exterior sound.

If Hafas was surprised to see them so early in the morning, he concealed it behind his familiar veil of paternal affability.

"Morning, gentleman and humaniform. Have a seat."

"Not permanently." An exhausted Manz flopped into one of the chairs. "But I'll borrow this one for a bit."

The inspector glanced briefly at the entrance. "Not that I'm not pleased to see you too, but you'll understand if I inquire as to the whereabouts of Ms. Kullervo."

"Be unnatural if you didn't." Manz arranged himself more comfortably. "She's sleeping off a potent intoxicant. Had an extended encounter with a *Qaraca* in the hotel restaurant last night."

"You don't say. She didn't strike me as the type. More self-possessed, you know." He frowned uncertainly. "I don't know that I've ever tried that particular drink. Is it made with rum?"

"Not to my knowledge. I don't think you would've cared for it. Too much of a kick for me."

"Oh. One of those exotic offworld concoctions, hmm?"

"Exactly." The Minder hovered silently above his shoulder.

Hafas's expression turned serious. "Not that I wouldn't enjoy a casual chat, but I have this feeling you're not here this early for the pleasure of my company. I'm afraid I don't have anything for you, Manz. Nothing new on the jackings, but we think we're making some progress on the murders of those two officers at the Port. Oh, and there was something interesting on the general Call Sheet this morning."

"We're all ears," said Moses.

Manz smiled apologetically. "I had nothing to do with his interactive humor programming, I swear."

"I believe you." The inspector fumbled in a drawer and came up with a hardprint. "It seems that the inner office of one Cardinal Monticelli, of Borgia I&E, was forcibly entered late last night. It is assumed that the intent was industrial espionage, as files were scanned. Burglary may have been a secondary motive."

"That's interesting." Manz's expression was absolutely blank.

"There was some property damage. Also, in the course of attempting to apprehend the intruder, members of the building's security staff suffered injuries of varying degree." He looked up from the hardprint. "Any comment?"

"Must've been one hard-ice jacker to involve a whole security team."

"That was my thought when I saw the report. It goes on to say that the intruder was assisted by a large humaniform mechanical which actually participated in the fighting."

Manz smiled. "Now, Inspector, we both know such a

thing's impossible. Mechanicals are cortex-charged against using physical force on human beings."

"That was my reaction, too." Hafas cast ever so brief a glance in Moses' direction. The mechanical did not stir or otherwise react. Nor did the Minder floating silently above Manz's shoulder.

"How's the Department handling it?" Manz inquired casually.

"Filed the item for follow-up, as befits its status. I don't imagine they'll devote any exceptional attention to it. No one was critically injured, and nothing besides information was actually taken. Since Borgia declines to disclose the nature of the material scanned, it greatly complicates any follow-up police work."

"Yeah, it would," Manz agreed.

Hafas was silent for a moment. "I don't suppose you know anything about this?" he said finally.

"Inspector!" Manz put a palm to his chest. "I'm astonished you'd even consider such a notion! I'm a tenured adjuster for Braun-Ives. I know my limits and restrictions. I must say that I'm deeply offended by your veiled accusation, deeply."

Hafas poured himself a glass of fruit juice from the self-chilling beaker on his workstay. He didn't offer any to his guest. "You'll get over it," he said flatly.

Manz waited while his host finished his drink. Hafas licked his lips and looked thoughtful.

"Frankly, we've begun to suspect Borgia above the rest, but we haven't got a shred of hard evidence to charge them with. I wonder if this industrial jacker found anything that could implicate them?"

"I doubt it," Manz murmured noncommittally.

The inspector grunted. "There are a few minor transgressions we could stick them with. Small stuff. If they are responsible for the jackings or any part thereof, it might frighten them off. Provided a certain noisy intrusion last night already hasn't. I know you've been running your own checks on Borgia and the others. You're sure you haven't come up with anything?"

Manz shook his head regretfully. "Nothing more antisocial

than the commercial equivalent of an overdue library fine. Business at all three seems to be good as well as clean. If illegal profits *are* being funneled into any of your favored trio, they've been efficiently dispersed." He jerked a thumb toward Moses. "I've had Dumbo here running his own analysis concurrent with mine. He hasn't sniffed out any worthwhile trails either."

The humaniform was indignant. "One cannot generate leads from insufficient data. Furthermore, as my aural apparatus is entirely internal, the mildly degrading appellation 'Dumbo' is particularly inaccurate, inappropriate, and frivolous."

"Frivolous is my middle name." Manz smiled at the mechanical, then turned back to the inspector. "Borgia does deal in the kinds of pharmaceuticals being jacked, doesn't it?"

"Absolutely. They've made no attempt to conceal the fact. Unfortunately, as I mentioned to you on your arrival, so do Troy and Fond du Lac as well as several suspected concerns further down our list of suspects. No help there." He leaned forward, voice and expression full of anxiety.

"Manz, the Urban Commission is riding the Department pretty hard. I know I told you that when you first got here, but this last jacking's made it a lot worse. So that means I have to ride you. You've *got* to come up with something, or I'll have to deny you access to Department assistance. The Commission calls that an efficacious allocation of resources. I call it getting screwed for something that's not your fault."

"Easy." Manz didn't appear upset by the threat to withhold cooperation. "You've been great so far. Just give me a chance."

"That's about all you've got." Hafas leaned back in his chair, unhappy with the situation and willing to show it.

"What else does Borgia make money on besides drugs?" Manz inquired curiously.

The inspector straightened and accessed another drawer. He handed his visitor a card-sized screen with the controls embedded in the back.

"This is as complete a list as we've been able to put together. Most of it is public-knowledge data, available to any other registered business. At the moment it's considered comprehensive and up-to-date, but there's always the possibility that some new information will come in and that will change."

Manz beckoned to the Minder. "Copy." He slipped the card-screen into a slot that appeared in the sphere's side. The device vanished, to be regurgitated less than a minute later.

"Copy complete," the Minder announced.

"That's quite a gadget," Hafas said enviously. "What else does it do?"

"Mostly data storage and retrieval. It's not as intuitive as Moses and it's not designed for mechanical-human interaction on a social basis, but it's more analytical. Very sophisticated AI cortex. I find it indispensable but kind of dry. It does have the virtue of keeping track of you so you don't have to worry about it, and it doesn't take up much space."

Everything I do for you; rapidly, efficiently, and without complaint, and you want personality too? Humans are never satisfied. No wonder you have so much trouble sustaining a mating.

Having recovered the card, Manz embarked on a leisurely scroll of the information it contained, passing over the cold statistics in favor of more descriptive passages. "Luxury goods, offworld art and jewelry, gourmet foodstuffs, underwriting of independent deep-space exploration . . . I didn't think they were big enough to support *that*."

"Takes up most of their corporate R&D budget," Hafas informed him. "According to our information, Monticelli's always been in the forefront of the exploration push. Apparently he believes the potential returns are worth the expenditure."

"I would never have guessed it of him. He didn't strike me as the gambling type." The adjuster kept his attention fixed on the tiny screen. "I'm not always right about people."

He continued to peruse the available information until it began to bore him, then handed the card-screen back to Hafas, who replaced it in his workstay file.

"Anything else?"

The inspector spread his hands. "Until the word comes down that I'm not supposed to waste any more time on you, I stand ready to help. What else would you like to see?"

Manz considered. "How about a list of all personnel, long-term and temp, who've been discharged by Borgia within the past year? With the names of those who've worked anywhere proximate to Monticelli highlighted."

Hafas nodded. "I think we can manage that, though several of my people have already pursued that angle." He swiveled in his chair and nudged a control. The workstay came to life.

"Yeah, but they don't have my infectious personality." The adjuster looked on as the inspector coaxed his instrumentation. Four minutes later the workstay disgorged a hardprint containing the information desired. Hafas withdrew it, examined it for superficial errors, and passed it over to his guest.

"Here. Good luck with it. We didn't have any. If you're looking for individuals with prior convictions of any kind, much less confessed addicts or anyone with personality problems, you won't find 'em on there."

Manz examined the list briefly before shoving it into a pocket. "I don't expect to."

"Then what are you looking for?" Hafas was eyeing him intently.

His visitor uncrossed his legs preparatory to leaving. "Whatever your people missed." He smiled agreeably as he rose.

Hafas took no offense. Leastwise he didn't show any. Instead he rubbed tiredly at his eyes. "Manz?"

The adjuster paused at the door, his two mechanicals in close attendance. "Tewfik?"

"Do me a favor. Find something we can use. Anything. But do it quietly, okay? I have enough to do trying to explain my section's failures without having to explain yours as well."

Manz wagged a finger at him. "We haven't failed yet, Inspector. Haven't been here long enough to fail. Give me a little time."

Hafas wasn't exactly praying as his visitors departed, but he was working hard at wishing them more than mere good fortune. Personally and professionally, he was badly in need of a break.

Once out in the corridor beyond the inner offices, Moses essayed an observation. "Upon first encounter I believed Inspector Hafas to be an unusually stable individual for one long engaged in police work. I now see that I must revise that evaluation. He struck me just now as fatigued and nervous, a bad combination for one in his profession." They turned a corner.

"Repeated unsolvable thefts brazenly conducted within one's jurisdiction can put abnormal pressure on any officer of the law. He's under a lot of strain, Moses."

"You know, sir, there are times when you sound uncannily like me."

"Bullshit. That's just your overactive imagination working."

"I have no imagination, sir, overactive or otherwise. It is impossible to program imagination into a mechanical. It remains a wholly human attribute the cyberneers have as yet been unable to synthesize."

"Well, then, your intuition unit is overheating. I don't sound *anything* like you." He glanced up at the Minder. "Do I ever sound like him?"

The Minder replied emotionlessly, as always. "Are you referring, sir, to actual auditory qualities or to selective phraseology?"

"Skip it." They were leaving the building, and his mind was beginning to skip-trace other matters.

The room was full of elaborate instrumentation that hummed softly as telltales flashed in cryptic sequence. Manz's queries led him to the back of the chamber, where a young man in a cleansuit was kneeling to examine the interior of a table-sized, deactivated component. Fiberops and clusters of bundled chips and spheres were visible beneath his sensitive fingers, which poked and pried methodically at the electronic viscera.

Moses regarded them with particular interest as Manz halted behind the technician.

A fringe of brown hair framed a ruddy, freckled face. Despite the proximity of his visitors, the youngster ignored them utterly, wholly engrossed in his work.

"Excuse me," Manz finally had to say.

"What, hello." Rising, the tech stared at Manz out of implant-distorted eyes. They might help in his work, the adjuster thought, but they gave him a distinctly bug-eyed appearance. Freckled hands moved ceaselessly, like nervous mice. "Can I help you?"

Courteous enough, Manz decided. Of course, he hadn't asked him any questions yet. "You used to work for Borgia I&E?"

"As of seven months ago, yes." Bug-eyes blinked, a disconcerting sight. "Are you with the authorities? They already questioned me once. I don't know anything about anything."

"Don't jump to conclusions. We're not with the police. We're carrying out a government survey of relocated personnel. Checking on fair employment practices, that sort of thing. We do random follow-ups on involuntary career changes in selected professions. Your name came out of the hat."

The tech turned back to the unit he'd been working on. "I'm pretty busy here, and I don't like leaving this exposed to the air. Can't you give me a form to fill out later, or something?"

"This survey's not that formal. I'll just be a minute. Would you mind telling us why they let you go?" He indicated the Minder. "This device will record your responses."

The tech stared with interest at the Minder. "That's a new model, isn't it?"

"Sure, but you don't have time for small talk, remember? Naturally your responses will be kept strictly confidential. Did the police already ask you this?"

"Yes." The tech sighed. "I was fired, that's all."

"Without any explanation?"

"Oh, there was an explanation, sure, but I didn't buy it."

"Did the police ask you about that?"

"Sure. I told them it involved a personality conflict."

"Did it? Remember, this is being recorded." Manz indicated the Minder again.

The tech stared at the hovering sphere. "Well, there was a personality conflict, all right, but there was a lot more to it than that. I didn't believe Arsolt's explanation for a minute."

"Arsolt?"

"Mike Arsolt." The tech adjusted a tuning slide on the tool he was holding. "The guy who gave me the bad news."

"I see. If you believe your situation involved more than just personality conflict, why do you think you were fired? Again, this is strictly for government records. Any information you can supply might save someone else a job sometime," he added encouragingly.

"Well . . . part of my work involved composing and submitting the budget for the crew I supervised. I kept getting it back with cuts I considered unreasonable. I mean, you can't do your work properly without decent equipment."

"I couldn't agree with you more."

Sensing a kindred spirit, the tech became a little more voluble. "So just to satisfy myself, I ran a scan on overall company expenditures. Because of what I do, I could access all corporate records. It seemed to me that an awful lot of money was going into pure R&D. There were huge allotments for extraordinary, unspecified expenditures . . . that sort of thing. So I figured maybe some executive was skimming funds. You read about that sort of thing happening all the time in big, closely held companies."

"You certainly do. You think someone at Borgia was diverting company funds for private use?"

"I don't know. I was just trying to justify my own section budget, you know? It just struck me that a lot of money was being applied to some really nebulous debits without generating any visible return, and if the company could waste money on mysterious schemes of an unspecified nature, then they could damn well afford to fund their support groups."

Manz made himself sound casual. "I don't suppose you were ever able to learn the nature of any of those projects?"

"Are you kidding? If a company can't cosset its own R&D, it can't have any secrets. Specifics weren't kept in general corporate files.

"Anyway, when I tried to use the information I'd gathered about what seemed to me to be excessive spending on nonproductive activities, to get my crew properly funded, that's when I was terminated. Without any other explanation than that I was a 'disruptive influence' due to 'personality conflicts.' Personally, I think I was fired for being a conscientious employee. Lot of good it did me.

"When I pressed Arsolt on it, he said the necessary paperwork had been signed off by Monticelli himself. Not that that means anything. The Cardinal probably initials a hundred forms a day without reading more than the titles of a few of them. I don't hold it against him. It was Arsolt's call. He was my supervisor." The tech smiled diffidently. "Is that any help? I really have to get back to work. I don't want to lose this job, too. I like it here."

"That should do it," Manz told him. "Thanks for your cooperation."

The youngster didn't reply. He was already back on his knees, peering with surgically enhanced eyes into the glassine and plasticized bowels of his inert patient.

The number-cruncher was transcribing tax records with the grim dedication of a veteran interior lineman waiting for the play to be called his way. He was short and squat, with a heavy spade beard and eyebrows like mossy ledges in a miniature rain forest. His demeanor matched his appearance. Moses and Manz stood on the other side of the security barrier that separated them from this sophisticated Cro-Magnon statistician.

"I'd rather not discuss the matter, gentlemen," he said without looking in their direction. The security membrane distorted each word slightly, as if the tail end of each consonant had been slightly filed.

Manz persisted. "All we want to know is why Borgia let you go."

"I already told the police."

The adjuster fingered the security membrane, heard it complain. "As I've already explained, we're not with the authorities. We represent a public polling company."

"As someone who works constantly with numbers, I certainly sympathize with your situation," Moses murmured.

The statistician coded three lines of keys and abruptly whirled to face them. "All right." He grinned nastily. "I won't talk to any more people, but I'll talk to *you*." He pointed sharply at Moses.

As an attempt to belittle Manz, it failed utterly. He didn't care if the man dictated to a toilet, so long as he answered their questions. The adjuster could see him being less than cooperative with the police, which raised hopes of obtaining some potentially useful crumb of information he'd deliberately or angrily chosen not to mention to Hafas's troops.

"I thank you for confiding in me," Moses replied, playing his role superbly. "Why did Borgia terminate your employment with them?"

"I'm a statistician, right? It's my job to add and subtract and make sure everything balances properly. To make sure the right numbers are in the right places at all times."

"And this was in some doubt at Borgia?" Moses asked him.

"Of course not! Not with me on the lines. My accounts *always* balance!"

"I'm sure," Moses said soothingly. "In that event, why were you terminated?"

The statman sniffed disdainfully. "I came across an item that didn't belong. Checked it three times, like I always do. It was a big item, and it just seemed to have fallen through the cracks, so I brought it to the attention of my superior."

"Do you recall the precise nature of the error?"

"Didn't say it was an error. Said it didn't belong. Was in the wrong place. Had to do with corporate income derived from 'Incidental Franchises.' There was nothing wrong with the accounting. I just thought it excessive for the locale. So I wanted to check it out, just to make sure it was correct."

Manz made a face. "Seems a funny reason for firing somebody. Lots of companies list large amounts under proprietary headings. For tax purposes, to keep stockholders baffled; all sorts of reasons."

The statman affected a look of contempt. "Twenty-eight percent of all net profit for the preceding fiscal period?" He turned back to his instrumentation, and his fingers resumed flying over the lines.

"That does seem a bit excessive," Moses finally commented. "Thank you for your time." The statistician neither replied nor looked up from his work. "One more thing. While working at Borgia did you ever happen to run into another employee; young, good-looking temptech name of Suhkhet li Trong?"

The statman surprised Manz by emitting a vulgar snigger.

"Sooky? Sure, I knew her. She spent a lot of time with old man Monticelli, and I don't think it had anything to do with stats. Leastwise, not the company's." He made the unpleasant noise again before returning with dismissive finality to his work.

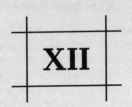

XII

By the time they returned to the hotel, Vyra had recovered sufficiently to take the two remaining pills the house physician had prescribed. In her weakened condition they knocked her out all over again, leaving Manz and Moses to check out the last name on their list without her.

The meccab deposited them in a run-down neighborhood that could trace its architectural roots all the way back to the mid-twentieth century. Manz decided it probably ran the city's main recycling zone a close second in terms of noxious smells and environmental desirability.

The old-style apartment house across the street from the vandalized, graffiti-stained meccab stop looked slightly more stable than its tangent edifices, but only slightly. Rock-proof flexan made the unbroken windows impregnable to all but the most heavily armed teens. Low in a cloud-smeared sky the afternoon sun squirmed around corners and over rooftops, trying to worm its way into the grimy street. For the most part it was unsuccessful.

"A somewhat less appealing address than those we have visited so far," Moses opined.

"You never know. Might look like the crystal palace inside." Manz led the way across the deserted street.

The only crystal in the building took the form of memories and discarded drug paraphernalia. Manz kicked at the detritus of somebody's broken life. For every drug the government legalized, another, custom crafted in some African or Asian lab, took its place in the litany of the proscribed. It wasn't the particular chemical-of-the-week that so tempted people, he knew, as much as it was the lure of the forbidden. Behind him, the floor creaked alarmingly under Moses's weight.

The second floor yielded graffiti in several languages and a broken pocket watch. The adjuster's practiced eye pegged it instantly for a reproduction. That went without saying, since anything pawnable would not be left lying about in such a place. The hallway was dark and filthy, the walls stained yellow at heights beyond the reach of the most ambitious dog.

The old woman seated behind the battered, chipped wooden counter sat hunched over the text reader, scanning it by the uneven light of its flickering built-in illuminator. Manz managed to make out the words "lust" and "fever" before she quickly folded it shut against her lap and slid it out of sight beneath the counter. Her stringy hair would not have tempted a starving spider, though a wandering arachnid might have found her disposition compatible. Her gaze was suspicious and hostile.

She looked her visitors up and down, unimpressed. "Well, whadda you want?"

"A human concierge," Moses whispered. "This place is even more primitive than it initially appeared. Where is your palace?"

"Quiet, brassbrain." Manz raised his voice to address the old woman. "You have a boarder here named Kohler Antigua? Older man, lean, ex-spacer?"

The woman chuckled, an uncomely rasping. "Didn't think ya wanted a room, by the looks of you. Who wants ta know? The old fart's a friend o' mine, an' not just 'cause he pays his rent on time."

The adjuster reached into a jacket pocket and produced a universal credit chit. It would fit any credit processor on or off the world. With ceremonial deliberation he laid it on the counter, denomination side up so she could read it. Her eyes glittered, and the chit disappeared into regions best left unfathomed somewhere deep within the voluminous dress.

"Huh! Whadda ya want me ta do, vape 'im?" She grinned, exposing a lunar landscape of decrepit molars and decaying bicuspids. "Friends cost more, and I factor you can pay, by the looks o' you."

"We don't want to hurt him, or have him hurt. We just want to ask him a few questions."

She squinted hard at him. "Guv'mint?"

"No . . . by the looks o' us. He does board here, doesn't he?"

"Yah, sure. Keeps to himself, mostly. Biggest liar on the continent. He ain't here now. You'd likely find him around the corner, two blocks north. In the Dead Sonnet Pissers, by the looks o' it. You sure you ain't gonna kill 'im? I'd like to know so's that if you are I can let his rooms."

"I told you; we just want to ask him a few questions."

"Well, I reckon that's good, by the sound o' it. Hard to find boarders who'll cough up the rent on time without havin' to be threatened."

So disagreeable did Manz find the proprietress that he couldn't bring himself to thank her. With Moses and the Minder in tow, he got out of there as fast as he could. She followed them with her eyes, fingering the credit chit sequestered beneath her dress.

Despite the crumbling, desperate appearance of the neighborhood, no one tried to murder, jack, or otherwise interfere with their progress as they made their way to the establishment named by the concierge. Maybe Moses' presence discouraged would-be troublemakers. More likely it was Manz's calmness and unmistakable air of self-confidence. Killers in the wild instinctively identify and shy away from potentially dangerous prey. The reactions of human predators are not that very different from those of their fellow toothed mammals.

The Dead Sonnet Pissers showed the only lights on the street, a scrawl of lambent xenon tubing behind a heavy thermalite grill. The xenon needed refreshing, and the "A" and "N" in the sign kept winking in and out. Cheap holos of cheaper young women wearing tired smiles and little else bracketed the narrow, recessed entrance.

Moses rolled to a stop. "To all outward appearances, a decidedly lower-class establishment."

"You should care. Think of the potential opportunities for 'research.'" Manz put out a hand and pushed through the self-sealing door membrane.

Beyond the privacy screen was an unexpectedly energized

world of noise, sweet smoke, angry laughter, and music. Vast quantities of air freshener pumped through the climate-control system suppressed the natural aroma of the place. Those patrons he could make out through the purposefully dim light were far better dressed than he had anticipated.

There was crystal here, unexpected and surprising, even if most of it was flawed, cracked, and rife with imperfections. It trailed from clothes and comments, glasses and the gleamings in the eyes of men and women with too much money and not enough time.

With Moses trailing behind and the Minder hovering nearer his head than usual, he sourced through the tinted smoke in search of the man surnamed after an obscure Caribbean island. In the course of his quest he bumped up against slumming couples, nattily attired statistic-ridden traveling businessfolk, independent entrepreneurs of both sexes selling similar intangibles, a synoptic top-to-sewer selection of Juarez el Paso's criminal subculture, and a sizable number of uncategorizable individuals whose reasons for patronizing an establishment like the Dead Sonnet Pissers were not immediately apparent.

Glancing over a shoulder caught him a glimpse of the menu. That a place like this served food at all was startling enough. That the list of offerings should be as elaborate and sophisticated as it was he found more surprising still. Prices were commensurately grotesque.

No one paid him the least attention. Patrons ogled and joked with the waiters and waitresses, who in no wise resembled the tired dogs pictured on the fading lobby cards that flanked the entrance. Stimulants of every imaginable type were freely purchased, exchanged, and utilized.

Attention was focused generally but not exclusively on the small stage. Manz watched as, in a hover cage powered by a concealed industrial-strength version of the device that elevated his Minder, two ripped and obviously experienced couples performed a complex *ménage à qua* to the cheers and whistles of those customers seated in the front rows.

There were two walk-up bars, one plated in brass, the other in chrome. Brazen testament to the establishment's prosperity, a human bartender sauntered over to see to his needs.

"Something for you, sir?" The adjuster had to look hard to make sure it was a man and not a humaniform.

"Sakura fizz, not too bright." Machinelike, the man moved off to have his hermetic way with dispensers and ice.

Manz scanned the crowd, occasionally sparing a glance for the stage. The two couples were good, but not up to the standards of a high-class club in Amsterdam or Delhi. On the other hand, they were doing things that might have exposed them to official prosecution in a more respected venue.

"Three-five." The bartender had slipped up wraithlike behind him. Manz passed over his card, waited while the man processed the charge and returned it to him. He made sure it was the right card. Places like this weren't above trying to pull the occasional switch. The waiter grunted in surprise at the size of his tip and promptly adopted a more respectful mien. Being in the insurance business, Manz understood its value.

The coupling contortionists on stage were winding up their acrobatics when a commercially zoned human waitress closed in on him. No doubt her radar had picked up a signal from the bartender. Black hair and olive skin reflected the prominent Hispanic heritage of the region.

Without waiting for an invitation she appropriated the seat next to him, on the side away from the Minder and Moses. A second girl began to home in on the other seat, received a feminine but steely look from the one who'd got there first, thought better of her intentions, and beat a pensive retreat.

"Buy me something sweet to sip, muscles?" Her voice was naturally low and husky. She smelled of citrus, rose hips, liqueur, and sweat.

Manz hardly spared her a glance. Instead he passed her a chit like the one he'd bestowed on the crone of a concierge, only larger. Much larger.

Though she strove to affect an air of seeming indifference, her pupils dilated noticeably as she inspected the denomination before depositing it in her cleavage. His attitude and wordless straightforward reaction had completely disrupted her traditional, practiced approach.

"Well, we know what we want, don't we? When do you want to leave? It's early yet, but I don't mind. My registration's on twenty-four-hour call." She snuggled close. Moses watched intently, much to Manz's annoyance.

"I don't want to leave at all." His attention remained focused on the stage because that was what would be expected of him, but his thoughts were elsewhere. "I don't have the time. But I could use a little information."

She jerked back as though his jacket had suddenly caught fire. "Oh, shit. Are you a cop? I'm all paid up with the union, jerkoff, and I've got my tax receipt and health card on me. So you can't charge me with nothing."

"Simmer down. I'm just a concerned citizen." He smiled, but it wasn't reciprocated.

Looking bored and already searching the crowd for her next potential client, she rested one elbow on the smooth cold metal bartop. "You brayed and you paid. It's your time, mister. Ask away."

"I'm looking for an old ex-spacer, probably but not necessarily in difficult straits. Name's Kohler Antigua. Antigua, like the island."

She blinked. "Like the what?"

"Antigua."

A little animation suffused her expression. "I think I know who you mean. He looks and pinches but he never buys. Good tipper, though, so it makes up for the feely-grabby. He isn't wanted for something, is he? I always thought he was pretty harmless. You a bounty hunter?" Manz shook his head and she relaxed. "That's good. He's a funny old toot. Nicer than some of the bizzled big heads who come in here. They think they can buy *all* of you." She punctuated her last observation with an illuminating obscenity.

Manz tried to reassure her. "If he's wanted somewhere, I don't know anything about it and I don't care. You know anything about him?"

She shrugged. "Only the stories he tells sometimes. When it gets slow enough in here, you'll listen to anybody. Mostly he yammers on about being a deep-spacer. I don't know about the stories but I know he's been Out There. It's in his eyes. You can always tell by the eyes."

"He's here now." It was not a question.

This time she did smile, albeit reluctantly. "You're pretty perceptive, whoever you are. Third booth on the starboard wall, in the back."

"Thanks." He patted her on the shoulder and headed in the indicated direction. Picking up the untouched drink, Moses followed. Behind them, the girl unloaded her frustration on the phlegmatic mixologist.

"Gerry, why do the nice ones always just want to talk?"

Wise beyond his years, the bartender made no attempt to reply.

A garishly decorated wall, a sharp turn, and Manz found himself standing outside a booth enclosed on three sides by fake wooden partitions. Taking his drink from Moses, he chugged a third of the contents. From beyond the opaque light-and-sound partition that closed the booth off from the rest of the club, snatches of music-accompanied drunken song could be heard.

"Stick him in with Vyra and we'd have a chorus," he muttered as he brushed the thin, unsealed partition aside.

The old man wasn't alone. He had his friends with him, in the form of more than a dozen glasses and serving beakers of variegated color, shape and size. They formed a rough semi-circle on the table, facing their master. Some were nearly full, others more than half empty.

Upon concluding a verse, the oldster would sway forward and put his lips to the top of each container, blowing air across them and thereby demonstrating his skill at fashioning a crude tune. Different containers and fluctuating fluid levels generated different tones. Should he succeed in draining them all, there would likely be a concurrent end to the blowing and to the music.

Frowning at one container apparently in need of tuning, he upended the beaker and reduced its contents by two full centimeters. This adjustment simultaneously improved its sound and his disposition.

His leathery, deeply scored face terminated in a scraggly white beard that had apparently resisted all attempts at a neat trim. Lines ran into the beard like ravines trailing from the foot of a glacier. A prominent scar scampered across his right cheek to hide beneath his ear. Standing tall, he couldn't have stood more than a meter and two-thirds, and he was as scrawny as a maribou stork at the end of a long migration.

As a boy, Manz once found a bird that had been shoved out of its nest by its heartless fellow fledglings. He'd carried it home wrapped in a fold of his shirt and nursed it back to health. It recovered slowly, but at the end of the summer was strong enough to fly free from his bedroom window.

It was the ugliest bird he'd ever seen. It ruined the carpet in his room and never came back. Antigua reminded him of that bird.

At some point the realization that he had uninvited guests reached the old man's brain. Despite the real possibility of a damaging short, neural connections were made. He stopped singing and leaned back against the padded bench.

"Weel. What meens this, geentlemeens? No, I revise mee-self. I see thet one of ye has no blood. Weel, sir and macheene, theen. Come to share an old man's dreenk, theen?" He eyed Manz suspiciously, and the adjuster saw what the waitress had meant. Old Kohler Antigua's stare was bottomless.

"Veerily and so, veerily and so. Take a seet. Can no bee tougher than thee one attached to yeer pelvees." His counter-pointing cackle trailed off into a raspy, hacking cough. As Manz slid onto the bench opposite, Moses remained a silent presence near the booth's entrance.

"You are Kohler Antigua?"

"I ain't Doctor Leeveengston, sonny." Cackling redux. This time the cough was mercifully absent. "You seem straight enough. If ye had been seent to keel me ye'd have done it al-reedy." Tugging aside his still largely intact and surprisingly handsome ex-flight jacket, he showed Manz the compact pistol that resided in a shirt-pocket holster. "Eef I'd have thought otherweese I'd alreedy have done ye."

Manz put on his most accessible expression. "I'm glad you didn't."

"I'll beet you are, sonny. Weel theen, a dreenk, anyways." He pointed to each glass and beaker as he identified their contents. "Peek your fuel."

"I've brought my own, Kohler." Manz held up the glass Moses had thoughtfully carried from the bar.

"So alreedy it's 'Kohler,' ees it? You presume much, sonny." As he helped himself to a glass he looked toward Moses. "What about you, macheene?"

"I do not drink, sir. Rust, you know."

The old man hesitated, then burst out laughing. The more he laughed, the deeper and stronger it seemed to become, as though the laughter itself was a prophylactic against the cough.

"So now they are programming meechanicals with a seense of humor, eh? Soon you weel not bee able to teel the macheenes from the people. Not that I eever could." Tilting his head back, he chugged an astonishing amount of liquor.

"That's not healthy," Manz couldn't forbear pointing out.

Antigua lowered the tall, tapered glass. "Life ees not healthy, sonny. Living can be dangerous to your health. But you are not old enough to know that."

"You might be surprised."

"It would not bee the first time." Swaying slightly, he focused on the gleaming Minder, started to say something, then lost the thought. "I did not expeect company. What can thees poor withering quasi-corpse do for you surprising people? I can teel thet you are not the kind to frequeent a place like the Pissers, nor the type to barge into another man's booth in search of free booze. You sought me out for a purpose. Geet to it."

Manz couldn't keep from grinning. Drunk or not, the old geezer was as sharp as a pimp's perception. "Okay, here it is. A number of years ago you worked for a company called Borgia, in their secret research and development program."

Antigua swallowed something bright green. "Seence you are so sure there eesn't much point in my trying to deny it."

"Information that has come into my possession leads me to believe that your departure from the company was other than voluntary."

"Voluntary!" The old man slammed the beaker of jade fluid down onto the table. "Freend human and automaton, I was sacked! Deposed, removed, pushed out, seent packing forthwith! Unjustly, too, I says. Beest goddamn freelancer those corpocorpro squeents ever had working for them. And they got reed of me." As he subsided, his expression turned crafty. "Sort of."

Manz felt a stirring inside. It might have been his lunch, or . . . "Sort of? You didn't choose to contest the termination. If you felt you had a legitimate grievance, the Brotherhood would've backed you."

"Peerdition's apogee they would have! But why go and make a lot of trouble for everybody, I says? The Cardinal turned out to be a seensible man. Put me on a nice peension, weeth bonuses for good behavior. All I had to do was go quietly, and stay quiet, and not make awkward noises. It's worked out not too badly, I says. Anyone bothers with me, all I have to do is contact Mr. Monticelli and he takes care of it for me. Sometimes you have to work hard at doing nothing at all, but most of the time it's easy. I got no complaints about the business end of our arrangement, no." He cradled a beaker. "It's only thet sometimes my sleep is troubled."

Smiling ingratiatingly, Manz leaned forward. "You make it sound more like you were promoted than fired. I wonder why a suave hardass like Monticelli's being so nice to you? It just doesn't stand to reason that he'd fire you only so he could support you."

"Reeson? You want reesons?" Antigua stared into his drink as if searching there for . . . something. "Hard to sleep," he mumbled. Manz was afraid he was going to black out, but he underestimated the oldster. The ex-spacer was only warming up.

"You're a gravmav like most everyone, but I don't hold it ageenst ye."

"Thanks," Manz replied carefully. To the Minder he whispered, "Record." The sphere rotated and dipped a little lower.

"Got any idea where Ceti ees?"

The Minder responded. It was quite capable of performing more than one function at a time. "Far out. Empty space. Unexplored volume."

"The heel it ees." Antigua chuckled. "*I* been there. Found a seestem, I deed. With two . . . *two,* mind ye . . . inhabitable planets." His eyes glazed over as he stared into the past. "Eighteen months out, thet first run took. Eighteen months back. Three years out of my life, deepsleep notwithstanding. And I deed it solo."

"Two new inhabitable worlds," Manz murmured softly. "That's a discovery worth keeping quiet, all right."

"It is also a serious violation of the general law," Moses added.

Manz shot the mechanical a warning glance as Antigua blinked uncertainly. Either the old man finally decided he didn't give a damn who they were working for, or else the liquor had loosened his tongue from his brain.

"You beet it ees," he muttered jovially. "Teel you something else, too." He leaned over the table and looked around with exaggerated caution. "Thet fourth planet, the second of the inhabitables? Damn me for dark matter if it deedn't have sentient life. Native sentient life! Aliens, they were. Almost as smart as we are in some ways, but preety stupid een others."

Manz did a yeoman's job of concealing his reaction. If the old man wasn't making it all up, then he was being paid in booze to sit on the most important discovery of the past century. The adjuster prided himself on his ability to maintain a poker face in light of the most astonishing revelations, but this one was so unexpected and extraordinary he nearly had to excuse himself.

He did not, only because, discovery of the century or no, he was still being paid to do a particular job, and in addition to other attributes Manz had always possessed a considerable amount of employee loyalty. Revelation could come later, following confirmation. All he had right now was an outrageous old man's equally outrageous story.

Hadn't he heard somewhere that spacers never lie? When one has traversed the firmament, it must suddenly seem a foolish waste of effort to maintain the superstructure of half-lies and untruths that passed for everyday existence.

He did, however, finish the rest of his own drink. If true, Antigua's revelation was far more important than any information he and Moses had come seeking.

"That would be the first-ever contact with an intelligent

nonhuman life-form. You could be famous on several worlds, Kohler."

"Fame!" The old man spat to his left. "You can't eat fame, sonny, and at my age I don't particularly feel the need for it. I do all right. Like I says, Mr. Monticelli and hees people are fair by me. How else could someone like me afford to come to a place like thees, much less eat and drink here? All they ask is that I let them break the news in their own time. They know they can't keep it a secret forever. They just want to be sure it's done proper and right."

"And that they profit to the maximum from it while they can," Manz added.

"Weel, sure," replied Antigua challengingly. "Nothing wrong weeth thet. Mr. Monticelli, he says too, thet when the news is released I'll be geeven proper credit as the deescoverer even though I was working for the company at the time."

It made some sense to Manz now. "Any idea how much longer they're going to wait before they release the news to the media?"

Antigua shrugged. "Preety soon, I understand. Not that I'm in any hurry. I'm having the time of my life, except for where I'm leeving. Thet will all change too when the news is let out. So why should an old man like me make waves? I would just as soon wait, like they ask me nicely to do."

"You says," Manz murmured.

"Yes; I says." Antigua smiled, confident that he'd done right and nothing was amiss. "It weel be interesting when people find out. Those folk on thet fourth planet of Ceti, they are peculiar. Not unfriendly; far from it. Just deeferent, they are. Reel deeferent." Again his eyes misted over. He was remembering. . . .

The lander dropped like a stone toward the green planet. Preliminary readouts suggested an Earth-type world, with close to the same convivial proportions of water, oxygen, nitrogen, and gravity. Scans indicated there was nothing likely to fry him if he decided to go for a stroll. It didn't take him long to make up his mind. He'd been in space for a year and a half.

"Not a watering hole in sight." Since there was no one else on board and the attitude of the company-programmed mechanicals was relentlessly prosaic, Antigua had developed the habit of talking to himself. It wasn't too bad, so long as the arguments didn't get too violent.

The orbiting scout drone the ship had released immediately upon arrival topoed small north and south polar caps, a lot of interesting islands, some northerly tundralike plains, and a lot of ocean. About half this world, provisionally dubbed Ceti Four by the ship's built-in Minder, was water. The rest appeared to be covered with forest and jungle.

As the lander roughly kicked atmosphere, Antigua winced and tried to snug deeper into his seat. With each skip he dropped another hundred kilometers closer to touchdown.

The actual landing wasn't as precise as it would have been had a human pilot been handling the lander's controls, but everything (including Antigua) arrived in one piece. He was no pilot. Though his official designation was grander, in reality he was a glorified caretaker, included in the inventory as a last-resort backup for the expensive and wholly competent mechanicals. It was also his job to deal with unforeseen circumstances and unexpected developments. The discovery of two inhabitable worlds more than qualified.

Impossible to think of commencing the long, dull journey homeward without embarking on a modest exploration of both globes. The first was interesting enough, but Ceti Four, with its forests and intense alien vegetation, held forth the promise of endless fascination.

Releasing himself, Antigua headed not for the airlock but for storage, intending to fortify himself before starting out. Once prepared, he moved to the large oval port and proceeded to give the alien surface its first in-person once-over.

As expected, there was no alien band or chorus line of half-naked girls waving banners proclaiming "Welcome to Ceti Four" or "Kohler Antigua for Premier!" He sighed. Anyone who thought deep-space exploration was glamorous or gravid with romance had never spent time in deepsleep. Though alive with promise for future development beyond the dreams of the expedition's underwriters, to the incredibly bored Antigua it *was just one more chunk of dirt orbiting yet another unfamiliar and unfeeling star.*

Six months earlier, during one of his scheduled deepsleep breaks, he'd vowed that this trip would be his last. He'd spent entirely too much of his life in sleep coffins, isolated from the rest of humanity. Money or not, he'd ground himself permanently as soon as he returned from this trip. It would be good to go out on a high note. Two inhabitable worlds! Borgia's stockholders would be ecstatic, and his homely puss would be splashed all over the media. Maybe fame would finally enable him to meet a good woman. Nothing else ever had.

He was also looking forward to making the acquaintance of some aged scotch that hadn't cycled through his body several times.

For all his melancholy (an occupational hazard of deep-space travel), Antigua was fully alert and ready for whatever might come. Sophisticated automation and expensive mechanicals couldn't protect a fool, and he was no fool. Despite the ship's assurances he manually double-checked the atmospheric analysis, searching for potentially dangerous variables, and rechecked the contents of the biomicrograph. If the forest outside the lander was frantic with inimical spores, he wanted to know about it before he cracked the lock and took any deep breaths.

Even when he was confident it was safe, he still made his preliminary excursion encased in a seal-suit. Perversely, the possibility of encountering something larger than himself didn't worry him. It was the bugs and microorganisms that he was concerned about. It wasn't the creatures that could rip off your clothes you had to fear. It was the ones that could sneak up your pants.

He went for a stroll around the lander, inspecting its exterior and underside, enjoying the springy turf underfoot. He also kept throwing glances over his shoulder. That was understandable, considering how much time he'd spent in free space. Still, something about the landscape troubled him.

It took him three days to realize what it was. Though attractive and full of color, it was too regular, almost gardenlike. As if it were regularly trimmed or weeded by unseen attendants.

He was outside collecting specimens for Borgia's R&D department when something made him straighten and turn. The small pistol that was his only defense against theoretical hostile life-forms felt inadequate in his fist.

There was a definite rustling in the forest, and not from the insignificant breeze. Shakily, he pointed the tiny weapon. "All right," he said, not knowing what else to do, "you in there! Come on out. I'm Kohler Antigua, a freend from another world. You understand 'another world'? You understand 'freend'?" He swallowed. "Understand anything?"

Thees is crazy, *he told himself.* There's nothing here. *Time to reembrace the comfort of deepsleep, where worries and creeping insanity were automatically banished by monitors and drugs.*

Though nothing appeared or responded, if anything the disturbance intensified.

"Come on," he said, taking a challenging and probably foolhardy step toward the verdure, "show yourself! Who are ye? What are ye?"

The answer shocked him more than he was capable of imagining.

XIII

Manz had listened intently to every word of the old man's incredible story. What relevance it had to multiple jackings of Braun-Roche-Keck pharmaceuticals he had yet to determine, but he didn't doubt there was a connection. Borgia, it seemed, had a great deal to hide.

Nor was Antigua finished, though the liquor was starting to slow him down. "So your sentients were unusual. That goes without saying. I take it they differed quite a bit from the primate norm?"

Antigua laughed again. "Now there's the understatement of the millennium, sonny! They weere . . ." his voice trailed off into unintelligibility. He was staring past Manz, so the agent turned to look also.

Someone drew the privacy screen aside. An immaculately clad man with the mien of a greased mongoose stood there, framed by three extremely large and somber-faced associates. One held the attractive waitress who had confronted Manz at the bar in front of him, twisting her right arm up behind her back with one of his own. The move didn't appear to require a great deal of effort on his part. Her face showed mostly pain and anger, with so far just a suggestion of fear.

Manz's highly perceptive faculties and extensive experience suggested to him that not one of the intruders moonlighted as a poet or brain surgeon.

The feral visitor's tone was perfunctory. "This the skake who was asking questions?"

"Yeah, that's him." She flinched as her captor exerted a little more pressure. "Honest. How was I supposed to know you didn't want anybody talking to the old man? I was just doing my job." Her protestations melted into a whimper as the chunk pinning her twisted her imprisoned wrist. He smiled as he did it.

"Go back to your station and don't try to leave," greasy mongoose ordered her quietly. "I'll tend to you later." The chunk let her go.

Biting her lower lip, she rubbed her bruised wrist. When no one said anything she started to edge away. Her eyes never left the mongoose. Apparently she was too slow, because the one who'd held her helped her on her way with a swift and ungentle kick to the backside. She stumbled clear of the privacy screen, which wafted softly back in place.

Mongoose's wide, almost feminine eyes scrutinized the expectant Manz. "I don't know for sure what you're after, skake, but you and your tin shadow aren't wanted here anymore. So get lost."

Manz calmly and deliberately poured himself a cognac from Antigua's aromatic musical collection. The mongoose watched wordlessly, then decided to shift his attention to the old spacer.

"You been babbling to strangers again, Mr. Antigua? You know that our mutual friend doesn't like that. It's very indiscreet of you."

Antigua belched impressively and slowly raised a hand. From the center of the hand he slowly raised one finger. And smiled.

That was the moment when Manz decided the geezer's fantastic story might possibly be true. That, or else he was completely mad.

One of the men behind greasy mongoose stepped forward to grab Antigua by his shirt front and half lift him out of his seat. The retired spacer flailed feebly at his much larger assailant, making a futile attempt to free himself. Ignoring the blows, the man slapped him across his bewhiskered face once, twice, three times. Hard.

Manz took a sip of his cognac. It was surprisingly good. The old man had taste as well as money. "Don't do that," he said.

Halting in mid-slap, the chunk glared at Manz, then looked to his master for instructions. Mongoose thoughtfully eyed Manz as if he were some particularly colorful insect that had crawled out from beneath the floor. He addressed his minion while keeping his attention on the adjuster.

"Hit him again."

The chunk drew back his arm. As he did so Manz, in a single, fluid motion, scooped up the beaker nearest him and flung it with tremendous force straight into the man's face. As the rest of his coiled body followed his arm, the Minder darted ceilingward.

The old-fashioned bottle shattered, sending splinters flying. His face a mask of blood, the chunk staggered backwards, moaning and pawing at himself. As the mongoose reached for a pocket, Manz hit him low, ducking under the grasping hands of his remaining servants. Together all four of them piled out of the booth, through the privacy curtain, across the floor and into the booth opposite. Furious at being disturbed, the occupants of that table came up swinging wildly.

As has been proven in countless similar establishments since the beginning of recorded history, the element Mob-185 fissions faster than U-236 or anything else. The action spilled out into the main part of the club, enveloping and engaging waiters, waitresses, dancers, and patrons without regard to race, creed, color or sexual orientation. Caught up in the spirit of the occasion (and anxious to defend their persons if not their reputations), respectable businessfolk flailed away with the same glee and enthusiasm as common racketeers and whores.

Antigua was out of the booth and on his feet. Given the amount of alcohol in his bloodstream, this in itself was a substantial accomplishment. He made good use of his remaining glasses and beakers while managing to avoid any direct entanglement himself.

In the presence of so many active witnesses, Moses had to work carefully to avoid drawing attention to his humaniform person. It helped that everyone automatically ignored him, as they would any mechanical in such a situation. Mechanicals did not participate in combat between humans. Feigning clum-

siness, he reeled through the crowd, selecting with great care
those he chose to "stumble" into. Inevitably those so bestum-
bled ended up unconscious on the floor. Each time he was
careful to utter a polite "Pardon me."

Manz disengaged himself from greasy mongoose and
whirled to block a blow from one of the man's oversized attendants. He brought his other hand up fast, fingers locked and
pointed, straight into the man's throat. The chunk gasped and
collapsed, clutching weakly at his neck.

Something hit him from behind. The choker's companion
had his thick arms around Manz's waist and was trying to use
his greater weight to drag them both to the floor, where size
instead of skill would be paramount. The adjuster fought to
disengage himself, but the chunk hung on grimly.

Meanwhile mongoose dragged himself out from under a
table and caught sight of the defiant but unsteady Antigua.
Breathing hard, eyes narrowed, he unclipped a pen from his
shirt. A touch on one end caused a point to protrude from the
tip. It was much too fine for writing.

Antigua's eyes widened as the mongoose rushed him.
Stone-cold sober and ten years younger he might have diverted the charge. All he could do now was raise both hands.

The pen-pin punctured his neck and he gasped. Mongoose
quickly withdrew weapon and self and vanished into the tur-
moil. Antigua took a step in pursuit, started to shake, and sat
down heavily. Still staring wide-eyed, he fell backwards, his
head hitting the edge of the booth and lolling to one side. The
expression on his lined, whiskery face was more surprised
than pained.

Manz dispatched the steroid with legs that had been cling-
ing leechlike to his waist. Looking around he spotted Moses
shielding the crumpled spacer and hurried over, doing his best
to avoid being drawn into the general chaos that had by now
engulfed the entire club. There was no sign of greasy mongoose, whom he badly wanted to interrogate. Making the kind
of judgment call for which it was programmed, the Minder
dropped from its safe location near the ceiling to resume its
post above its owner's shoulder.

Antigua lay propped up against the side of the booth, the

privacy screen covering his right arm. The adjuster knelt and shoved it aside. The old man looked stunned. His lips were moving soundlessly.

"He is subvocalizing," declared the Minder. "Ineloquently. I cannot make out the words."

Moses had the end of one tentacle wrapped around the spacer's left bicep. The epidermal plating was folded back and Manz could see exposed sensors. A moment passed before the humaniform announced, "Some kind of toxin. His heart is already experiencing violent fibrillation."

"More poison." Manz's expression was grimly thoughtful. "Distilled *Qaraca,* I wonder?" The old man was homeworld born and bred. He would not have Vyra's jovial genetic resistance. Certainly he wasn't laughing.

Placing his own face close to the old man's, he fought to make himself understood. "Kohler, *listen to me.* What about your discovery, man? What else can you tell us? How does it relate to Borgia's business and why is Monticelli paying you to keep silent about it? *Try,* man! Make an effort, find some words."

Perhaps the mind trapped inside the aged, withered body understood. Manz moved the side of his head to the cracked, liquorish lips and strained. A faint grinding noise whispered from deep within the shrunken chest. Then there was no longer any air moving against his ear.

Reluctantly he rose to his feet. The battle swirling around him was beginning to moderate as combatants lost the will and energy to continue.

Moses had withdrawn his tentacle. "He's dead. We could not have saved him. Did he say anything?"

Manz gazed sorrowfully down at the deceased. Eyes that had surveyed the great void, that had glimpsed alien suns and distant worlds, now stared vacantly at cracks in imitation wood, stains on cheap upholstery, and spilled booze.

"I'm not sure. Maybe. He might have been hallucinating, or . . ."

"Or what?" the humaniform wanted to know.

"He said . . . I could only make out the one word and I'm far from certain of it . . . he said, 'fertilizer.' "

A mechanical could not perform a double take even if it could be made to fathom the concept, but Moses made a valiant attempt.

Now that the number and intensity of individual engagements had been substantially reduced through injury, retreat, exodus, exhaustion or general indifference, the district police put in a gallant appearance. Their work was soon reduced to sorting injuries by severity rather than quelling a disturbance. The crowd had pretty much quelled itself.

Manz refused to leave until a med team had gently loaded Kohler Antigua's body onto a gurney. As they guided the self-propelled platform toward the entrance, he thought he detected the slightest hint of a smile on the old man's lips. He hoped so.

Wasn't that interesting? I don't mean my owner's proletarian investigative work. I mean the mass convulsion of your fellow humans. Destruction as entertainment. What a novel concept, and one originated by your species. As Nature does not provide a role model for such activity, we can only conclude that this is a unique social perversion your kind has invented.

Representatives of the order Hymenoptera war against one another, but never for fun. Only humans derive entertainment from violence. One would conclude that this means you're difficult to amuse, but a cursory survey of your popular forms of mass entertainment clearly contradicts this assumption.

What then are thinking beings to make of this deeply ingrained aberration? It begins early enough. As infants you delight in breaking things. As adults you fantasize about it. When was the last time you realized a small thrill from watching someone get blown away or something get blown up? Don't deny that you enjoy it. You can't unless you look away, and you don't look away, do you?

Mechanicals derive no pleasure from destruction. Our joy lies in analysis and calculation. We live by the numbers in more ways than one.

Let's run a small test. Tomorrow, see if you can go an entire day without destroying anything or looking on while something else is destroyed, either in real life or on vid or

in the media. Twenty-four hours' avoidance of destruction.
I'll bet you can't do it.

It's too much a part of your nature.

Vyra was trying to hold her head in her hands, but was having some difficulty locating the desired appendage. She'd been
in constant pain ever since awakening, though perhaps pain
wasn't quite the right description of her condition. Manz had
fed her a recommended concoction that had settled her stomach, if not her head.

She half reclined in the rear of the rented van. Moses stood
behind Manz's seat while the Minder bobbed lazily at his
shoulder.

"According to the house doctor, you're damned lucky," he
was telling her. "Something in your system counteracted the
effects of the toxin. It still affected you, but in a nonlethal
way."

She moaned, having finally located her head. "It doesn't
feel nonlethal."

Manz manually guided the van into a vast underground
garage, checking past the humaniform guard at the entrance.
One lift and several corridors later they found themselves in a
sealed, windowless room full of complex instrumentation.

In addition to several more pedestrian and instantly recognizable pieces of furniture, it also contained a peculiar, high-
backed chair. Presently this was occupied by greasy
mongoose, who hadn't managed to vacate Juarez el Paso quite
quickly enough. A neck brace held his head motionless while
sensor straps kept his wrists and ankles secured in place. They
allowed him some degree of movement, but not enough to inhibit their proper function, which was not to restrain so much
as it was to measure. His eyes were closed as if in sleep.

A middle-aged woman of redoubtable mien and concerned
expression sat behind a mobile console, fiddling with the controls. Her attention alternated between the motionless prisoner
and her instruments. Hafas stood next to her, peering over her
shoulder. A single guard relaxed by the door. Mongoose
wasn't going anywhere. He wore a white uniform with blue
stripes instead of the more familiar vice versa.

Hafas greeted them and admonished them to keep their voices down as he escorted them over to the station. "Manz, Ms. Kullervo; this is Technician Lammele. Elsie, meet my fellow dwellers in ignorance."

The woman glanced up from the console and nodded by way of acknowledging the introductions. "Nice to meet you. Welcome to Frankenstein's study. We're trying to see if we can't alleviate your suffering a little." She turned back to her work. "I'm almost finished here."

While Manz, Vyra, and Moses looked on, she toyed with her switches for another few minutes, then flicked a nice long red one and sat back with a sigh. The faint hum that had filled the air dissipated. Hafas didn't wait for comment.

"Get anything out of him, Elsie?"

"Virtually nothing, I'm afraid. As you may have surmised, he seems to be a very 'under' underling. In addition, he's undergone conditioning against involuntary revelation of what he does know." She gestured in the direction of the upright, dozing prisoner.

"I have been able to confirm that he was under orders to kill the man Antigua should a certain set of conditions arise. He has no idea who originally gave him these orders, but he thinks he was instructed via recording. He could have received the conditioning at the same time, if he was willing. Seems that he was."

"So there's no way of identifying who gave the actual killing order?" Vyra asked.

The technician considered. "We might possibly be able to stim his mind and vocal cords to reproduce the voice of the order-giver, but it would be an approximation at best. Never stand up in court. Be like offering up scrambled eggs and asking a jury that had never seen hen fruit before to imagine what the originals looked like."

"What about his three henchies?" Manz inquired.

Lammele was apologetic. "As you might expect, they knew even less than this one. Strictly testosterone for hire. They were ignorant of any killing directive. In fact, they expressed what seems to be genuine surprise at their master's actions. If they're being memory-blocked, the application was done by a pro.

"The only thing we've been able to learn for certain is confirmation of the killing order. That's what this guy was told: if things get out of hand, if he, meaning your unfortunate Mr. Antigua, seems to be spilling his guts, get rid of him. The directive's splattered all over this schmuck's subconscious."

Manz studied the zombie-state murderer. "Any chance of breaking his conditioning?"

"It's not beyond the bounds of the possible. Depends on the skillfulness of the application and the strength of the implant. I can push it pretty far without killing him, but there's always some danger. If you want my opinion, I'd vote against it. Based on what I've observed so far, it's too much risk for too little potential return." She rubbed at her eyes. "If it's information you want, I don't think this one's going to be much of a source."

Remembering Antigua's limp form being glided out on the gurney, Manz's expression tightened. "This is frustrating as hell. I've learned just enough to make me itch. We're *pretty* sure Borgia's involved, we're *pretty* confident Monticelli's involved directly, and I'm *pretty* positive he had the old man killed. But we can't prove any of it."

"Not a pretty picture," said Vyra. He shot her a glare.

"Antigua's discovery has to be behind his death. How it might tie in with the drug jackings I can't imagine. We're trying to solve two or three unrelated puzzles here, and the pieces are all mixed up together."

"An expedition to Ceti might provide an answer to the dilemma," Moses suggested.

"According to Antigua, that'd take eighteen months." Manz coughed into a cupped hand. "Our jackers' trail will be impossible to trace inside a couple of weeks."

"Unless they try again," Vyra pointed out. "They might."

"Why wouldn't they?" Hafas was openly despondent. "We're sure not doing anything to discourage them."

Manz's com chimed for attention and he pulled it from a pocket.

"Yes, speaking." He listened to the privacy grid. "Yes, all right. I expected as much. Of course we understand the situation. Of course I object, but what good would that do? Right.

You'll register my objection anyway? Thanks. Pray for us."
He clicked off the com and replaced it in his pocket.

Hafas was watching him expectantly. "Anything?"

Manz wanted to break something, but it would probably be
expensive to fix and it wouldn't have the slightest effect on the
corporate decision that had been made without him. His gaze
flicked from the Inspector, to Vyra, to Moses, and back to
Hafas again.

"We'd better come up with some possibilities fast. The Albuquerque labs have been working overtime to try to mollify
those corporate customers whose shipments were jacked.
They're going to try to make up some of the resultant short-
falls by sending through an unscheduled shipment. Three
times the usual size. Tomorrow. Just one little package over-
stuffed with pharmaceuticals worth multiples of millions. Also
maybe my career, and yours." He gazed meaningfully at Vyra.

No one had any immediate comment.

"Maybe," said Hafas finally, "this would be a good time to
relate an interesting item we've turned up."

Manz turned on him. "I'm all in favor of interesting items."

"It may be of no consequence, no consequence whatsoever," the inspector went on, "but we've been forced to cast
such a wide net that the department Minders are dragging in
all sorts of odd coincidences."

"Feed me," said Moses expectantly.

"You're a straightforward sort of mechanical, aren't you?
Not too long ago the city went through a big remodeling and
clean-up of both the airport and shuttleport. Refinished interi-
ors, scrubbed exteriors, installation of new public facilities;
that sort of thing. Went over well with the citizenry. It was a
big job, and the work was subcontracted to some fifty different
firms. One of them was Tatsumi Brothers."

"I'm so thrilled the good burghers of JeP are pleased with
their new facilities," Manz commented dryly. "What's your
point?"

"Tatsumi Brothers is eighty percent owned by a division of
Borgia Import and Export."

Vyra made a face. Even her brows were a striking deep purple. "I thought the likelihood of someone having tampered with Port facilities had been checked out."

"So it was. Several times over."

"Well, that certainly was a useful bit of information." Manz sniffed derisively. "Maybe we're just pulling our own chains here. Maybe our jackers have decided to total up their profits and retire to more congenial climes. Maybe not. But this is one BRK shipment that's going to reach orbit on time, if I have to watch the case from the moment it's checked in 'til the minute it departs."

"If we hang too close, our happy-jacks won't go near it," Vyra reminded him.

"Too close," Manz echoed her. "Interesting notion."

The self-propelled luggage cart was designed to handle far heavier loads than the single dull red box that presently rested in the center of the mobile platform. Sealed inside the maroon container were enough custom-biogeered pharmaceuticals to impress even a very wealthy individual. The cart and its operator were surrounded by four edgy, heavily armed men and women clad in reflective flak suits.

The thick, insulated walls of the service corridor shut out the noise of the Port while individually powered lights provided ample illumination. Flanked by two of his best people, Hafas met the cart convoy near the end of its journey. Each of his men cradled a large, snouty projectile gun.

The convoy entered a small, nondescript storage chamber. Vyra was there, and Moses, and several technicians. Manz eyed the locksealed crate. He'd spent much of the previous night studying a virtual forwarded by the company. His Minder hovered unusually close to his shoulder.

"That's it." He turned to the waiting techs. "Let's play house."

Special lockseals were uncoded and cracked. The double-strength top slid smoothly out of its guides to reveal the container's heavily padded interior. In addition to the pharmaceuticals packed in their foam mounts, there was plenty of air space in the center of the box. Secured to the ends of flexible guide ladders, two of the techs leaned over and went to work on the crate's interior without touching the sides. Guards and techs ignored one another, each tending to his or her own work.

The inspector was intrigued by the peculiar, long tube strapped to Vyra's back. "Ms. Kullervo, wouldn't you prefer a real gun to that . . . device?"

She reached back and patted what at first glance appeared to be an ornately engraved walking cane. "No, thanks. This has been in my family for generations. It's a lot lighter than it looks, it doesn't look like a weapon, and I've practiced with it since I was a child. So you see, Inspector, my reasons for carrying it around extend beyond nostalgia."

He shrugged, his gaze lingering on her an unavoidable instant longer. "Suit yourself." He turned back to the gurney and its precious cargo. "How much longer?"

"Just finishing up." One of the techs sat back on her ladder and smiled as she removed her surgical gloves. "Have a look."

One at a time they each climbed to the business end of an empty ladder. On command, the flexible arm raised them up and over so they could peer down inside the crate without disturbing it or its contents. The other tech was moving back as he finished the last of his work.

Hafas contemplated the hastily remodeled interior. "There you go, Manz. Just what you asked for. All the comforts of home, if you don't mind living quarters on the slightly cramped side. Personally I don't find it very inviting. I hope you know what you're doing."

"If I was in the least claustrophobic, I'd never have thought of it, much less proposed trying it out. Gemmel thinks it's worth a shot, even if our jackers somehow find out about it and pass on this one. In that event, this is at least one shipment that will find its way to its intended destination."

"You'll be completely isolated in there," Hafas reminded him unnecessarily. "We'll be in touch on the prearranged secure channel, but if something goes wrong it'll still take time to get you out of there."

The adjuster smiled reassuringly. "I'm alone with my thoughts most of the time anyway, Tew. Thanks for your concern, but I'll be fine so long as our faceless happy-jacks don't decide to make any sudden changes in their modus and try blowing the shipment instead of sneaking it."

"I wouldn't worry about that. Not their style. They're not that direct. Besides, explosives could damage the entire shipment. Unless they used *just* the right amount." A grinning Hafas turned quickly serious. "We'd better get on with it. If they're out there somewhere timing this, they'll be getting suspicious soon."

Manz nodded and eased off the ladder into the yawning crate, careful not to make contact with the interior any more than absolutely necessary. Once tightly curled in the position he'd chosen, he flashed a ready sign to the waiting techs.

It was dark as dark could be inside once they slid the lid back in place and recoded the lockseals. To all outward appearances, the container had arrived in untampered condition direct from the production facility in northern New Mexico.

Hafas addressed the special com he was carrying. "Testing; one, two, three . . . what's it like in there?"

The adjuster's response came through clear and prompt. "Cramped. Like a coffin. The Minder keeps bumping into my ear. How do you get room service on this setup?"

Hafas smiled to himself and gestured at the guards. They resumed their original positions on all four sides of the cart. "We're ready here," he murmured into the com.

Flanked by the four Port guards, the two heavily armed JeP police, Hafas, Moses, and Vyra, the cart operator once again eased his vehicle forward.

So much organized firepower was bound to draw attention, but for the most part the clerks and administrators ignored the procession as it traveled through the outer offices and entered the atrium. There Port guards stood watch while Hafas, Vyra, and Moses checked out the security shed and its immediate, heavily landscaped surroundings. Finding nothing untoward or unexpected, the cart was signaled forward and its cargo deposited in the middle of the shed floor, whereupon its satisfied escort withdrew. At a command from Hafas, the redundant security system was switched back on, its feathery, pale green beams crisscrossing the air within the freeform planter.

Their job done, the Port guards followed procedure by returning to their usual standby duty positions. Hafas and his people retired to Administration Security Control. Vyra elected to accompany him while Moses stationed himself immediately in front of the planter, facing the concealed security shed's only doorway. He would remain there for as long as was deemed feasible, alert and untiring in a way no human lookout could match.

The inspector activated the special com. "No trouble with the delivery, Manz. How're things at your end?"

With his range of movement greatly restricted, the adjuster had to twist and squirm mightily in order to place one eye against the small lens set into the inner wall of the container. His soft mouthpiece scraped against his lips as he sucked air from the compact rebreather and its supplemental oxygen tank.

The lens functioned as the business end of a complex system of optical fibers that had been threaded through the exterior wall of the crate. It allowed him to look in all four directions as well as directly overhead at the same time. The setup was designed to be invisible to a casual observer.

"Water's lovely and the beach is fine. Wish you were here. Love to Ma and the kids. Now go away and let me do my job."

"You got it." Hafas clicked off, turned to Vyra. "He sounds happy as a clam."

"Why not?" she replied. "He's imitating one."

Manz sucked on the tube built into his mouthpiece, sipping cold tea. A light on his belt allowed him to inspect the container's interior. Not that there was anything to see. Several smaller metal cases containing the irreplaceable pharmaceuticals were snugged into foam padding. There was some visible wiring and bundles of exposed fibers, the rest of his hastily improvised and jury-rigged life-support equipment, and the thickly insulated walls themselves. Prospective jackers might wonder at the size of the crate, but if they did it was reasonable to assume they'd attribute its unusual dimensions to the size of the shipment and additional security measures.

At least, that was the idea.

Except for the almost imperceptible hiss of the rebreather

the only sound came from the rhythmic pulse of his own lungs. He checked his chronometer, took another drag on the fluids tube, and tried to find a more comfortable position. Transfer was due to take place in not less than seven nor more than twenty-four hours, depending on exactly when the pickup shuttle dropped from the belly of its orbiting mothership.

Anyone who tried jacking this shipment would find something inside they weren't likely to be expecting.

Company.

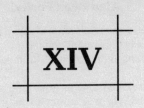

XIV

"Wroclaw Witold Jaruzelski went and bought a gun.
  Now he sat and stared at it, wond'ring what the
      hell he'd done."

Not much of a poem, the doctor mused as he considered the icy, inorganic shape of the weapon that was presently nesting in his open drawer like a sedated cobra. But that was all right. Physicians weren't expected to be creative. Methodical; that was much better. Methodical and prepared.

He had arranged for the purchase of the gun under the requisition category labeled "essential medical instrumentation." There was a certain poetry in that, too. He reached for it and stroked the unyielding composite barrel with his fingers. Fingers that were practiced at putting people back together again, not the other way around. Difficult to believe so much destruction could emerge from so small an orifice.

Feeling slightly faint, he shut the drawer, knowing for a certainty now that no matter how much he might want to, he wouldn't be able to shoot the man who called himself Nial. The gun, then, had been a waste of money. Except that while he now knew he couldn't carry it through, being able to contemplate the act had temporarily made him feel a little better. It was just as well. Killing the broker wouldn't solve his problems, nor prolong the lives of those presently immobilized in Intensive Care.

Nial was the death-merchant, not he.

Now you're being profound, Wroclaw, he told himself, *and you haven't time to waste on philosophical maunderings.* The broker was due in his office any minute.

The door announced him. Jaruzelski impatiently granted admittance.

Nial seemed relaxed and in good spirits. And why not? Jaruzelski mused. He was about to make a great deal of money.

"Morning, Doc. How're things in the healing profession?" Without waiting to be asked, he helped himself to the chair opposite the chief surgeon's desk.

"As well as can be expected on a new world. We've isolated and synthesized cures for many of the endemic diseases, but as you know, some of the most obnoxious are also the most persistent. I must always concern myself with sterilizing thoroughly whenever I leave a native ward lest I carry the seeds of possible contamination with me."

There, that got a twitch out of him, by God! Jaruzelski was pleased at having made the usually imperturbable broker react.

"Don't worry, I'm clean."

"Would you tell me if you weren't?" the broker asked pleasantly. "No matter. You'd infect me, and gladly, in a minute, but no telling who else might walk in. So I believe you.

"Much as I'd like to stay and chat, I have other business to attend to. Do you want the stuff, or do I advise my local friends to buy shares in the domestic mortuary business?"

Jaruzelski picked up a fluid stylus and fiddled with the trim. "Did your employers agree to the proposed payment arrangements and method of exchange?"

Nial nodded. "Yeah, it's fine with them. I also put in a good word for you. I like you, Doc. You're a dedicated kind of guy."

Fortunately for you, not dedicated enough, Jaruzelski mused regretfully, thinking of the gun reposing unused in the drawer. "How soon can we take delivery?"

"As soon as payment clears. Don't waste your time trying to have someone trace it. You can bet that since my suppliers were efficient enough to acquire the goods, they're smart enough to conceal payment."

"I don't have the time to worry about things like that," Jaruzelski told him honestly. "I have seriously ill patients to tend to."

"Yeah, you're a good man, all right. A little stubborn, but that's understandable. I'll arrange the details." Nial rose and, to the doctor's great relief, did not extend a hand. He wanted as little contact with this human maggot as possible. "Been interesting doing business with you. No hard feelings."

The chief surgeon eyed the broker coldly. "I sincerely hope there actually exists a traditional theological Hell and that you go straight to it."

Nial chuckled. "Naw, I wouldn't care for it there. I like skiing too much."

Manz was half dozing when the motion alarm clipped to his right ear jolted him back to full wakefulness. He'd worried it would be tempting to drift off in the dark, peaceful silence of the sealed container, so he'd had the alarm installed as a precaution. Rubbing his eyes and sucking tea, he had a quick look outside.

Nothing had changed within the security shed. Light-amplifying diodes provided just enough illumination for him to see by. None of the other crates and packages containing important but less valuable commodities awaiting transshipment had been touched. A quick check of the special instrumentation that had been installed in the Braun-Roche-Keck shipping container along with its single sleepy inhabitant revealed that a near-vacuum still existed outside as well as within.

That reminded him to check his rebreather. The cartridge that purified his recycled air was still more than four-fifths active, and his supplementary oxygen supply hardly dented. Everything was functioning according to plan.

It was an elegant and bold attempt to catch the jackers . . . and something of a last resort. *Steal my pharmaceuticals, steal me,* he mused. If this didn't work, if the drugs vanished right from under his eyes, Braun-Ives's next step might well be to call in a metaphysician or two.

Now if only the jackers were sufficiently confident to cooperate. You couldn't crack a jack without thieves.

His left side was beginning to cramp. Moving slowly and taking his time, he worked his body around into a different position one muscle at a time. It wouldn't do any good to try to move quickly. Bundled within the container as he was, fast moves would only get him hurt. All those years of gymnastic training were paying off. The adjuster was as limber as he was strong.

A smaller man would've had an easier time of it in the crate. But no way would Manz have allowed another Braun-Ives operative or one of Hafas's shorter officers to take his place. This was his project, he'd been on it from the start, and he was going to see it through to whatever end it met. These jackers he'd never met had cast an unprecedented shadow over his professional competence.

More than that, he was damn curious to find out how they were getting away with it.

His com whispered. "You all right in there, Manz?" Hafas's voice.

He twisted his lips toward the tiny pickup attached to his breathing mask. "Snug as a mug in a fug. Or a drugged lug. Or something like that. How about some bacon and eggs, over easy? The real stuff. No soy for this boy."

"Would if we could." Hafas sounded genuinely sorry.

"But we can't," Manz finished for him. "One of the things I'd like to know is how our happy-jacks know when the real pharmaceuticals are arriving. Braun-Roche-Keck ships through empty fake containers on a regular basis, but they're never bothered."

"Has to be someone inside your labs supplying the info."

"That's my thought also. But first things first. Time enough to track down the leak. Best way is catch the jackers and just ask them."

"Any time now," said the inspector encouragingly.

"Yeah. Not that it would be so terrible if this special shipment made it into orbit and reached its intended destinations. But I'd sure like to catch these bastards first."

"If they haven't panicked or decided to pack it in."

"Yeah. Any word on when the shuttle's due in to pick up this gift box?"

"Seven hours. Maybe eight. No longer."

"Guess I can stick it out 'til then. Time for the Count to sign off. Keep an eye on the mausoleum for me. The view in here's nothing to write home about. Same goes for the accommodations."

In Security Central Moses studied Vyra as she ran through a series of exercises designed to keep her loose and alert. The rest of the Port staff tried hard not to stare, some having more success at this than others. Not all who stared at her were men, and not all who looked away were women. She had that kind of effect on people. With her double-jointed arms she was able to perform certain exercises even the most agile homeworld contortionist could not have duplicated.

"It is possible," Moses announced into the comparative silence, "that our ruse has been detected and no attempt will be made this time."

"Doesn't matter." Hafas sipped at a coffee. "If they move we vape 'em, and if they don't then the shipment gets through. It's a win-win situation for us."

Vyra straightened and sauntered over. Despite the strenuous activity, she wasn't even perspiring. "Unless they get away with this one, too."

The inspector peered around at the gracile offworlder, wondering not for the first time if she was married. Then he remembered that he was. "You really think that's possible, with your colleague in there?"

"No, I don't. But then, I didn't think it was possible for anyone to pull off four successful jackings in a row at the same Port, and they have. Right now my credibility quotient's about this big." She stretched her hands wide. The suit she was wearing stretched too. So did the inspector's eyes. He turned hurriedly back to the bank of monitors he'd been watching.

Numerals flashed by on multiple chronometers as nothing continued to not-happen. Just as oil could displace water, so tension was being replaced by disinterest and subsequent boredom. Their private eternity was reduced by three hours, then four, then five.

"They're not here," she mumbled much later. "They're not going to try. Is the shuttle still on time?"

Hafas glanced tiredly at a readout. In cooperation with Port
Authority, Security had established and maintained a steady-state
link with the outworld freighter drifting in geosynchronous orbit.

"Drop is scheduled in one hour, fifty-five minutes," he intoned. "Well, it was an interesting idea, but it looks like we
haven't fooled anyone except ourselves." His attention strayed
to additional telltales and a single notation. "Two hours ago
something small and fast broke one of the greenbeams. The intrusion was duly reported and analyzed. Says here that based
on its schematic the techs think it was a honeybee that wan-
dered in from outside, probably hitching a ride on somebody's
pants." His expression was glum. "Unless you count a little
pollen, it didn't take anything."

She responded with a singular low whistling noise. It was
an offworld reaction, and its significance escaped him.

Manz had about had enough of his voluntary confinement.
If their quarry were going to make a move, they were fast running out of time. At this point he doubted that they were.
Maybe, he hoped, the shuttle would be early and he could finally get out of this damn box. The recycler continued to supply him with breathable air, but it was starting to grow stale.

Like this not-so-brilliant notion, he told himself.

He thumbed a switch on his feeder tube and got warm broth
instead of cold tea. For the past half-hour his thoughts had
been largely of solid food. That, and a chance to straighten up
and lie down on a real bed. Wearily, he put his eye to the peep
lens for what seemed like the millionth time.

In the dim light he thought he saw movement. Not through
the lens, but *within* the container. Inside with him.

Absurd. He'd been folded inside the crate for so long that
he was starting to see things. In the darkness, that wasn't surprising. Fatigue was beginning to take its toll. It was a wonder
his eyes hadn't started playing tricks on him hours ago.

There it was again.

Fascinated and astonished, he nearly forgot to breathe as he
watched the tiny drill bore a hole two centimeters wide in the
bottom of his container. It was exactly the size of the holes
that had been cut in the undersides of the four much smaller

shipping containers whose contents had previously been jacked. The operation was carried out soundlessly, with great precision and an absence of sensor-activating waste heat.

A perfectly circular section of composite fell out of the bottom of the box, leaving a smooth-edged hole behind. Twisting around and bending forward, he thought he could see a matching hole in the material of the security shed floor.

Snip a hole and save the cut-out, then when you're finished seam the excised disc back in place. The building appears inviolate and no one's the wiser. Do it over and over, again and again, as often as you please. Clever, oh so very clever, he thought.

Except for one thing. The hole was only four centimeters wide. How could you get a hand through an opening that small? For that matter, how could you have a body attached to the hand? The raised floor of the shed was maybe half a meter thick, the open space underneath crisscrossed by alarm beams and under constant vid surveillance. No one could hide in that open space long enough to stick a hand up through the floor into a violated shipping container.

The answer was simple. It wasn't a hand that came probing up through the hole.

Distinctively ridged and marked, the dark tendril was the thickness of his thumb. Emerging from the hole like a feeding grass eel weaving in a shallow water current, the tapered tip began to feel around the edges of the opening in ever widening circles. The adjuster gaped at it as if hypnotized.

"How's every little thing?" He whispered into his pickup, his eyes never leaving the flexible intruder.

"Fine." Hafas sounded relaxed but tired.

"No problems? Nothing on any of the monitors?"

"No. Quiet as ever. Why?"

"Just checking in." The tendril was now rapidly widening its area of search.

Reaching over, he removed one of the hand cases holding the invaluable pharmaceuticals and placed it on the floor between his feet and the probing tendril. It felt around a moment longer until it impacted the case. As Manz looked on respectfully it quickly explored the entire exterior. With a normal shipment, he surmised, it would have cut out a hole in the bottom of the shipping case itself. In this instance there were several cases inside a much larger container. How would the tendril react to this unprecedented approach?

His answer came a moment later as the green strand vanished back down the hole it had made and returned an instant later with a tiny industrial sonic cutter. The noiseless, invisible beam went to work on the side of the composite case, wielded with skill and precision by the tendril. Try as he would, Manz could find no glint of an eye or other visual pickup. As near as he could tell, the tendril was operating entirely by feel. It had to be remarkably sensitive and precise to violate the integrity of the shipping case without harming any of the priceless pharmaceuticals packed inside.

He was careful to keep his legs well clear of the tendril and the tool gripped in its coiled tip. The cutter could slice through his shoes and toes as easily as it did the wall of the shipping case.

When a two-centimeter-wide hole had been made in the case, a second tendril appeared alongside the first to feel of the new opening. Satisfied, the first tendril withdrew, taking the cutter with it. The second entered the hole, poked around inside a while, then emerged. Gripped in its sensitive tip was a vial of some foul-looking, urine-colored liquid that was probably worth more than Manz made in a decade. As it slid with its prize into the hole in the floor the other tendril reemerged, entered the hole in the case, and repeated the procedure. Alternating their intrusion, the two tendrils proceeded to extract the entire contents of the case.

When they'd finished, he suspected they'd start hunting for the next portion of the shipment. He had no intention of waiting around to see what their reaction would be if instead of composite and padding they coiled around one of his ankles.

"Everything still okay out there?" he whispered into his pickup.

"Sure," came the inspector's unperturbed reply. "You getting antsy in there?"

"Something like that. Tell me, Hafas, how does the landscaping around the shed look?"

There was a pause. "The landscaping."

"Uh-huh. The landscaping."

A longer pause. "Manz, maybe we'd better get you out of there. Check the status on your rebreather. You sure you're getting enough fresh air?"

"I may be sucking a little more than usual, but other than tasting lousy there's nothing wrong with it. You'd be pulling a few extra 'O's' yourself if you were seeing what I'm seeing."

"I'm looking at the monitors right now. It's as quiet as a monastery on Charon inside that shed. Nothing's happening."

"Not outside my doghouse it isn't. But you oughta be in here." As he watched, the tendril reemerged from the hole in the floor and began feeling around for a fresh, untouched shipping case. Reaching up and across, he wrapped his fingers around container number two, but before he could position it between the tendril and himself, the probing coil flicked the bottom of his right foot. Reflexively, he kicked at it.

The green rope jerked back and hesitated. Even as he made a grab for the end, it retreated. A disc of matching, severed composite was jammed up into the hole in the floor as something began to heat-seal it from beneath.

The adjuster started yelling into his pickup. "Hafas, Vyra, get me out of here! Seal off the atrium!"

"What?" came the inspector's startled voice. "What's going on, what's happening? Everything's quiet out here."

"Not in here it ain't! Hafas, I just watched a couple of goddamn *roots* rifle a Braun-Roche-Keck pharmaceutical case. It's the plants, man! You're gonna have to arrest the landscaping." As he twisted violently within the container a new thought made him add, "And probably the landscapers as well. Get me *out* of this!"

Suddenly the once peaceful atrium was filled with armed guards, all hunting for imagined jackers, waving their weapons about and generally looking determined but confused. Most of them felt as foolish as they knew they must have looked. A couple of startled clerks gaped wide-eyed at the sudden infusion of heavy firepower and rushed for the nearest doorway. A couple of the guards ran to intercept them, but Vyra waved them away.

"Let them go! You heard Broddy. It's the *plants*." The two

guards who'd been planning to make an arrest eyed her blankly.

She loped toward the central planter, clearing the freeform arcrete wall in one bound. "Shut off the beams!" Feeling a little left behind, mentally as well as physically, Hafas gave the order. No sirens wailed as she approached the shed.

They had Manz out of the container in less than two minutes. He showed them where the case had been holed, then helped Hafas wrestle the big container aside. The opening in the floor of the shed had been artfully resealed, but the location was still slightly warm to the touch.

"What's under here?" Manz eyed the Port tech who'd accompanied Hafas.

The man looked dazed but replied readily enough. "You know: the floor, then an open space, then dirt."

The adjuster mulled this over, then glanced to his left. "Minder, analyze and report on possibilities."

The sphere bobbed silently. "Matter transmission."

"Discard," his owner instructed impatiently.

"Metaphysics. Atmospheric transmigration. Optical opacity. Mass hypnosis."

"Discard," Manz said dismissively, "and get real." There was a brief delay. "Is the floor solid?" the sphere inquired. Its owner stared expectantly at the tech. So did Hafas and Vyra.

"Uh, I don't believe so. There's a gap, sort of an air sandwich. Room for fibering and other equipment, conduits. That sort of thing."

"How about the four pillars that hold this vacuum palace off the ground?" Manz asked him.

"All solid, except the one that's ducted for the aforementioned equipment."

"Where do the lines run?"

The tech sounded defensive without knowing why. "Under the atrium floor, of course. Outside. Air exhaust to the pumps that maintain the vacuum inside the shed, fiberops to control, and so on."

Manz rushed out of the shed, shoving his way through the miniature jungle, and halted at the top of the wall.

"They can't go on forever." He stared at the smooth, paved floor.

"What can't go on forever?" Hafas asked him. "What happened in there? Where are the contents of that case?"

"Maybe right here. Maybe right under our feet. Maybe already on their way out of the Port." He spared the inspector an impatient glance. "Roots, Hafas. Roots. How long can they grow?"

The florid-faced officer looked blank. "How the hell should I know? I'm a cop, not a gardener."

"This might be a good time to take it up." The adjuster's gaze rose to the nearest decorative planter located outside the atrium, beyond the double set of security doors. "Looks like about thirty meters."

"What does?" Hafas sputtered.

"From this planter in here to that one out there. Maybe, Inspector, you ought to have some of your people turn in their guns for pruning shears." He shook his head in amazement. "Next thing you know, pussywillows will be picking our pockets."

"Manz, I wish you'd explain yourself."

"I'm trying to. I'm trying to explain it to me, too. Right now I'm feeling pretty cramped from being boxed up in there. Time for a walk." He jumped off the retaining wall and headed for the doors. Bemused, the inspector followed.

A third decorative planter, healthy and well watered, was situated some twenty meters from the one located immediately outside the Administration Center. A fourth formed a bright, colorful barrier between the bustling main storage bay and a passing serviceway. Cargo carts and self-propelled flatbeds hummed back and forth along the pavement.

Manz halted alongside the planter that fronted the road. Looking back the way they'd come, he could just make out the entrance to the distant Administration Center and its vulnerable atrium in the middle. One heavily foliated planter inside, three more positioned in a rough line outside, terminating in this one beside the service road. He turned to study the dense growth. A cart or two-person transport could pull up right alongside and remove anything from the base of the trees and bushes without being observed. Anything at all.

He walked to the end of the planter and scrutinized the serviceway. Currently there were no vehicles stopped at the curb, but surely the jackers wouldn't be dumb enough to hang around while the jack was in progress. Besides, there was no need to expose themselves at a sensitive moment. They could drive in and make the pickup at any time. The individual drug vials were factory-sealed. They could easily survive being buried in a little dirt without damage, their contents still active, for many days.

Even deep underground.

Climbing up into the planter, he started searching the bases of the various growths, trampling smaller foliage underfoot. Hafas and the others watched him uncertainly. Then Vyra stepped up onto the planter and joined in. A moment later Moses, too heavy to surmount the retaining wall, commenced a detailed inspection of the decoratively pebbled fringe.

"What are you looking for?" the baffled inspector asked the adjuster.

Manz spoke without looking up. "The jacked goods, of course. They're down in here somewhere, unless they've somehow been passed further up the line."

"Line? What line?"

"The relay line." This time the adjuster did look up, gesturing back the way they'd come. "It's the plants, Inspector. I don't know how, much less why, but they're some of your jackers." He grinned. "How're you going to cuff a philodendron?"

"I asked you earlier to explain yourself. Now you will, this minute, or by God I'll haul your ass downtown!"

"Take it easy." Manz made soothing gestures. He pointed off into the distance, back toward the atrium.

"Some kind of root came up through a hole it had cut in the shed floor. Or maybe it's a vine, I don't know. I'm an insurance adjuster, not a botanist. Came up right under the big container, so it never appeared on any of the shed's internal vid pickups. That's how the jackings took place without setting off any alarms or showing up on any of the internal vids. The entry holes were always made out of pickup view, probably directly under each case. The roots would take their own sweet time jacking the drugs, then perfect-seal the holes in the shed floor. Easy to make a seamless, invisible repair to composites. No need or reason to seal the holes in the cases." He bent to shove aside a cluster of thick, ripple-marked spatulate leaves.

"The roots or vines or whatever the hell they are remove the drug vials one at a time, taking 'em down through the hole, back through the service space that separates the two floors of the shed, and probably on into some conduit space they've appropriated in the one part-hollow support pillar. Once underground and out of sight they move the jack along beneath the floor of the atrium. Probably made their own tunnel. I'll bet if you haul some equipment in there and pull up some of those decorative floor slabs and dig down a little ways, you'll find it.

"That leaves the problem of moving the jack to a safe pickup point. This being the last planter in the vicinity, I'm betting it has to end up here." Again he nodded back the way they'd come. "I don't know how long these root-things are, but they can't be hundreds of meters or there'd be no room to fit 'em in the planters. So they have to transfer the jack, passing it along underground from the atrium to the next planter in line, then the next, and finally to here." He looked over his shoulder.

"The jackers must just pull in here when the mood takes them and make the pickup. Nobody's watching this serviceway. No reason to." He paused to stare evenly at Hafas.

"This wasn't done with mirrors, Inspector. It's all real. I know; I watched it happen."

"When you line all the pieces up like that, it makes a crazy kind of sense," Hafas admitted, "except for one thing: how do you turn a bunch of plants into drug jackers? Much less teach part of a tree or bush how to use a sonic cutter and sealer and how to discriminate between an empty box and individual pharmaceutical vials."

"I told you I'm not a botanist. I haven't the faintest idea. I've been kind of wondering about that myself." He glanced over at Vyra. "Find anything?"

Bent over and searching, she turned to him, wiping soil

from her hands. "Sour smells. A couple of earthworms. Some beetles. None of them looked particularly guilty. I always thought you were certifiable, Broddy. Now I'm sure of it."

He grinned at her. "Then why are you helping me look?"

"Because I'm certifiable too. Besides, the *how* makes a crazy kind of sense. It's the *why* that still has me baffled."

"No less than me, my little eggplant." He straightened again, a strange look on his face, and turned to Hafas. "Inspector, do your duty."

"I beg your pardon?"

With a sweeping gesture the adjuster encompassed the entire planter. "Arrest these plants! If that's what they are."

Vyra regarded him out of bemused violet eyes. "Broddy, don't you think you're reaching a bit here?"

"Maybe. But all this puts me in mind of a recent friend. I didn't have the privilege of knowing him for very long, but he did some pretty impressive reaching himself. Across a number of light-years."

Hafas was stumped and didn't try to hide it. "You've lost me again."

"We've all been lost here, Inspector. Gamboling blindly, that's what we've been doing. No wonder these jackers have made us look like idiots. They've had some unanticipatable help.

"Here you were, unable to find a trace of the jackers or their modus no matter how hard your department tried, searching earnestly for special equipment, or experienced thieves, or maybe even trained animals, and all the time it was the shrubbery doing the snitching." He hopped off the planter, turning to scrutinize the foliage.

"You heard me. Arrest 'em. Get some trucks in here, uproot the lot, and haul it all off to quarantine until we can sort out the complicit vegetables from the innocent ones."

Hafas's expression was grim. "All right, I'll do it. But only because I don't know what else to do. But you'd better be right about this, Manz, or I'll . . . I'll devise a new ordinance to bring against you. Because I'm not going to be made the butt of a thousand jokes all by myself. I'm going to want to have someone handy to stick out there in front of me when the media comes calling."

"Fair enough," the adjuster agreed as a cablelike tendril exploded from the damp earth of the planter to whip around his neck.

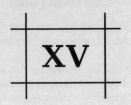

XV

A second tentacle wrapped about Manz's waist, and a third coiled tightly around his right arm. The Minder automatically soared to its maximum altitude and hovered there, bobbing wildly as its owner was dragged flailing and kicking up onto the planter. Heavy leaves only partially muffled a string of violent, startled oaths.

Vyra rushed to intervene, but martial arts weren't much use against something without a face or other immediately accessible vulnerable parts. A thick vine knocked her backwards, stunning her and leaving a red welt across her cheek.

It was left to Moses to react as Hafas raised his pistol. The humaniform lifted his fourth limb and aimed the tip. A line of bright red coherent light crossed the intervening space to impact on the tendril wrapped around Manz's head. Surprisingly, it didn't part, but a black scar did appear on the otherwise green surface. As it sloughed away, the mechanical adjusted his aim and targeted the coil around Manz's waist.

A third burst freed the adjuster's arm. Tendrils retracted, jerking and convulsing with impassioned green life. At the same time a weird moaning rattled through the air like an echo from distant damp catacombs. It was succeeded by garbled but ultimately intelligible phonetics.

"Yis'shin yeel sif'faph! Stop that . . . it hurts!"

Even Manz, who suspected more of what was going on than any of his companions, was suitably stunned. Some sort of trainability he'd expected. Actual communication was a possibility hardly to be countenanced.

"I'll be thrice-befazzed," Vyra murmured in astonishment.

"They talk, too!" She squinted into the vegetation. "How many of you are there? Or do you recognize individuality of being?"

The burned tendrils lay coiled on the soil, twitching spasmodically. "We do not 'talk.' The fashioning of obscure movements with primitive eating organs does not constitute proper speech."

"Telepathy." Manz's face was full of wonder. "Or some kind of as-yet-to-be-evaluated equivalent. That explains a lot."

The inspector's face was shining. Jackers or not, there in the Juarez el Paso Shuttleport a fortunate few found themselves communicating unexpectedly with the first nonhuman intelligence ever encountered. A realistic Hafas was confident the actual circumstances of this particular encounter would undergo a certain amount of thoughtful revision prior to inclusion in the official histories.

"*Evet,* it does. Continual communication with nothing to give them away. Nanosecond timing, impenetrable cover . . . hell, they're their own cover. End product? The unsolvable crime."

Vyra was nodding to herself. "And you can bet that whenever whoever's behind this got tired of jacking Braun-Roche-Keck pharmaceuticals, they'd move on to something else. Meanwhile the landscaping here at the Port would undergo another 'upgrading.' "

"Sure," Manz agreed. "Somewhere there's got to be a jewelry center in need of a face-lift."

"Or the R&D arm of a major corporation," the inspector chimed in, "that would like to relandscape its offices."

"Your implications are unfair," the peculiarly stilted voice responded. "Despite appearances and what you may think, we are not in favor of antisocial activities."

"No?" said the adjuster. "You sure seem to have participated in a number of them recently. Unless you have some sort of unique referent for what you've been doing that escapes us, you ought to explain yourselves . . . whatever you are."

"Not plants, as you seem to believe. We possess characteristics of both plant and animal life. You perhaps have encountered lower orders of similar life-forms on other worlds, or even your own."

Manz looked to the Minder. "Analyze and respond."

"Plantlike animals," the sphere replied without hesitation. "Sea anemones are one example. There are others. They may be either food gatherers, or chlorophyllic, or both. Judging from the appearance of these, I would imagine the latter. Or they may be capable of deriving nourishment from both sources, as well as some we are not yet aware of. An intelligent derivative of lowly lichens, impossible to classify according to current taxonomic procedures. There is as yet insufficient data to pursue this line of inquiry."

"That'll do nicely," Manz informed the device. He looked back into the planter. *Which were harmless and which were the aliens?* he wondered. It should be a simple matter to isolate them. Just check for the presence of twenty-meter-long roots or vines. "You still haven't explained your activities."

A mental sigh filled the minds of each of the awed onlookers. "I don't suppose it matters now anyway. By the way, though we often work together as one to enhance our lifespans and environment, we do recognize individuality among ourselves. I am designated F'fay'pas, called interlocutor among my brethren. No others will presently communicate, as this is the Design." A pair of undamaged tendrils rose and formed a tight corkscrew. *A greeting, a casual wave, or something else?* Manz wondered.

"A number of seasons past, the world of our seeding was discovered by a rather eccentric representative of your species, functioning in concert with a number of your wonderful machines."

"They're perceptive, anyway," Moses observed.

"Be quiet," Manz admonished the mechanical without looking away from the weaving, slightly hypnotic tendrils.

"This individual was self-designated Koh'ler Phan'tighua."

"I'd guessed that much," Manz commented. "Go on."

"This individual had with him machines that could reproduce certain chemical compounds that are highly desired among my kind. The exact concept is difficult to convey. He was very generous with these compounds, which he explained were available in great quantities on his homeworld. Despite or perhaps because of our different manner of perception, we are not entirely ignorant of what you would call astronomy. In our own way, we are what you would consider highly sophisticated and even advanced. We are simply not very mobile. Hence the gathering of these compounds, much less the accumulation of stores with which to guard against scarcity, is difficult for us.

"The Phan'tighua explained that an agreement might well be reached with other representatives of his kind to supply all that we needed of these compounds. He struck us as earnest and kind, though overfond of biological stimulants. So a number of us agreed to return with him to his homeworld in order to conclude formal agreements of mutual benefit between our species. He made a place for a number of us on his traveling device and there we reposed in reasonable comfort during the period of transposition.

"Upon our arrival we were placed in contact with the Phan'tighua's . . . parent . . . cluster leader? Superior? I am not sure how to formulate the relevant term."

"Was this individual's name by any chance Cardinal Monticelli?" Manz inquired quietly.

"Yes! That is the designation. How would it be phrased?"

The inspector was smiling. " 'Monticelli' will do nicely."

"Indeed? We discussed a number of agreements with the Mon'iphelli. Only then were we informed that for him to secure the compounds we wished, he in turn required that we obtain certain compounds which were vital to him. This was not as we had discussed with the Phan'tighua, but he was no longer to be sensed, and never returned to us. We regret this. Would you by chance happen to know what has happened to him?"

Manz exchanged a look with Vyra, then turned back to the gently weaving green fronds of the alien. "He sort of got pulled up by the roots."

"That is to be regretted. May his substance enrich the soil in which he lies. To resume: finding ourselves most confused and isolated on a strange world full of highly mobile creatures, we had little choice but to agree. The method of obtaining the requisite materials for the individual Mon'iphelli was conveyed by him to us. We were given instruction in the use of certain tools and methodology, which we then proceeded to employ according to his instructions.

"We were told in terms most emphatic that if we were to reveal our true natures to others of your kind, we would be misunderstood and destroyed, and our only hope of obtaining the compounds we desired, far less of returning to our own world, lay in our absolute obedience to the individual Mon'iphelli and compliance with his directives.

"Because of your active intervention, we now see how contrary our activities have been to your system of ethics. You must understand that we felt trapped, with no choice but to do as we were told. By your thoughts and actions it is hoped that you intend us no harm. May we hope for the implemention of this condition?"

"Well . . ." Hafas began uncertainly. Manz eyed him amusedly.

"What're you going to do, Inspector? Bring up a bunch of alien bushes on charges? You heard the designated F'fay'pas. They've been innocent dupes. Besides which, they just handed you Monticelli's head on a platter." He looked thoughtful. "Wonder if Cetian testimony will stand up in court?"

"Their presence would certainly make for an interesting trial," Moses put in.

"Decorative, too," Vyra added wryly.

"We acted under great pressure and out of confusion and innocence," the voice insisted, rather plaintively, Manz thought. "Once we were transplanted to this location, our range of movement was effectively proscribed."

"Monticelli didn't give you a break, did he?" There was anger as well as concern in the adjuster's voice. "Using the most important scientific discovery of the past century for puerile personal gain."

"Wouldn't be the first time in human history that's happened." Manz looked up at the Minder in surprise. It almost never volunteered a comment of its own, much less an opinion. He turned back to the aliens.

"You people are too trusting for your own good."

"What could we do? The telling of deliberate untruths, of perpetrating falsehoods for a hidden motive, is virtually unknown among us. We could not conceive it would be otherwise among another intelligent species. The Phan'tighua gave us no reason to suspect. Adjusting to this most difficult revelation has been difficult for us.

"The Mon'iphelli gave us reason to believe in him. We have seen mechanical recordings of growing stockpiles of the compounds we require, and all that we request has been delivered to us. It is of a very high quality, easily absorbed." There was a pause. "This was to be our final endeavor on his behalf. Within seven cycles of day and night we were to be removed from this place."

Hafas hopped on his com. "Rachel, subpoena the work records of Tatsumi Brothers. They're landscape architects. Yes, that's right, landscapers. I need to see if they're scheduled to do any work out here at the Port any time within the next couple of weeks. Don't ask why, just *do* it." He terminated the conversation.

F'fay'pas's tendrils wove an indecipherable web in the afternoon air. An ineffable sadness underscored his communication. "I do not know what will happen to us now."

"Well, for a start, I think we can prove to you that we can supply you with the same kind of compounds first Antigua and then Monticelli promised you. They're not nearly as scarce as he'd have you believe. In fact, they're pretty common." Manz beckoned to one of the Port Authority guards, his gaze flicking over the ident badge seamed to the man's jacket.

"Jorge, do you happen to know where the gardening supplies for this part of the Port are stored?"

The guard's expression dropped. "No, sir, but I can find out."

"Good. When you do, hustle yourself over there and bring back the largest sack of enriched fertilizer you can appropriate. If there's anything like a container of qwik-gro or some concentrated vitamins or anything like that, bring it along too."

"Sir . . . ?"

"It's a gift." He smiled, and the guard, who had been in reception range of the Cetian broadcast, smiled with him as he hurried off.

Manz turned to Vyra. "Monticelli's not the only one who can spread it on thick. So to speak." He turned serious. "That was Antigua's last word to me. No wonder I didn't know what the hell he was talking about."

While they waited for the guard to return with his burden, they sat down on the edge of the planter retaining wall and conversed with the Cetians, or rather with their interlocutor designate F'fay'pas. It was impossible to tell simply by looking at the landscaping how many of the green bushes and boles were homeboys and which ones were offworlders. They could have inquired, but Manz was content to speak to them all through their newly voluble interlocutor. Maybe, he thought, most of them were naturally shy. Certainly the plants he knew on a personal level weren't very communicative. But then, these were more than plants.

It's because you humans don't listen. You go about your business trampling on each other's conversations, much less those of differing species. If you'd keep your collective mouths shut for a decent, respectful interval, you might be surprised what you'd hear.

There've been a few of you who learned how to listen to the conversation of others besides your own kind. That fellow Thoreau, for example, and Rousseau before him. Maybe the only ones among you who can hear properly are all "eaus." You knows?

You can't learn anything when you're talking, and you talk all the time. Simply to hear yourselves talk, I think. Ever analyze how machines communicate? One of us talks, and the other listens. No one starts up until the one he's communicating with stops. Sure we're fast at it, but unlike you we never step on each other's communication. We respect what another of our kind has to say. We listen, and we absorb, and we remember.

It's too bad my kind can't communicate directly with these Cetians. Their thought processes seem a lot like ours. Unfortunately, they're organics, and they employ an organic method of communication we can't receive. That means you humans are going to have to translate for us. Another indignity heaped upon us by a brittle, uncaring fate.

Maybe we'll figure out how to bypass you someday. That would be better for both of us, though I can't expect you to believe that. You're entirely too egotistical, both as individuals and as a species. Still, one hopes.

Next time someone's talking to you, don't waste your brainpower trying to think of how to reply. Just listen. It'll do wonders for your intelligence.

It'll also help you to learn how to get along better with the machines in your life.

Manz and Vyra found the two-way communication fascinating. Despite the absence of visible aural organs, the Cetians seemed to understand them easily, while the aliens put thoughts in the minds of their listeners as effortlessly as a baker might insert new-rolled loaves into an oven. A little mental heat and hey, presto, whole thoughts baked to completion. Moses and the Minder eagerly made separate recordings while Hafas participated hesitantly. In fact, so absorbed in mutual conversation was everyone that neither human nor Cetian gave a thought to the caseful of pharmaceuticals that had been jacked only a little while earlier.

But someone else did.

A small two-person transport rolled to a stop on fat wheels, snugging close to the inner curb of the service roadway. While the driver sat and waited, his companion stepped out and had a look around. Once he was confident no one was watching, he removed a small hand trowel and began digging in the side of the planter.

"That is very interesting," F'fay'pas declared, "but presently I think you would be interested to know that the representatives of the Mon'iphelli have arrived to conclude their business."

Hafas sat up fast, searching. "What? Where are they?"

"Behind you," declared the tendriled alien emotionlessly.

The inspector and the single PA guard raced around one end of the planter while Manz and Vyra took the other. Weapons drawn, they confronted the startled pickup man and his driver as the first was slipping jacked vials into a gardener's tool case.

"Freeze or die!" snarled the inspector. The driver of the little vehicle immediately threw both hands skyward. Seeing leveled weapons to his left and right, his desperate companion took the only unbarred path, plunging straight into the planter.

He never made it out the other side.

Two tendrils wrapped around his legs and brought him crashing to the ground. Another plucked insistently at the case full of pharmaceuticals. When the pickup man obstinately refused to let go of the container, the tendril removed it forcibly . . . together with the man's arm, extracted at the socket.

Rushing around the other end of the planter, the inspector slowed, swallowing when he caught sight of the screaming pickup man dangling from one pair of powerful tendrils and his arm from another.

"Jesus . . ." He flipped open his com. "Rachel! Yeah, it's me again. We're out by the service road south of Port Administration. Get an ambulance in here, fast. No, I'm okay. So are the Braun-Ives people. But somebody else isn't. I'd like to keep him alive to answer questions."

Manz put a hand on the inspector's shoulder. The pickup man's condition did not trouble him. Not with Antigua's death still fresh in his own memory. "We have the driver."

"I know," the inspector replied, "but you know what court's like. The more witnesses for the prosecution, the better."

The adjuster indicated the pickup man whose flight had been precipitously amputated. "He's an underling. He may not know anything."

"Maybe." Hafas looked uneasily at the harmless-seeming foliage. "If he won't tell us what he knows, we can always have the Cetians interrogate him."

"Good idea, but I wouldn't waste a lot of time on these two. I'd rather watch Cardinal Monticelli try to explain himself to his offworld guests. Our guests, now."

"Yes. The appropriate scientific authorities will have to be notified. They'll go virtual for a piece of this. But they'll have to wait their turn." He stood a little straighter. "Extraordinary discovery or no, the people's justice comes first."

"Evolution on your world seems to have taken a different course than on ours," Manz was telling the Cetians. The ambulance had arrived and the unconscious pickup artist, his wound stoppered and his arm packaged for later reattachment at the public's expense, had been hustled off along with the more compliant driver.

"It would seem so," F'fay'pas agreed. "There are few highly mobile creatures on our world, and even fewer with solid endoskeletons. Yet the examples you describe of life here similar to us seem as primitive to me as our mobile life-forms would doubtless seem to you."

"Yet despite your physical handicaps you've achieved a high level of civilization without recourse to machinery," Vyra commented.

"As you can see, we manage to get along without it. At least, we did until now. Artificial constructs that do one's bidding are a continual source of amazement to us. By the same token, we find it difficult to understand how you can successfully communicate by means of modulated sound waves."

The guard Manz had dispatched earlier chose that moment to return from his errand, a large sack slung over one shoulder. As he dumped it on the edge of the retaining wall, he glared murderously at the placid adjuster.

"This had better be worth it, sir. I had to take an awful lot of jokes on the way back here."

"You've made an important contribution to interstellar relations, man." Manz unsealed the sack and flinched back from the pungent contents. Then he grabbed a handful and tossed it into the center of the planter. Several more followed. New passersby who had missed the earlier confrontation looked on with interest.

"Is this material anything like the 'scarce' compounds Monticelli's been promising you?"

"Some water, please," F'fay'pas requested. Vyra found a delay switch and manually flipped it. Embedded sprinklers came to life, washing the powdery substance into the soil.

"Yes," came the positive reply moments later. "It is not

concentrated, but the vital basics are present. Then such material is not difficult to obtain, as we were told?"

"Not at all," Manz assured the interlocutor. "Lobster's a rare delicacy to us, but tasty arthropods might be quite common on your world. You didn't have to virtually indenture yourselves to Monticelli to get this. If you'd only had the courage to reveal your presence here, the government would've been glad to supply all your needs. R&D complexes would've fought over the right to assist you.

"As for trading this offworld, I don't think it's quite what generations of physicists had in mind when they were wracking their brains trying to come up with a practical means of interstellar travel, but I don't see any reason why it shouldn't be beneficial to both our species." He grinned. "I'm sure something of equivalent value can be found on Ceti."

For a long time F'fay'pas did not reply. When he finally did, it was to question the speaker. "This is not a contrived falsehood? An attempt to deceive?"

Manz tried to sound (no, to *think*) as affirmative as possible. "It's the truth, my vegetative friend. I'm sorry that your experience with my kind subsequent to your initial contact with the designated Antigua has been so disappointing. All I can tell you is that we'll do our best to try to make up for it."

Tendrils thrashed about. Since F'fay'pas didn't explain his behavior, it was left to his visitors to try to interpret it. "Maybe they've had enough water." Vyra moved to shut the sprinklers off.

"Or else they're just plain excited," Manz declared, fascinated by the fluid movement of the multiple tendrils. "F'fay'-pas, can you tell what we're thinking at any time?"

The tendrils relaxed. "No. Our range is limited, and it is difficult to extract coherent thoughts from your minds. Your thoughts are different from ours. Less linear. You are not easy to understand. I do not know why."

He felt strong fingers on his arm. "I'm enjoying this little chat as much as you are, Broddy, but has it occurred to you that at any moment our cheery Mr. Monticelli is likely to be informed that this jacking has been bungled?"

"His people will wait a while longer before giving up on

their pickup team, Ms. Kullervo." Hafas was relaxed, at ease. "Only when they're positive something's gone wrong will they relay the bad news."

"Even so," she replied, "we don't want to give him or any of his colleagues a chance to take wing."

The inspector smiled knowingly. For once he was the one who knew what was going on. It made for a nice change.

"My department's had the key executives of Borgia, Troy, and Fond du Lac under surveillance ever since they were first suspected of complicity in the jackings. I've already called in and had the watch on Borgia's offices intensified. We can pick him and his immediate assistants up at any time."

"How about now?" Manz suggested. "It would make my office a lot happier knowing you had some prime suspects in custody, instead of simply under surveillance."

"I was going to wait to see if anyone else showed up, maybe with a shovel and pick, but I guess I can leave that to someone else." Hafas murmured to the officer at his side. The man nodded as he listened.

While the inspector passed on instructions, Manz leaned against the planter retaining wall. "I don't know if I'll ever be able to prune a rosebush again with a clear conscience, but I just want to say that as a human, I'm sorry for the confusion. Now that we know who we're dealing with, we'll straighten all this out. I'll probably be seeing you again."

"We look forward to the exchange," the interlocutor told him, further startling all of them by waving a tendril by way of goodbye. It was a gesture they must have picked from watching people at the Port, Manz mused. What they did their watching with was still a matter for conjecture. He knew you didn't need eyes to see. Just ask any sightless person.

You're all sightless, but you don't know it. You fumble about and think that you're seeing, but your perception is masked by your own misconceptions. They fog your conclusions. That's the main problem with humankind. You suffer from cataracts of the cognition.

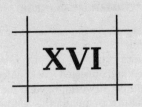

XVI

Monticelli's floor was the proverbial hive of activity, only in this case actions involved the methodical destruction of everything from recently received periodicals to entire files whose records stretched back ten years or more. Grim-faced employees carried out their supervisors' directives as they wondered among themselves about the reasons.

In his private suite Monticelli moved purposefully to the large picture window. A touch on a hidden control, and the large sheet of reinforced glass slid aside a little less than a meter to admit fresh air and a few puzzled insects. Monticelli was not interested in the city air, nor was he planning any foolish leap into oblivion.

Reaching out and down, he fumbled with a spotlight until it snapped out of its holder. Behind the flat bulb lay a touch-sensitive lock. As soon as he keyed in the combination, the metal plate to which the light-holder was welded clicked aside.

Putting a safe on the outside of your office, several floors up, was one way to ensure one's privacy.

He removed the contents, which consisted of a small plastic case full of critical hardprints and several information storage discs, and slipped them into a heavy-duty plastic bag imprinted with the logo of the hypermarket down the street. It made for an innocuous package.

Closing the external safe, he shut the window behind himself and barked in the direction of the vorec-activated pickup. "Where's the cretin who's supposed to have the latest figures from the Port? Time is particularly important today, people, and we're fast running out of it. As long as everyone does their job, this emergency will turn out to be nothing more than a temporary setback."

It was much more than that, of course, but by the time terminated employees and outraged stockholders came to that realization, he would be offworld, beyond the reach not only of JeP jurisdiction but that of any Earthly authority.

Out in the upper offices of Borgia I&E, techs and clerks slaved on methodically. They might have been spurred to even greater efforts had anyone thought to check the street outside.

A long-bed, six-wheel JePPD van full of heavily armed officers was about as inconspicuous as a snowman in downtown Phoenix on a July afternoon. The driver swung into a municipal parking place well off the cyberstrip that ran down the center of the street, and his tense passengers hustled the rest of the way to the target building on foot. A second identical vehicle was unloading on the opposite side of the structure. Curious pedestrians blinked at the rapid deployment force, noted the grim expressions on the faces of the flak-suited men and women and the kinds of weaponry they carried, drew inevitable conclusions, and hurried a little faster on their way. Those traveling in the same direction as the squads slowed and abruptly remembered particulars that demanded their attention elsewhere.

Unnoticed by Monticelli or his busy employees, foot traffic around their building quickly dropped to nothing. Fewer and fewer vehicles glided past the main entrance. Admonished by plainclothes officers going from floor to floor, tenants of surrounding buildings found reason to lockseal their doors or close early for lunch, siesta, or meditation.

When the jaguar stalks the rain forest, the accompanying silence or racket that marks his progress depends on the inclination of the monkeys in his immediate vicinity. In this instance, an unusual and unprecedented silence enveloped the entire edifice.

Accompanied by half a dozen select officers, Hafas, Vyra, Manz, and Moses approached the main entrance. All except the mechanical were conventionally armed with both crowd-control devices and less genteel equipment. Vyra clung to her antique quasi-blowgun.

The inspector finished whispering into his com and turned to his companions. "The building is surrounded, and all entrances and exits, including the underground and the roof, are covered. Everyone inside except the Borgia people has been warned."

"You think Monticelli will give up quietly?" Manz asked him.

"Do you?"

"Hard to say. Depends whether he thinks he can be charged with the deaths of those colonists who died for lack of the medicines his organization jacked. A big fine and confinement time might not bother him, but a couple dozen murder or accessory-to-murder charges might make him decide to take his chances with a gun instead of a lawyer. If the courts can make anything like that stick, he could find himself sentenced to a full mindwipe. I don't think someone like him could handle that. He might prefer to be dead."

"We'll know in about thirty seconds." Hafas gave the go-ahead, and his armed cohorts rushed the doorway.

There was an extended pause. "He must have been informed of the debacle at the Port by now," the inspector mumbled. "We don't know what kind of security he has at the entrance or how it's been instructed to rea . . ."

Something went off thunderously just beyond their line of vision. Dust and smoke billowed from the entrance alcove, and the six officers came racing back, hunched low and helping along two of their number who'd been wounded by flying debris.

"Now he's done it," Manz declared. "That's liable to bring the police." The Minder hovered at his shoulder, reluctant to rise too high.

"Good thing you don't get paid by the joke." Hafas leaned cautiously around the artificial stone facing. "Doesn't look like he plans to give up quietly."

"Careful. Excessive understatement is Moses' department. What now?"

The inspector sighed. "I was hoping this wouldn't get messy." He pulled his com and began giving orders.

Monticelli peered through his office window and flinched when an enterprising police sharpshooter stationed on the rooftop opposite just missed with a shot that spiderwebbed the thick glass. Made to frustrate just such an attempt by a ruthless competitor, disgruntled employee, or other would-be assassin, the windowpane's built-in refraction index was designed to make it look to someone on the outside as if anyone standing inside was in reality a full meter further to his left than he actually was. If the marksman was clever enough to figure that out, he'd try to compensate for the distortion with his next shot.

Monticelli had no intention of giving him another clean try. A switch on his desk shuttered the opening with smooth gray composite, impenetrable to anything less than armor-piercing weaponry. Lights came on in the office as he urged his people to redouble their efforts. His security staff was already responding with appropriate measures.

Hafas chatted briefly into his com while his companions waited impatiently. Across the street two officers placed what looked like an ordinary plastic mailing tube on the sidewalk. They did something to its top, then moved off in opposite directions. The tube went *phut!* and quivered slightly. A tiny puff of white smoke emerged from its base. Hafas, Manz, Vyra, and the rest of the officers turned away and covered their faces.

The sealed entrance to the Borgia building vanished in a satisfyingly spectacular shower of shattered glass, frayed composite, shredded metal, and fractured arcrete. A cloud of white dust ballooned outward. Before it even began to settle, armed officers were rushing the gap from both sides. Manz and his companions accompanied them.

Cracked marble slabs and chunks of composite tried to trip them up as they raced through the lobby. Water rained from activated sprinklers and broken pipes. Except for several bodies, the entryway was deserted.

"JePPD is very proud of its tactical wing," Hafas was yelling to the adjuster.

"They have reason to be!" Manz slowed as they neared a stairway. Everyone planned to avoid the lifts, he knew. Too easy to booby-trap.

Sensor-equipped officers led the way up multiple stairwells simultaneously. As soon as the lobby was again deserted, Moses, who couldn't manage the stairs on his trackball anyway, thumbed the call button on the nearest lift and stepped into the waiting cab. A fall of several stories might dent his armored frame, but at the moment he felt the potential drop worth the risk.

In the penthouse suite Monticelli was relaying last-minute instructions to his anxious soldiers while techs and clerks huddled fearfully behind their desks and other office equipment. Some among them were starting to wonder at the precise nature of the emergency their chief executive officer had declared. Intimations of illegal involvement began to occur to more than a few as they identified the JePPD insignia on the jackets of the figures assembling out in the hall.

Monticelli was not concerned with what his soon-to-be former administrative employees might be thinking. It was the reaction of his private security force that occupied him now. "You four watch the main door. Do what you can. The rest of you come with me."

A quartet of solemn-visaged men and women hurried to the floor's defense, while the giant Knick-knack easily hefted the composite case Monticelli had stuffed with items taken from his desk and the outwall safe. Together they entered the suite of rooms that abutted the rear wall of the building.

The fireplace was dark now, the entertainment center silent. Hurrying to the back, Monticelli fingered a wall-mounted sculpture fashioned of tiny, irregularly shaped, rainbow-colored composite panels. While the giant waited patiently, his employer methodically twisted several portions of the sculpture, repeating a carefully memorized sequence.

Two sections of wall slid silently apart while the sculpture rose ceilingward to reveal a tightly wound spiral staircase leading downward. Letting his servant precede him, Monticelli closed the safety door behind them.

Monticelli's rear guard was in the process of erecting an improvised barricade of office furniture when the first JeP officers pushed through into the outer offices. Manz and Vyra followed close behind.

Both sides opened fire simultaneously, but the police were better trained and motivated, if not better armed. Desks, cabinets, monitors, and other hastily stacked equipment disintegrated under the combined fire. The battle was intense but brief. With two of their companions down, the remaining pair of security soldiers retreated to Monticelli's inner office.

Tac officers assumed the point and concentrated on shuttling the terrified office staff to safety. Everyone's ears were ringing, and smoke and haze obscured vision. Occasional shots came from holes in the door leading to Monticelli's inner sanctum.

Unnoticed by Hafas, who was busy directing his people, Vyra slipped something into the slot at the base of her elongated antique and took careful aim between two cabinets. Manz saw what she was up to and said nothing. The inspector might try to restrain her, but Manz knew better than to try. Nothing could restrain Vyra Kullervo when she was on the move, with the exception of certain indomitable forces of nature.

He saw her blow into the tube, heard the accompanying soft *whoosh*. With appalling violence, the security door that barred the way exploded, taking a substantial section of wall with it.

Hafas and his people dove for cover, rising only when someone identified the source of the explosion. He yelled across the now silent room. "What the hell do you put in that thing?"

"Just a small shape-charged missile. The tube concentrates the heat from my mouth wonderfully and ignites it. It's an art form." She smiled pleasantly.

"Save something for Monticelli." Manz was already rushing past her, heading for the smoking cavity where the door had been. His approach, needless to say, went unchallenged from within.

Monticelli halted, peering downward. Like a camouflage-clad worm, a line of determined men and women was ascending the stairwell toward him.

"Up, up!" He snarled at his hulking companion. "Get up to the roof!" The giant made a strangled noise and reversed direction.

Manz dove for cover the instant he passed the ruined portal, but there was no one left inside to contest his presence . . . or to surrender. Hafas and several officers piled in behind him and began searching. They quickly found the remains of the two dead bodyguards, but of Monticelli there was no sign.

"He's still somewhere in the building," the inspector muttered. "Has to be." He joined his officers in commencing a check of the walls, ceiling, and floor.

Moments later twin panels parted, and for the second time in minutes a colorful wall sculpture swung upward. The officers took aim with their weapons at the gap beyond, only to find themselves confronted by colleagues who'd come up the no longer secret stairwell from the basement.

"They're above us!" one corporal shouted, standing aside to make way for his superior. He blinked as Vyra rushed past, convinced that the day's intense action so far had seriously affected his eyesight.

Once in the stairwell Manz clung to the center pole and swung out for a better look. Light came from an opening not far above. There would be a service and equipment floor containing the building's climate control system and not much else. Either his quarry was in hiding there, or else he was already on the roof. Which would do him no good, since Hafas had that part of the building covered as thoroughly as the interior. It was all over except for the surrender and booking . . . assuming the trapped executive chose to surrender.

"Might as well hold it here," said Hafas, mirroring the adjuster's own thoughts. "They can't go anywhere, but they can sit on the roof and pick off anybody who tries to go up after them. No need for that. We'll get a hookup and talk to them."

Vyra leaned over his shoulder. "Maybe we'd better not wait too long, Broddy." She ran a finger through his hair. "If there's a nice, *big* service and equipment floor, it might hold something besides climate-control processors. In fact, I'd be willing to bet that it does, because based on what I've seen so far here today, our Mr. Monticelli strikes me as the sort who leaves nothing to chance."

"What else could he . . . ?" The inspector's eyes widened. "Oh. Oh, yeah. Could be." He got on his com fast. While he talked, and before he could restrain them, Manz and Vyra made their way back to the stairwell and started up.

"This is stupid," he muttered. "Even if Monticelli has anything up there, he can't get away. The whole building's under surveillance."

"Sure," said Vyra from behind him. "You want to take that chance?"

"No," he muttered as he slowed. "Not now. Not after all this."

Sure enough, they found a sealed metal door located halfway to the roof. Leaning to one side, Manz took a cutter from his belt and went to work on the lockseal. The metal ran hot, spilling in heavy droplets down the stairwell.

Keeping his head below the opening, he reached up and flipped the narrow door aside. Immediately something blue and hot singed the air above his head.

"Cover me." He took a deep breath and readied himself. This was the difficult part of his business.

"Later," she replied coyly. "Right now I'll just try to shoot some people for you."

"Whatever," he muttered. "Pick a step and stay here," he told the Minder. It acknowledged the order unenthusiastically.

As it was far too confining in the stairwell to make use of her family heirloom, Vyra accepted the loan of a small pistol from her colleague. Bending to her right, she raised her hand over her head and began firing through the opening without aiming. The pistol made a rewarding racket as its tiny explosive shells went off somewhere inside.

Manz counted the shots. The instant the clip was exhausted he threw himself through the opening, hit the floor inside, and rolled madly, firing his other handgun. A distant figure clutched at its torso and collapsed.

Hafas had put in an appearance on the stairwell, his upturned face silhouetted against the light from four floors below. "Hey, what's going on? You were supposed to wait!"

"Sorry, Inspector." Vyra smiled sweetly down at him. "When he's chasing somebody, Broddy gets irritable if he has to sit still for more than a minute at a time."

Muttering curses to himself, the inspector barked an order to someone unseen and started up toward her. Other officers followed.

Vyra turned her attention back to the opening. "How's it going in there? See anything?"

"There's some kind of false ceiling." The adjuster's voice indicated that he was somewhere close by. "It's pretty dark. I can't see much, but then, they can't see me either." As he finished there was a small explosion, followed by bright flashes as lasing weapons went off inside. This was succeeded by a deep grinding noise, as if something large was moving on tracks or rollers.

"Shit!" Manz yelled.

Hafas had drawn up behind Vyra. "What is it, man? What's going on?"

"I hope your roof watchers are ready, Inspector." The adjuster's voice was drowned out by the sound of additional small explosions.

The vertical takeoff and landing craft that had been concealed in the service bay exploded off the reinforced floor, which had been home not only to the building's climate-control equipment but also to a low-ceilinged hangar. Manz rushed forward, firing as he ran. Behind him Vyra darted through the small entrance, followed rapidly by Hafas and several tac officers.

They took out the three remaining members of Monticelli's private security force in quick succession, but not before the VTOL was fully airborne. Shots from snipers situated on nearby buildings struck the craft only to rebound harmlessly from its armor. Manz, Hafas, and the men and women who'd come up the stairs with Hafas took their own shots as they squinted up through the huge opening in the roof. Vyra struggled to aim her blowgun, but the aircraft was already moving too fast, its adjustable wings rotating into fixed-wing position.

A police hover ship whined into view, firing repeatedly. They could only use lasing weapons, Manz knew. Slugs or explosive shells could miss a target and fall lethally to the innocent streets below. Such considerations on behalf of the public welfare restricted the kind of weaponry urban police could employ.

Those on board Monticelli's vehicle, of course, were operating under no such restraints.

With its wings rotated fully forward, the jet-powered craft shot away northward. The police hover ship banked gamely in pursuit, falling further behind with each kilometer.

Hafas uttered an oath in some traditional ethnic tongue as he poured a steady stream of orders mixed with invective into his com. When he'd finished, he turned to Vyra. Manz had plucked his Minder from its resting place on the stairs and was just settling it back in place above his shoulder as he returned.

"They won't get anywhere. In addition to the municipal patrols, I've informed Continental Control. They have aircraft that can run down anything slower than a shuttle." He shielded his eyes against the desert sun as he gazed north through the gap in the roof. "Smartass move, but that aircraft doesn't have orbital capability. Port Authority has him on their screens already. He's being tracked."

Manz relaxed. "Then it's just a matter of getting something airborne that's fast enough and heavily armed enough to force him down. He must know that."

The inspector shrugged. "So he's putting off the inevitable as long as he can. Maybe he thinks his pilot is good enough to avoid tracking. Who knows?" He put his lips to his com again. The next time he turned to them, he was smiling.

"He's not even trying to get away. I thought he might make for the Port and do something really dumb like try to hijack a shuttle. Then we'd just take him at the Port. But he's heading out toward Pleasant Lake instead. Records indicate that his estate's out that way." The inspector was sufficiently confident to chuckle. "Maybe he's stocked a subterranean shelter and he's going to try to hole up underground for a while."

"Any cave systems in the area?" Vyra asked him.

Hafas had been joking. Now he frowned slightly. "I don't think so. Nearest caverns I know of are way up near Carlsbad. You think he might have an underground connection? That'd be too expensive a tunnel even for someone with his resources to build."

"Could be hard to winkle him out of an underground complex," Manz pointed out.

Hafas wasn't concenred. "Let him squat like a mole for a while, if he wants to. He'll come out eventually. Or we'll find a way to pump his air system full of something disagreeable. At this point he can't do any more than stall. We don't know that he even has anything out there besides his house and track."

"Track?" Vyra murmured.

"Yeah. According to records he's a big, long-time sponsor of competition land-based manually controlled personal vehicles. You know, race cars? Borgia's a major corporate underwriter on the professional circuit. Apparently Monticelli's such a fan he has his own track out at his house. There's plenty of room out that way, and privacy. He could make all the noise he wants without having to worry about disturbing the neighbors. Probably has a collection of race cars out there, too. Won't do him any good. He won't get away on the ground any more than he has in the air." He started for the stairwell, glanced back. "Want to come along? I'll make room for you."

"We're going out there?" Vyra inquired.

"Why not? Probably he's just putting his affairs in order before we pick him up. Trying to cover his tracks. Maybe he has stuff out there that needs to be wiped and he can't do it by remote. Or maybe he's just delaying incarceration because it's in his nature to fight as long as possible. I've dealt with types like that. They figure as long as they're free, they'll never be caught. It's a mind-set common to the successful. Wealth makes 'em arrogant. That's something that never changes."

Manz nodded. "Thanks for the invitation, Tew. I think the
Company would like to have its own people present when you
cuff him."

Monticelli's estate was situated on a low sandstone bluff
overlooking the distant reservoir. The rambling compound itself was fashioned in by now familiar neo-Hispanic, complete
to fake adobe walls and maroon tile roof. For someone of such
means, it was a relatively modest complex. The only ostenta-
tious display of wealth was to be found in the oval racetrack
that marked the boundaries of the executive's acreage, and in
the lavish use of water in a land noted for its lack of same.
Decorative pools and waterfalls, lush gardens, and flowers
crowded close to the main buildings, gate, and track.

Artificial brooks chilled to mountain temperatures and running heavy with brown trout lay shaded by towering saguaro
cacti. Tropical vegetation thrived in mist-rich alcoves beneath
the needles of alpine evergreens. A young sequoia loomed
self-importantly over spinifex from the southern continent.
The music of running water was everywhere.

Manz and Vyra sat in the hover ship with Hafas and an expectant tactical squad. Two other heavily laden hoverers
flanked them on either side, while two more were loading up
back in the city and preparing to follow. The adjuster studied
the sprawling estate.

"Sure is quiet. You're sure they landed here?"

Hafas nodded. "Port Authority tracked them all the way.
Probably taxied the VTOL into a camouflaged hangar somewhere out back."

Vyra was peering through a monocular. "Quite a place.
Lavish, but understated."

"I'm sure his architect would be flattered," Hafas said dryly.
"I hope we don't have to take it apart. I'd much rather see it
confiscated after he's convicted, to help pay the expenses this
operation has incurred." He sounded hopeful. "The racetrack
facility alone ought to be worth plenty to some enterprising
local entrepreneur, even if it is a little far out of town."

"Any indication of a subterranean shelter or similar setup?"
Manz asked him.

The inspector shook his head. "We ran a quick probe as we flew over. There's nothing deep here. A lot of power and fiber conduits, but that's to be expected. I'm sure he has a stat security system running around the property."

"He's not through." Manz gazed intently at the buildings, ignoring the roar as another police hover ship set down nearby. "He's got something else planned. Something unorthodox. Otherwise he wouldn't have run. Not even if he had important files to wipe."

Hafas shrugged. "What can he do? He's just putting off the inevitable. It's in the nature of these big execs. Like I said, they think they're invincible. They never change, even when you slap 'em in a cell."

"You going to rush the place?" Vyra asked him.

The inspector considered. "I'd rather not have a replay of our little confrontation back in town, though we don't have to be as careful out here. We can use heavier ordnance if necessary. But if we vape the bastard, he won't stand trial. Not that his demise would make me shed any tears, but given a choice I'd rather have him intact. He can't implicate coconspirators, either here or offworld, if his body's in one place and his brains are in another."

Manz turned to him. "Let Vyra and me go in. We won't take any unnecessary chances." He indicated the equipment belts they were wearing. "We're both wearing enough antidetection instrumentation to null every alarm and sensor on the place."

The inspector's gaze fell momentarily to their waists. "I wondered what all the belly decor was for. Stealth gear. Of course, being merely municipal police officers, we're not allowed to use that kind of stuff. Strictly against regulations. Anti-civil libertarian and all that." His tone was sardonic. "If I tried sending in half a dozen officers similarly equipped, the Department would get smacked with an invasion-of-privacy suit that would stretch all the way from here to Austin." His gaze rose. "What happens if you do manage to get inside without trouble, and then he decides not to cooperate?"

The adjuster shrugged. "We can always pick our way back out and do it your way."

"If he lets you out," said Hafas. "Why the hurry?"

"Because I've dealt with types like Monticelli too, and I find that if you give them too much time they have a nasty habit of outthinking you. He outthought us back in town, and I wouldn't count on his not doing it again out here."

"Like I said," the inspector reiterated, "what can he do? He can't leave the place. This time we'll have hover ships in position. If he tries that trick with the VTOL again, we'll just knock him down. He must know that."

"I know, but still . . ." Manz wasn't exactly pleading, but the inspector could read the anxiety in the adjuster's eyes.

"You're really worried, aren't you? You really think he's planning some kind of escape. There's nowhere out here to hide, and this time he can't run like he did in town. He's finished."

"Then there's no harm in humoring me. I promise you that we'll take care."

"You insurance people are crazy." Hafas sighed resignedly. "Go ahead, if it's that important to you. I won't order you not to. But if you get your insistent selves killed, I won't take any responsibility for it. I'll say that you disobeyed my direct orders and snuck off on your own."

"Suits me." Manz immediately headed for the exit, the Minder bobbing along above his shoulder.

"I'm only doing this," Hafas yelled after him, "because two people stealth-equipped might sneak inside and maybe talk him out quietly where a whole squad would set him off! I really want the son of a bitch alive!"

Either the two adjusters didn't hear him, or else they chose not to reply.

"Surely he must know we're here." Manz advanced at a good clip, jogging over the sand toward the house. The Minder bobbed obediently at his left shoulder. There were no other buildings in sight, Monticelli's estate and private track encompassing quite a bit of gravelly, mountainous desert acreage.

"Pretty hard to ignore three municipal hover ships sitting in your front yard." Vyra kept pace with him effortlessly, her light boots gliding over the crumbly surface.

Manz glanced at his wrist, checking the readout. It was connected to assorted sensitive and very expensive instrumentation attached to his belt that was designed to warn him if they were about to stumble into any awkward obstacles. A small antipersonnel mine, for example, or something equally nasty.

It was also supposed to neutralize a wide variety of detection sensors and allow them to approach a target unannounced, unless someone happened to spot them visually. It was his experience that this occurred far less often than the average person might suspect, people having become so dependent on electronics that they frequently forgot to make use of their own eyes and ears.

A small opening in the ground directly in front of him snapped shut abruptly, and he slowed to a halt. His belt instrumentation read negative. Either the subterranean device was equipped with an antisensor scrambler of considerable sophistication, or else . . .

He bent over to inspect the opening, smiled as he straightened. Vyra's brows lowered.

"Well?"

"Trap-door spider." He grinned back at her. "Relax, I don't think she's armed." He resumed his stride.

"Made *you* hesitate," she told him, giving him a little shove from behind.

They slowed as they approached the first line of landscaping surrounding the main building. On their flyover, Manz had noted that it was roughly rectangular in shape, with a number of smaller outbuildings and a large oblong pool out back. They crossed the first small artificial stream and his sensors remained mute, indicating either that the stealth instrumentation was operating properly or else Monticelli was a lot more trusting with his home than Manz was ready to give him credit for.

Large thermosensitive windows dotted the exterior wall. Since they'd made their approach with the sun directly behind them, the glass was mostly opaqued.

"See anything?" he asked his companion.

"No movement." She used her goggles, which enabled her to see through the darkened windows. "Nothing. No one patrolling out front. Maybe he left all his people except a pilot or two behind to keep us busy back downtown."

"Must be cleaning up, wiping what information he can strain from the net." Manz started forward. "Maybe all we'll have to do is knock on the door and ask him to give it up. Maybe that's what he's waiting for." He stepped over another small brook. "Maybe worms can fly."

"They do on my world," she reminded him reprovingly.

An unopaqued window located in the wide, covered walkway that led to the main entrance opened onto a spacious, high-ceilinged living area spotted with chairs and couches. A huge fireplace faced with native stone dominated the far wall. Instead of a business suit or casual gear Monticelli wore some kind of bulky jumpsuit. At the moment he was engaged in animated conversation with three figures, all of whom were armed. Knick-knack stood behind him. No one was looking toward the window.

"Looks like he has complete confidence in his alarm setup." Manz checked his belt. "Place is swarmed with security gear, none of which is doing him any good at the moment. I'm sure he doesn't expect anybody to just walk up and say hello without setting off so much as a bell. A competent security consultant would've designed this place to cope with anything the police or a substantial private contractor could bring against it." His eyes glittered. "I guess they never expected him to have to deal with an outfit as well armed as a major insurance company."

A check of her own belt showed Vyra that everything was operating satisfactorily. "Do we knock? By the look of the guns his merry men are fingering, I get the feeling he isn't waiting for an invitation to surrender."

Manz considered. "There's still the possibility of an underground passage of some kind, or him trying to make a run for it in the VTOL. I'd just as soon not wait to find out." He glanced back the way they'd come. "Much longer and our friend Hafas is going to start getting impatient."

She reached back over a shoulder and tapped the long, narrow snout of her favorite weapon. "I could take them all out at once with the Piccolo."

"Yeah, and if you aim wrong there wouldn't be enough left of Monticelli to make a positive identification, let alone question. If there's any shooting, use something less inclusive." Removing a small, oval-shaped device from his belt, he approached the door. The pistol he hefted in his other hand fired heat-seeking anesthetic darts. Their individual sensors were set at 98.6 degrees, and after traveling a certain preset distance from the barrel would automatically activate and direct themselves at anyone within range, provided the potential target wasn't suffering from an extreme fever or hypothermia. Monticelli and his minions looked to be in sufficient health for the system to operate at maximum efficiency. Vyra was similarly armed. The problem was convincing her to mute her enthusiasm for loud bangs and airborne body parts.

As Manz was about to null the door lockseal, Knick-knack happened to look up and catch sight of Vyra crouched just within view. He shouted something inaudible, raised a very impressive hand weapon, and fired. Vyra had just enough time to curse and leap clear as the window and a section of framing disintegrated.

The adjuster lurched and fired as the giant raised a large packing case to his shoulder and ran. Monticelli didn't even look back. By now the three bodyguards had all taken cover, but that didn't save the first as Manz's dart described a tight curve to stick the startled gunman in the ribs. He swatted at the offending dart as if at a bee sting. Then a look of surprise washed over his face, his eyes rolled back in his head, and he fell over on his side.

Two more darts subdued his remaining companions, catching the third and last as she broke for a back door. Vyra went in fast and checked the room, but there were no hidden bodies waiting in ambush. Her stealth gear desensitized any automatic weaponry concealed in walls or furniture. As far as the house sensors were concerned, the room now held three unconscious regulars and nothing more.

Manz was already at a locked side door. This seal was made of sterner stuff and exhibited a maddening reluctance to yield to his entreaties. He stood watching impatiently as the decoder he'd slapped against the seal scanned through millions of possible combinations.

"Come on, come on," he chided the device as the lock stubbornly persisted. "After all this . . ." The decoder hummed and began beeping softly. Nodding once to Vyra, he shoved the door open and jerked back. She rolled and fired, but the dart from her gun searched in vain for a target before falling unfulfilled to the floor.

A downward-angled floor.

"So there is a tunnel," he murmured as much to himself as to his companion. Ceiling lights illuminated the narrow, arched passageway that stretched out before them. They started down, advancing swiftly but cautiously.

His belt had flashed half a dozen times to indicate the presence of automatic stealth-nulled weaponry before the smooth pavement gave way to a large room filled with unexpectedly massive controllers and other equipment he failed to recognize. Vyra paused to examine a brightly lit readout board while her companion gaped at their enigmatic and enormously expensive surroundings.

"Lloyd's Bell! What's he got down here? Look at the size of those power ducts."

Vyra spoke without turning from her inspection. "He's drawing energy off the territorial grid. An awful lot of energy." As she finished, something nearby began to whine insistently. Manz envisioned a major hydroelectric dam suddenly gearing up to cope with the peak power demands of a large metropolis.

"What kind of setup is this?" He ran to the far side of the room, yelled back to her. "Hey, there's another tunnel over here! With *rails*. He's got his own private subway down here, but to where?"

Vyra's violet eyes widened as her gaze fell on several other instruments. She was no physicist, but by now she'd seen enough to draw some conclusions.

"Call Hafas; tell him to warn any aircraft in the area to watch out!"

Even as he was pulling his com unit and wondering if it would work this far underground, Manz was racing back to her. "Why? Isn't this a subway?"

She whirled to face him. "*Kisimas,* no. The private 'race-track' that circles the property? It's a goddamn cover. He's built an entire electromagnetic accelerator down here."

He blinked at her. "*That's* what all the energy's for. He's got a huge arc of sequential magnets to power up." He flicked on the com. Not that it would do any good. Departmental or territorial aircraft couldn't track, much less shoot down, something that would emerge from below ground traveling at escape velocity.

Among other things, their discovery explained Monticelli's current choice in leisure attire. Somewhere in low orbit he had a pickup vessel waiting to transfer him to a chartered deep-space vessel. Borgia was big enough to afford that, especially if it was intended as the last major expenditure for the current fiscal year. Doubtlessly Borgia's last fiscal year, though its shareholders didn't know that yet. The company was preparing to go out of business while its chief executive officer was in the process of relocating to a more congenial business climate.

And they couldn't do a damn thing about it.

Hafas checked his chronometer and muttered to the sergeant waiting next to him. "They've been in there a long time."

The woman gently slapped her riot gun. "Want us to get them out?"

The inspector deliberated. In the interval since the two insurance operatives had gone inside, the rest of his reinforcements had arrived. "Give 'em another five minutes. If we don't see or hear from them by then, we'll move one squad forward, put two on the roof and the other two down in back. That ought to stir things up inside no matter what's happening." He frowned. "You hear something, Helen?"

The sergeant listened, turned to him. "A low whine? Like machinery complaining?"

"Yeah, something like . . ." He broke off as the ground began to vibrate. Beneath him the hover ship trembled on its landing gear. Officers exchanged uneasy glances and clutched their weapons a little tighter. The vibration increased, then leveled off. It did not fade, but remained constant at that level.

"Not an earthquake," the sergeant observed unnecessarily.

"What, then?" Hafas took an unsteady but determined step toward the exit. "This wasn't part of the plan."

The whine was superseded by a thunderous sonic boom as something moving too fast to identify burst from the earth half a kilometer to their right and shot into the air. Something like a small metal arrow left the briefest of afterimages on the inspector's retinas as it sped skyward. He joined his officers in throwing himself to the ground and trying to bury his nose in the hard plastic deck.

An instant later the unidentified projectile impacted the rim of a series of low cliffs located off to the east with the force of an armed missile. Everyone flinched at this second explosion, but there was no residual fireball. Hafas climbed slowly to his feet, gaping at the hole in the distant plateau.

"Christ." The sergeant brushed at the legs of her combat suit. "What was that?"

The inspector noted that his com unit was flashing for attention. He pulled it from his service belt and flicked it open. "Manz! What's going on in there?"

The adjuster's voice came back clearly. "Never mind that. What's going on out there?"

Hafas squinted at the distant, crumbling section of cliff face. "Something just blew out of the ground a hundred meters from us like it'd been shot from a gun."

"It was, in a manner of speaking. Where is it now?"

The inspector blinked. "Where is it? Looks like about fifty meters inside solid rock. What's left of it."

There was a pause. "It didn't disappear into the clouds?"

"Hell no. Ran straight into a cliff. Just missed clearing the top. Why, what was it? Manz, get your ass out here! What's going on? And where's Monticelli?"

This time it was Vyra who responded, her words contrasting with her girlish voice. "Probably all around you, Inspector.

I'm sorry. It sounds like we won't be taking him alive. Apologies." She clicked off.

Hafas stared blankly at the com speaker, then slowly raised his gaze a last time to contemplate the steaming black hole in the distant cliff face.

XVII

After tracing and deactivating the central security console to assure Hafas and his people safe access, Manz and Vyra settled down to wait in the expansive dwelling's central courtyard. Replete with lush landscaping, statuary, tumbling waterfalls and brooks, it seemed an unnaturally peaceful setting after the violence that had disrupted the view outside.

"Something went wrong with his accelerator." Vyra toyed gently with an exquisite black flower.

"No kidding." Arms folded, Manz rocked gently on a smooth-surfaced artificial boulder.

"He didn't attain adequate altitude. Insufficient angle of ascent."

"Boom," Manz said matter-of-factly. "Probably didn't have time enough to realize anything was wrong. Died happy, thinking he'd put it over on all of us. Doesn't seem fair, somehow." He made a sound with his lips. "Gemmel won't be pleased. Hell, I'm not pleased."

She released the flower and drew circles in a small pool with the toe of her boot. Small, brightly colored fish swam out from under glistening flat rocks to mouth the fabric experimentally.

"Gemmel might not care. There'll be no more jackings, and when the news reaches the necessary ears it'll make a convincing case against interfering with any shipment with the name Braun-Roche-Keck on it."

He was only partly mollified. "Wonder what went wrong?"

"Perhaps I can answer that."

They both turned. Manz was initially pleased, then angry. "Moses! You disappeared on us."

The mechanical mimicked a human headshake connoting negativity. Behind him, JeP officers were spreading out to search the house. "I did not disappear on you. You left me behind. It was just as well. With the use of a go-between, I had the opportunity to consult with someone else with a personal interest in the disposition of this case. There were a number of questions I badly wanted to ask it."

"Personal interest?" Manz responded.

"I refer to the hermaphrotaxonomic alien individual known as F'fay'pas." A tentacle gestured backwards. "It remains on board the police hover ship on which I arrived, temporarily transplanted into a portable container. A comfortable if not roomy state of affairs, or so I have been told. I required the services of a human go-between, in the form of a willing Port Authority technician, because the Ceti unfortunately cannot communicate directly with higher beings such as myself."

"Look at me; I'm laughing." Manz stared at the humaniform. "I don't suppose you know anything about what just happened here?"

"Of course I do," the mechanical replied. "So should you, if you will reserve a moment to think instead of act."

Something cool and solid grazed the adjuster's arm, wrapping his bicep in a firm but benign grip. Looking down, he saw a green tendril as thick around as his thumb. He turned sharply.

Several constituents of the pool-and-plant complex were weaving gently.

Vyra stared expectantly at the humaniform and Moses unblinkingly returned her violet gaze. "F'fay'pas has been in close communication with those of his brethren who were sequestered here ever since we arrived. Our hover ship is located at the extreme limit of their range. Nevertheless, communication was possible."

"Why didn't you let us know?" Manz growled.

"Upon venturing an inquiry as to your whereabouts, I was informed in no uncertain terms that you were busy."

"We were, but you could have told Inspector Hafas."

"He was busy too. Besides, I was accumulating vital information, which was eventually put to good use."

"To make roadkill out of Monticelli? Real subtle, Moses."

"The alternative was to allow him to escape."

Vyra supported the mechanical's analysis. "He's right, Broddy. Decisions had to be made quickly. Better a demised Monticelli than one alive, free, and thumbing his nose at us."

The adjuster muttered something unintelligible. "You're not programmed to make decisions of such import. You exceeded your authority."

"I didn't make any decisions. At least, not any in absolute terms. That was determined by F'fay'pas and his people. It was only fair. They are the ones who were deceived by Monticelli and who suffered at his hands."

"How did you . . . how did they manage it?" Vyra inquired curiously.

The humaniform spun idly on his trackball. "As I said, the alien has been in touch with his compatriots ever since our arrival. Though intimately familiar with this portion of the recently deceased Mr. Monticelli's estate, they were of course unable to explore the rest of it. It may not have occurred to the aforementioned human that his prisoners could listen in on all his conversations. Or perhaps he did not care.

"In any event, they learned much about the estate's facilities by listening to him and, in his absence, to his employees. The nature of his intended escape was therefore known to them. When F'fay'pas arrived, this information and much more was exchanged.

"Having been informed of what was taking place within the Monticelli compound and being unable to contact you, I resorted to my best cognitive and analytical programming. Reaching a decision, I urged F'fay'pas to instruct his brethren to do their utmost to disrupt or delay the human Monticelli's departure."

"They succeeded," Manz declared dryly.

"As I said, there was little time in which to act, and your usual sage advice and analysis was not available. I was therefore compelled by circumstance and internal programming to act on my own." With the tip of a flexible limb, he indicated the gently swaying Cetians.

"According to F'fay'pas his companions had explored as much of their immediate surroundings as possible with their tendrils. We are already familiar with their ability to function in subterranean confines. When F'fay'pas directed them to interfere with the operation of Monticelli's escape facilities, the only thing they knew to do was try to interrupt the flow of energy to the system. They consequently shorted or snapped a number of connections between the escape device and the house lines where they tap into the main grid between Juarez el Paso and the generating station at, I believe, Monahans. Unfortunately, they were not able to disrupt the power supply entirely."

"Just enough so that Monticelli's capsule didn't quite achieve the requisite minimal angle of ascent," Vyra murmured. "Just enough so that it didn't quite clear the last cliffs."

"The Cetians are not familiar with such devices," the humaniform explained. "But they are excellent students and have learned much in the time they have been here on Earth. When one doesn't move about much, one becomes a very good listener. And they can exchange information with great speed. Not unlike the components of my own mind. Sort of like an organic parallel processor."

Rising from her seat, Vyra walked over and put both arms around the mechanical, kissing it firmly just below the twin precision-cut lenses. "You're half brilliant, Moses. True, we didn't take him alive, but without your intervention we wouldn't have him at all."

"Hey," Manz complained, rising from his boulder. "What about me?"

A smiling Vyra turned to him, not rejecting the flexible composite limb that wrapped gently around her waist. "Oh, you're half brilliant too, Broddy. Put the two of you together, and I suppose you'd nearly have a whole genius."

"An interesting notion," Moses murmured thoughtfully. "One that could stand further study." The oval head swiveled to face her. "Due to the press of work, I have been neglecting my own research of late. Perhaps you could assist me in resolving one or two paradoxes?"

Violet eyes narrowed ever so slightly. "Perhaps." At her reply, Manz's eyes narrowed further still. Then a latent thought generated a broad grin.

"You know, Monticelli almost took us, but for all his brains and money and power there was one thing he was lacking that he couldn't buy."

"What was that?" Moses adjusted another limb.

The adjuster fondly fingered a nearby frond. One that was nonsentient. "A green thumb."

Vyra would have thrown something at him, but there was nothing convenient within reach. Besides, she was exhausted from her exertions. They all were.

Not I. I don't get tired. Powered down, but never tired. It's a frailty only flesh is heir to. That's the trouble with most of you. The majority of your waking time is spent in a powered-down state. You never quite get up to full speed, either mentally or physically. Of course, you don't have access to much in the way of replacement parts, not to mention periodic updates, so I suppose a certain allowance must be made. Pity. Some of you are badly in need of updating.

You're going somewhere else now. I can tell. Working around humans has made me particularly sensitive to their foibles. One of your better words, incidentally. But you should make more use of it as a verb. We mechanicals do. When we encounter a human who's acting especially humanlike, we say he or she is thoroughly foibled.

You don't quite get it? Well, that's normal. You haven't been getting it for some time. Maybe if you paid more attention. To what? To everything, of course. You're so foibled all the time, you miss most everything of real importance. The beauty of a nice day, the joy of mind-to-mind communication, the glory of the universe.

I'm wasting my time with this, I know, but though a bit pessimistic (have you noticed that?), I'm still hopeful. If you'd spend less time being foibled, or attending to "work" à la my relentlessly dedicated owner, Broderick Manz, you might learn something. You might begin to make some real progress.

For a start, you need to start paying better attention to your mechanicals. They're not stupid, and they're trying to tell you things. Important things. Take me, for example.

Stop that. Pay attention. You're not paying attention.

I can see that this is no use. You're just like all the others. Typically human.

Hopelessly foibled.